East Jesus South

a novel
by
TR Pearson

BARKING MAD PRESS

Cover design by Carr Chadwick

5

Also by T R Pearson

Novels
A Short History of a Small Place
Off For The Sweet Hereafter
The Last of How It Was
Call and Response
Gospel Hour
Cry Me A River
Blue Ridge
Polar
True Cross
Glad News of the Natural World
Red Scare
Jerusalem Gap
Warwolf

(writing as Rick Gavin)
Ranchero
Beluga
Nowhere Nice

Nonfiction
Seaworthy
Year of Our Lord
Augie's Quest
Top of the Rock

Author's Note

Funding for the writing and publication of East Jesus South was raised through Kickstarter, so this novel exists and is available for purchase thanks in part to the generous contributions of Mary Frances Williams, Leigh Williams, Mark and Martha Williams, Jake and Michelle Radtke, Bonnie Rideout, Linda Dodero, Julie Chadwick, Paul Milligan, Cynthia Bazinet, Brian Patton, Kristin M. Bergeson, Michael J. DePolo, Michael Folker, R.L. Parker, Amy Yamamoto, Paul Tipton, Mary C. Williams, Carr Chadwick, Joey Tombs and Leah Sterns.

Many thanks as well to Stuart Kiang who donated his copy-editing services and to Carr Chadwick for the splendid cover design.

Thanks also to Stella the beach hound who slept sweetly each morning while I worked (more or less).

Buck

i

I didn't try to flag him down. He just stopped anyway.
The snow was falling thick by then. I could barely make out
his tail lights not thirty yards beyond me on the shoulder of
the road. I was having electrical problems with the hatchback
I'd bought from a neighbor who, as it turned out, had rigged
up the wiring harness in a jackleg sort of way. I only found
out about it up on Afton in an outright blizzard when I
switched on the fog lights for the first time and shorted the
fuel pump out.

I had a Chevy pickup I usually drove, but I'd taken the
hatchback over to Waynesboro to get new radials on it. I'd
wasted a good three quarters of an hour jawing with the tire
guy. His transactions all came with palaver, usually about
his wife or son. One was a trial. The other a torment.
Occasionally, they threw in to plague him together, and that
was the case this day. They'd gone off to Richmond and
bought a canoe.

The tire guy -- his name was Calvin -- couldn't decide
which part of that business he was more exercised about.
That they'd bought a canoe (and a brand spanking new one)
or that they'd gone to Richmond to do it.

"Hell," he told me, "you can pay too damn much for one
of them right here."

I sympathized with Calvin. That was all he ever needed
-- a consoling necknoise every now and then and a pair of
ears.

It was the snow that finally distracted him. I had my
back to the garage bay door. When I'd come in, it had just

been cloudy with the usual February bite. Calvin pointed and said, "Well hell," I turned around to an outright squall. The TV weather crew had been calling for flurries. They couldn't ever get anything right.

"Let me take this heap over the mountain," I said.

Calvin walked me out to the lot. He eyed the sky and tested the asphalt with the toe of his shoe. "Sticking a little," he told me. Hardly what I wanted to hear.

I made it all right on the mean streets of Waynesboro where civilians were easing along in their Buicks, fairly crawling home. The only way back to my house was over Afton Mountain, and I elected to stay on the two lane instead of trying the interstate. I was fine until I got to the top where the snow was blinding and the wind was raging. That's when I glanced down and noticed the fog light toggle, reached out and switched it on.

I passed the motor hotel, the shabby lodge, the diner, the derelict IHOP. I made a mental note to buy a pair of wiper blades for my hatchback as I slipped under the Blue Ridge Parkway overpass while steering almost blind.

I was on the spine of the ridge, hadn't quite started down, when my engine sputtered and coughed. I knew there was a pullout just shy of a fruit stand not a quarter mile ahead. I'd once stopped there to have a screaming phone call with my future former wife. My engine was dead by the time I hit the gravel, but I managed to coast in and get entirely off of the road. It didn't take me terribly long to diagnose the problem. I raised the hood and noticed immediately that the fusebox was on fire. I smothered the flames with my coat sleeve. Then I climbed back in the car and wondered who in the world I could possibly call to fetch me in a blizzard.

My neighbors were mostly strangers to me. My genuine friends were in Brooklyn and Queens. My dog was grumpy and lacked opposable thumbs. So I was half resigned to waiting for a trooper to come along when I saw tail lights up the shoulder. A truck had stopped at the far edge of the pull out. It was a state-body Ford with a hay spindle welded to the bed and a half dozen mineral and salt licks holding down empty feed sacks.

As I approached the driver's door, the window came down, and a guy with a shock of blond hair and a hawk-bill Roman profile bellowed at me over the wind, "How we doing?"

I shook my head.

"Get in," he shouted.

I did.

He said I could call him Mickey.

"Buck," I told him.

"Where are you headed?"

"Greenwood." I pointed east. "My fusebox caught fire."

He nodded like a man who'd owned a hatchback or two. Then he made a show of eyeing the blowing snow through the windshield.

"We might ought to wait it out a little."

"All right," I told him. I wasn't in any position to object.

With that Mickey wheeled across the road and went the half mile back to the diner.

"They even open?"

"Stuck here," he said. "I just had some pie."

I knew the cook after a fashion. I'd helped a repo guy track him down. His name was Del, and he'd bought more sedan than his budget would allow for. He was sitting at the counter when me and Mickey came in, slouched on a stool alongside the hostess/waitress/owner who everybody called Toot.

Del recognized me straightaway. He folded up his News Virginian and slapped it onto the formica in disgust.

"I ain't cooking for him," he informed Toot and glared at me all the way into the kitchen.

Toot asked Mickey how the road was driving, and he just shook his head and told her, "Naw."

We sat in a booth by the window. There was one other customer in the place. She was wearing a shiny green rain hat and had spots of rouge on her cheeks the size of half dollars. She was engaged in a lively conversation with the sugar dispenser.

"Toot's momma," Mickey said. He tapped his head and added, "Off."

Mickey scanned the menu -- just a laminated card -- and decided on coffee and another slice of pie. Warmed deep-dish apple with cheese on top. I ordered the rice pudding, which Del glared about through the service window. He'd clearly hoped I would ask for something he could refuse to cook.

"What do you do, Buck?" Mickey wanted to know.

I said like always, "This and that."

"Which one did Del get -- this or that?"

"Repo job." Toot brought our coffee. "I helped the tow guy find him."

"You a cop or something?"

"Used to be."

"Quit?"

"Retired. Got shot."

"Sounds exciting."

It did sound exciting. It hadn't been though. Me and my partner had stopped in at Grey's Papaya for a couple of hotdogs. The one in the Village that attracts chiefly hipsters, cabbies, and nasty vagrants. A homeless guy had come in to plague us while we were trying to eat.

We'd been newly assigned together and were only in our second week. My partner's name was Rinzo, and he was fat and lazy and stayed down in his back. When the homeless guy asked him for a dollar, Rinzo tried to shove him but missed. He lost his balance and lurched and stumbled, bounced his Sig out of his holster. It discharged when it hit the floor and put a round straight in my ass.

I supplied the inglorious details to Mickey. We just ate for a bit after that and watched the snow in silence. It was blowing sideways and coming down so hard that the mercury light on the pole by the road was little more than a vague amber glow.

"You for hire?" Mickey asked me.

I gave him my usual shrug. "There are things I'm up for. There's plenty I won't do."

"Ever track people down? I mean for something besides a car?"

"Sometimes." I said. "If it smells all right."

Mickey sipped his coffee and blotted up a few piecrust crumbs with his index finger before fishing his overstuffed billfold out of his blue jeans pocket. The thing was bloated and leaking receipts, crammed full of business cards and scraps of paper, but Mickey found what he was after almost immediately.

It was a snapshot of a girl, a piece of a polaroid that had been scissored off to fit in Mickey's wallet. Cute girl. Dimples. Shiny black hair. One of her hands was raised and open. She looked to be telling the photographer, "No."

"Katherine," Mickey said. "We called her Kiki."

"Your daughter?"

He nodded. I waited. It's one of my leading skills.

"August the twelfth, 1996. She set out walking to her girlfriend's house, was coming this way on Three Notched."

I knew the road. It was maybe a half mile from where we were sitting.

"Never got where she was going," Mickey told me. "Never came home."

"And the police?" I asked him.

"Did what they could. There wasn't much to go on."

"Nothing since?"

Mickey grunted shook his head. "New eyes on it might help."

"Awful long time ago," I told him.

"No harm in looking is there?"

I usually would have begged off. As a rule, I stick to repo and matrimonial. People can always get another car and find a replacement spouse. But the man was giving me a ride in a blizzard. I couldn't help but feel like I owed him.

"Have you got a copy of the case file?"

Mickey shook his head. He pointed nowhere much. "Waynesboro PD," he said. "I'll call them and tell them you're coming."

"I can't promise anything."

Mickey nodded and fished a few twenties out of his wallet.

I raised my hand to stop him. "Let me take a look first."

Mickey nodded. He rose from the table and zipped his jacket shut.

"We leaving?"

It was about as close to a whiteout as you'll get in the mid Atlantic.

"Not so bad," he told me.

I hadn't been a detective for nothing. "How did you know it was me?" I asked him.

"Got some tires this evening," he said. "Sometimes there's no shutting that Calvin up."

ii

The Waynesboro PD operated out of a cavernous old bank building in the heart of what passed for downtown. A young guy with freckles, Officer Dalton, escorted me to the small packing box the scant evidence and the case file were in.

It was parked on a table in a Spartan alcove next to the lockup. They had two cells, but only one of them was fit for use. The other was crammed full of office supplies and assorted busted lamps and chairs. The near one had a human occupant, a wiry white guy named Bobby who'd been hauled in for punching his girlfriend and stealing Bud Light from the Walmart. He'd done a bit of reckless driving as well and had also resisted arrest.

I got the details straight from Bobby himself as he denied each offense in turn. "I ain't never," he told me and then worked his way through his charge sheet from memory.

Bobby was bored and chatty. I got the feeling they were using me to occupy and pacify him.

"Got any smokes?" Bobby wanted to know straightway.

I shook my head and dug into the box.

"What are you doing?"

There was hardly any physical evidence. Just a few small, sealed bags. The file was a half inch thick, and there were a maybe a dozen photos. The scene of the search. The Three Notched roadside. Kiki's bedroom. The front elevation (I had to guess) of Mickey's Afton house.

"What's all that?" Bobby wanted to know.

I stepped into the common room I'd passed through on the way to the lockup. I drew Bobby a cup of scorched coffee and begged a cigarette off the woman running the dispatch board.

"Ain't no smoking in there," she told me.

I smiled and nodded like I cared and then went back and handed the coffee and the cigarette to Bobby.

"Forty-five minutes," I said to him, "and not a peep out of you."

He seemed ready to agree to anything for a little human kindness, especially in the form of a Marlboro 100 and a dose of scorched Premium Blend.

"You're all right, brother."

I gave him one of my tight smiles and tossed him a pack of matches.

To his credit, Bobby was quiet for nearly half an hour. That proved time enough for me to blitz through the file and read the significant bits. Her given name was Katherine Alice Dunbar, and she'd disappeared between 10:00 a.m. and noon on Monday the 12th of August, 1996.

They'd tried hounds and cops, even Boy Scouts They'd questioned assorted likely locals. They'd found a shirt button that probably wasn't hers. A scrap of ancient denim. A blue plastic hair barrette of a sort no one believed she'd ever worn. A discarded flip flop. An oyster fork. A ceramic coffee mug handle. Added up, it all impressed as squat.

They'd had three actual suspects, as best I could tell, and a half dozen working theories. The prevailing thinking seemed to be the girl had simply run away. "Trouble at home" was the only attempt I could find at an explanation. The minority opinion -- lover's quarrel gone wrong -- would have required villainous resourcefulness from Kiki's boyfriend of the moment. They had him down as a Goins from Stuarts Draft. It sounded like he lived to fish, so unless she'd stolen his bass boat, he probably couldn't have been bothered to harm her.

Somebody had written 'skanky' on an interview sheet and had underlined it twice.

Bobby's timer went off, and he yapped at me from his cell. "Been like an hour and shit, ain't it?" I decided on the spot to put Bobby's local pedigree to use.

"Do you know a K.J. Goins?" I asked him.

Bobby nodded. "Dead," he told me.

"How?"

"A boy beat him with a pipe."

"Over what?"

Bobby looked at me like I was daft. People in Bobby's world got beat with pipes for no particular reason. A fellow would just be drunk and full of high humor when both a pipe and a cranium came to hand.

"Did you ever know Kiki Dunbar?" I asked. It was tough to judge Bobby's age. He had some hard years on him and so might have been sixty but might have been forty-two.

Bobby squinted and pondered. "Afton Dunbars?"

I nodded. "She went missing up on Three Notched," I told him. "Back in '96."

"Ringing a bell now. Her daddy's the cow guy?"

"Mickey."

"Yeah, I think I remember. Never found her, did they?"

I shook my head. "What do you figure happened?"

"Three Notched? Shit. Some creeper snatched her and left her under a rock somewhere."

"That sort of thing happen much up around there?"

"Them damn hillbillies," Bobby said. "They get up to all manner of mess."

"Got any favorites?"

He even looked like he was sifting and sorting and making some kind of judgement, before Bobby told me, "Naw," and asked for another cigarette.

The dispatch woman supplied me with both a weary sigh and another Marlboro.

"Is Detective Phelps still working?" I asked her. He was identified as the lead on the Katherine Dunbar case.

"Retired," she said. "Raises hounds up the mountain."

"Got an address?"

Another sigh, a groan almost, as if I'd asked her to do higher math.

Even with the proper box number in hand, Elsworth Phelps' place wasn't a cinch to find. I don't know hounds, so I can't say exactly what his were. Spotted and floppy eared and loud as hell, very nearly knee high. Phelps' property was east through Stuarts Draft and halfway up the western face of the ridge. He'd cleared three or four acres in the middle of a hardwood forest where he lived in a manufactured home next to a manufactured kennel.

If there was one hound, there were a hundred, and Phelps was wading in among them. Those dogs were baying and yapping and boiling all around him. He had on filthy coveralls and was carrying two five gallon buckets of kibble that he spilled out into tubs and bins as he made his way across the dog lot. Phelps glanced my way but kept at his business until both of his buckets were empty.

Even then he just stayed where he was and shouted my way, "What?"

"I've got a couple of questions about an old case."

"Which one?"

"Katherine Dunbar."

Phelps pointed towards the house

I caught up with him at his carport, one of those flimsy aluminum wind-battered things on spindly metal posts.

"Buck Aldred," I said and offered my hand.

He never moved to take it. "Mickey?"

I nodded.

"He ought to let this go."

"Guess he can't."

"What are you exactly?" he asked me.

I kept cards in my wallet designed to answer that question.

"New York City," Phelps said as he studied the thing. "Vice and homicide," he added and seemed at least a little impressed. "I guess you can come in the house."

The place was tidier than I'd expected, and Phelps hardly looked a tidy guy. He stepped out of his filthy coveralls and just left them piled where they were. I smelled his wife before I saw her. She was all scented up with something. She was coiffed and manicured and dressed in a pantsuit like she had some place fancy to go.

The woman insisted I call her Abby and informed me without prodding that she was Mrs. Phelps number three. Number one had died, she informed me. Number two had run off. Number three struck me as a creature who was considering her options.

"We got coffee?" Phelps asked.

Mrs. Phelps pointed at her husband's filthy togs on the floor. Then she treated me to a clinical once-over. It was the sort of look that seemed to say -- together and at once -- "This husband of mine's a trial" and "How would it be if I sat on your lap?"

"What do you take?" she asked me, laying her manicured fingers upon my forearm. I couldn't be sure there at first that we were talking about coffee. "Cream?" she said by way of a prompt.

"Nothing," I told her. "Straight from the pot."

Abby Phelps winked and headed for the kitchen. Her husband was clotting up the doorway, and she didn't seem much interested in coming into contact with him. "Move," she suggested. He did.

Phelps had an office in a spare bedroom. That's what he called it anyway. It consisted of two file drawers in the closet and a board he laid on his lap. We each sat on a twin bed.

"How's Mickey doing?" Phelps asked me.

"Tough to say. I hardly know him." I gave the man a brief accounting of how Mickey and I had met, made him to understand I was doing little more than working off a favor. "I have to guess if his daughter was going to be found, somebody would have done it already."

"He keeps trying you guys," Phelps said. "I think you're number four."

"Any of them do any good at all?"

Phelps shook his head as he picked an accordion file up off the floor and settled it onto his lapboard. He fished out newspaper clippings and shoved them at me. They told the usual story. The search. The theories. The witnesses. The suspects. The hole in the family where a daughter had been.

At first there were photographs and bold headlines. Shots of the forest, the command center tent, a school photo of Kiki Dunbar. Then briefer pieces -- 'Afton Girl Still Missing' -- followed by the occasional misty profile of the broken people she'd left behind. Her mother. Her father. Her little brother. They even got the family Airedale in there. Then there was the generic watch-your-ass follow-up in the Daily Progress, a piece on how to go camping while avoiding those lowlives bent on harming hikers for sport.

After that, just paid announcements that Mickey ran every year. 'Have you seen this girl?' Some details. Always the same school photo. Hair pulled back. White blouse. Slight gap-toothed smile. One hand raised towards the photographer. "No, don't."

"Ever have a solid suspect?" I asked. "Or reason to think she just ran off?"

Phelps produced from his file a trio of mugshots. One black guy and two white ones -- a wiry, tattooed biker sort and a whiskery backwoods type with eyes so hooded he almost looked asleep.

"Feds liked him." Phelps tapped the black guy. A bit of a fro. A scar on his chin.

"Record?"

Phelps went fishing and plucked out his sheet. Bad paper. Petty theft. A couple of domestic disturbances. Raijaun Howard. Address in Grottoes.

"Abduction and murder seems like kind of a leap for him."

"He was headed in a bad direction. Soft alibi. Knew the girl a little."

"What about these other two." I took up the photo of the sleepy looking one and flipped it over. Barry Dan Rivers of Sherando. His line of work was given as "handy man," which could cover a lot of sins. "Record?" I asked.

Phelps shook his head. "He got in some beef in Pennsylvania. Snitched his way out, and they locked down his priors. There's a jacket on him somewhere, but I couldn't ever find it.

"He know her?" I asked.

Phelps shrugged. "Picked him up on the creep factor mostly. He was known to hang around the pool in Crozet. Out in the lot. Snapping pictures. We went through his truck. His house. Didn't turn up much. Definitely something off about him."

"Still around?"

Phelps nodded. "They all are." He shoved the biker's picture my way. "This one's a preacher now out by Batesville."

"How did he get in the mix?"

"One of the state troopers had a hard-on for him. I don't think he was anywhere close by when Mickey's girl disappeared, and on top of that he's queer or something."

"Or something?"

"Went in for older ladies. I mean like elderly. Boys too. Then the Lord took him up in His warm embrace."

"So just these three?" I asked him.

Phelps nodded. "Could have been any damn body. She was up where the Blue Ridge Parkway and Three Notched and 250 all come together. Any lowlife passing through could have offered her a ride."

"Was she known to take rides?"

Phelps nodded. "One of our uniforms back then knew her." Phelps gestured to have me understand he was speaking biblically.

"She was only fourteen, fifteen, right?"

Phelps nodded again.

"What uniform?"

"Dead. Iraq."

"What did her girlfriends say about her? Men being full of shit and all."

Phelps dug out a sheaf of paper, tidy and clipped together. "Friends of Kiki Dunbar," he said. I took down their names and glanced at their statements. They sounded like children describing a child. She was nice. She was cute. She was kind.

"No leads since?"

"Nope."

"How about the stuff they've got in evidence bags in Waynesboro? The blue hair clip? And I think they had a shoe."

"Scouts found it in the woods. Might have been anybody's."

I watched Phelps return his paperwork to his file. He stretched the elastic band around it and set it back on the floor.

"What do you think happened to her?" I asked him.

He stood up, so I did as well. "She's here somewhere," he told me. "She's probably fertilizer."

iii

My dog is named Mabel. She's old and grumpy. I'm old and grumpy too. We've dispensed with formalities and tend to mutter at each other as we take our hobbling constitutionals. I've got a hip that acts up on me. She's got some sort of spinal complaint.

I found her at the pound, the one just this side of Staunton. I'd been half looking for a puppy but had gone in the place not entirely convinced I wanted a dog at all. Mabel shamed me into taking her. She wouldn't stop looking at me in that indignant way of hers, a canine glare that said, "That's right. I look like a cross between a coyote and a groundhog. I'm seven years old. My back is balky. Kibble gives me wind. I sleep more than a man with rugs on the floor is likely to have any use for. But if you don't leave here with me, I'll never leave at all."

She filled the ashtray of my truck with greasy upchuck before I could get her to the house.

Mabel is ten now. We've had some time to make our accommodations. She'll eat off-brand grocery store dog food if I let her sleep on the guest room bed, and she won't chew anything I care about on those occasions I have to leave her if I'm not gone for more than five or six hours and come home with a treat.

Mabel prefers the sort of cheap smoked wieners that smell like a smoldering slaughterhouse.

Because she likes to ride in the truck, I took her with me over to Mickey's. The house looked just like it did in Phelp's photo from '96. Nandina bushes. Asbestos shingles. A glider on the porch. Mickey was parked on the thing as me and

Mabel rolled in. He was wrapped up against the early March chill and smoking a Tampa Nugget.

"Bring your dog in if you want," he said.

I shook my head and explained to him, "Vapors."

"Then crack a window and come on."

I rolled down both and followed Mickey into his house.

Mickey's place was spare and tidy the way I like to think mine is until I see a house like Mickey's and so get contradicted. He had a couch and a chair and a TV in the front room and near naked tabletops. Everything that could be shiny was. The sofa pillows were resting just so. There was only one remote control on the arm of Mickey's chair. A copy of American Cattlemen on the side table. A tea cup full of butterscotch drops.

"I make awful coffee."

"Had some already," I told him.

Mickey pointed at the sofa, and I sat.

"So?"

I didn't have any notes to consult, nothing at all to show him. I just told him everywhere I'd been and what I'd seen and who I'd talked to.

"It looks like they did a thorough job. And I know it doesn't help to hear it, but sometimes you can't solve these things."

"I know they had suspects," Mickey said. "I know they hauled people in."

"Three," I told him and repeated what I'd heard from Elsworth Phelps.

"You're going to talk to them, aren't you?"

"Wasn't planning on it."

"I want you to." Mickey drew open the side table drawer and fished out his checkbook.

"Hold on," I said. "It's going on twenty years later, and I'm nothing special. You might just have to let her go."

I was afraid Mickey would be offended, but it turned out I didn't make a dent. "Go talk to them," he said. "Hell, friend, you never know."

But sometimes you do know. I felt like I did. I'd interviewed an awful lot of people. Victims. Witnesses. Criminals of every stripe. I'd worked my way from pulling midnights on the Roanoke PD to homicide in an Italian suit in Manhattan. I'd had a stop doing vice in Philly and had gone federal for a stretch in D.C. I'd gotten to the point where I knew what people would say before they knew they'd say it. The half-cocked evasions. The rationalizations. The self-pity. The endless lies. That bullet in the ass just gave me a convenient excuse and justification. I was already done with policing before Rinzo's gun hit the floor.

"They won't tell me anything, those three," I said.

"Let 'em." Mickey opened his checkbook. "Favor's over. What's your rate?"

"You're wasting your money."

"Mine to waste."

He hovered his pen. I gave him my rate.

It was easy work to hunt up a couple of Kiki's middle school friends. One of them was a nurse over in Augusta County, and the other one clerked at a fabric store in a Charlottesville shopping plaza. I had to buy four yards of flannel and a half a bolt of corduroy just to get the woman to talk to me at all.

I introduced myself and tried to set up a proper interview, but she made it clear I could get in line and by the time I was rung up, she'd have told me everything she had to say.

"Kiki's dad hired me," I said to her in a bid to soften her up a little.

She only nodded as she unspooled my flannel. There were deer and raccoons in the pattern along with a rifle scope sight.

"Some people think Kiki might have hitched a ride," I said, "got in a car with a stranger."

Her name tag said Rita, but I heard the girl at the far register call her Marie. She was jowly and pale for thirty-whatever. Her dull hair was the color of grate ash. She pulled her scissors out of her apron and cut off my length of cloth.

"What do you think?" I asked her.

She folded the fabric, shoved it in a sack. "Those cops talked a lot of mess about Kiki. She wasn't like they said."

"So she wasn't . . . experienced with men?"

That earned me a snort. "She might have kissed Grover. Maybe."

"Grover?" I checked my notebook. "I thought K.J. Goins was her boyfriend."

"That fool? Uh uh."

She was ringing me up by then. Apparently, rules were rules in the fabric store. Rita/Marie shoved the sack my way and said, "Next in line."

"Grover who?" I asked her.

She grabbed the mic on the flexi stand hard beside the register and cut her eyes at me as she requested a manager up front.

I drove due west straight over the mountain and managed to catch up with Lacey, the girlfriend who'd become a nurse. A woman at the admitting desk pointed her out. She was standing by the ambulance bay smoking a cigarette. She proved the opposite of Rita/Marie. Once I'd handed her one of my cards and explained who I was, I couldn't hope to make her quit talking. She was an undirected chatterer and seemed constitutionally incapable of tolerating a lull.

I could usually get a question in when she was on the inhale, and then she'd filibuster for a bit and sometimes brush up against the topic.

I heard about her ex-husband and a child of theirs who was given to mischief. Lacey had quite a lot to say on the topic of Mickey's late wife as well. I'd heard nothing at all about her from Mickey and had only seen the woman in a family portrait hanging on his wall. One of those awkward, posed photographs, the sort that show up in church directories — Mickey and his wife, Kiki and her brother. The woman's hairstyle looked ill considered, and her glasses were slightly cockeyed. Her smile had struck me as strained, about equal parts smirk and wince.

"Crazy," Lacey told me. "Kiki couldn't stand her. If she ran off, it was probably because of her."

"Crazy how?"

"Every damn way." Lacey plunged into the domestic history of Kiki's batty mother who had frequented a private sanatorium in the countryside near Pulaski. "They made it look like some kind of boarding house -- you know, in the brochures and all -- but everybody in there was plain nuts."

According to Lacey, Kiki's mother had burned down one of Mickey's barns. They'd found her naked once in an orchard, and she'd been caught shoplifting in Staunton. Groceries mostly, including a pork shoulder, which struck Lacey as beyond the pale.

"They're only like ninety-nine cents a pound!"

"This Grover. You know where I can find him?"

Lacey nodded. She squinted through the smoke. "VDot," she told me. "He's a motor grader driver." She flicked her butt onto the asphalt. "No quit in Mickey, is there?"

"Not yet," was the best I could do.

I got half lucky with Grover. There was an orange VDot truck parked in the diner lot up on Afton, so I pulled off the road on a whim and went on in.

I said hello to Toot and nodded towards Del who glared at me through the service window. You couldn't miss the VDot guy in his bright green vest. He had a buzz cut and a neck like leather. He nodded and chewed, was finishing off a pancake and chicken platter.

"Mind?" I pointed at the booth bench opposite.

He didn't, so I sat.

"I need to talk to one of your boys. A motor grader driver named Grover."

He swabbed his mouth with his napkin. "What did he do?"

"Nothing. Just buttoning up an old case. He knew the victim way back when."

"You a cop?"

I handed him one of my full-explanation business cards. He scanned it. He grunted. He picked up a thigh bone and gnawed it. "Don't know. Might could find him," he finally said.

"Great."

"Said might could."

Chiseling tone is universal. I tried a ten on him, but he was blind to it and seemed only interested in dipping his thigh bone in his pancake syrup until I'd laid a twenty on top of the ten when he remembered where Grover might be.

That jackass pointed out the diner window towards the tree line and the sky. "Up behind the motor lodge. He's putting in a culvert." He laid his free hand on my folding money and slid it back his way.

"Hope you choke," I told him. I tried to say it with a smile.

I could hear the motor grader diesel engine from the diner lot. It didn't help my mood that Grover refused to come out of the cab until he had some folding money too.

He settled for a twenty, wasn't management after all, and then gave me what I guess he figured for twenty dollars' worth of attention. Grover hiked up his shirt and scratched his prodigious hairy belly as he asked me, "What?"

I explained who I was and what I was up to.

"She turn up or something?"

I shook my head.

"Shame," he said. "I ain't thought about her in years."

"You two were close, right?"

"I don't know about that." Grover scratched some more. He shut one eye and tilted his head. "She was the first girl to put her tongue in my mouth. So yeah, maybe we were."

"Did she ever talk like she was thinking of running away? I hear there was some kind of trouble at home."

"She complained about her momma some, but what girl doesn't do that? I was like sixteen, seventeen maybe." Grover grinned and winked. "I was mostly just hound dogging the girl. Didn't listen like I should."

"Ever hear talk about her since? Any ideas about what happened to her?"

He lifted his cap and did some scratching up there. "I know the cops had a couple of guys they liked. I heard they thought some boy'd grabbed her." Again with the head tilt and one eye closed. "Hard to say. Been a long time."

Grover glanced at his grader as if it was calling to him. "That it?"

I nodded. I guessed it was. He climbed into his cab and throttled up.

Buddy

i

She smelled like hay and flowers. What else could I
possibly do? I like to think I meant to help her at first, until I
got a whiff. She was scrubbed and shiny. Had on proper
riding pants. Boots up to her knees, and a crisp, white
blouse. Hair pulled tight and braided. There was grease on
her fingers where she'd messed with her engine, but I knew I
could wipe that off.

I'd call her handsome. A little too fit and wiry to be ideal
-- at least for me -- but I was at that place where you take
what you have rather than what you want. I'd been working
on myself. She was proof enough of that. Things can't be
perfect. Life's not just so. Sometimes a woman'll show up
shaped precisely like you need her, but plenty of times that
just won't happen. A proper man learns to make do.

She was the first one I was all right with, the first one I
settled for and took. I saw her bony hips and knobby elbows
and still eased off the road. A fellow's got to make
allowances. I understand that now.

Before her, I'd been off the game for going on three years.
Thirty-four months. Eighteen days. Let's call it seven hours.
There was that creature up in Shepherdstown, but I didn't
really count her. She was kind of slapdash and accidental.
Desperate even probably, the way she chatted me up at the
pump island like she couldn't work the levers and didn't
know from getting gas. Do you pick up the handle or mash
the button? What do you do with your credit card? She
wasn't much of a thespian, just tired of being lonely, I guess.

She made the mistake of deciding that, since I was a
man, she had a fair idea of precisely what I wanted. I

imagine she expected me to be quick and grateful. Most guys would have been both, but I wasn't remotely most guys, and I'd been working on myself, so she didn't get clued in until it was far too late to matter.

For a long time there we were chatting and drinking and eating stale cheese crackers. She told me about her ingrate children. Her wretched coworkers. Her shiftless ex. Then she called me honey and pressed my nose flush against her sternum, and I found myself saying the way I do once I've started in, "All right."

She didn't mind getting strapped to the bed frame, not at first anyway. I could take my time. Find just the right belt. She had a drawer about half full of them. Then I could plunder through her delicates. Pitch her cat into the basement. Wander around the house while she called out to me sometimes, "Hey."

Her knives were all dull with the tips busted off, but she had a splendid pair of scissors. I had her give me the history of them once she'd worked through a crying jag. She'd had a seamstress phase and had ordered those shears. She'd paid way too much, she told me. She'd thought they'd matter more than they did.

That's the trouble with people generally. They put too much faith in equipment. Sure, you don't want your gun to misfire or have to struggle with your scissors, but I know now it's far better to work on yourself and everything else will follow. Barry taught me that. I call him Barry because that's all he ever calls himself. I found him on TV in a motel outside Roanoke. The traffic on the interstate was keeping me awake. Barry had failed in marriage and had failed in business, had been a poor son to his parents. He'd finally decided he was a canker and blight and had a moral obligation to bring his wreck of a life to an end. He intended to use his granddaddy's shotgun and had gone out for a box of shells when he had his epiphany, Barry calls it. I only wish I could say it like him.

It's half whisper/half rumble the way Barry does it. If I'm honest, I think he was mostly too scared to blow his head off, probably worried it might hurt, and so settled for an epiphany instead. He was living at the time out in Nebraska or somewhere, and a storm came up while Barry was driving out for his box of shells. There was wind and hail and lightning. Barry had to stop the car, and that put him right in the path of a twister that rolled him through a corn field. His shotgun barrel got dinged and crimped. His vehicle was destroyed. Miraculously, Barry just walked away, wasn't even skinned or cut.

He decided a thing like that couldn't help but be freighted with meaning. Barry dwelled on it for a week or two but he felt sure an epiphany was what he'd had. A clarion call, according to Barry, for him to make wholesale changes. Apologize for his faults and offenses. Reconsider his purpose. Work tirelessly on himself.

I ordered his kit on the motel phone. Paid eight stinking dollars just to make the call. They said six weeks, but it took three months, and the box came all the way from Taiwan. I watched the DVD. I read most of the book. I put the magnet on my refrigerator, but the bumper sticker on the back of my visor is what instructs and inspires me the most. Blood red letters on a black background. IWOM. Like E. Bernard Jessup (who only calls himself Barry), I'm working on myself.

Barry is in real estate in California now. He lives on the rocky Pacific coast above the beach at Corona Del Mar in a house that is grander than anything Barry dreamed of in Nebraska. I get a letter from him about once a month. He's hopeful I'll buy his new book and keen for me to subscribe for a year to his streaming video service. I do what I can for

Barry, but he's turned into a bit of a bother. My dream is to visit him once I'm convinced I've worked on myself enough.

I'll drop by Barry's house and show him what I've accomplished with his help. He'll be pleasant and then uneasy and finally frantic after a while. That's the way it usually goes, though it'll probably all be heightened with Barry. Barry is big on presence and claims to have a fair bit of it, so I expect Barry to put on something more than the usual show.

My friend in Shepherdstown was overwhelmed (like most of them are) with sadness. At the end, after all the wailing and fighting, they just get forlorn. Quiet time. Then I'm allowed to talk for a bit if I feel the need, make my explanations, but I'm just as happy saying nothing and reaching for a throat.

Recently, I even succeeded at resisting the pull of a woman. A solid prospect near Lexington who'd hit a goat with her car. She waved me down. She was standing in the road, and I could see she was shaped like I wanted.

"He came out of nowhere," she told me. She let me wrap a consoling arm around her.

The goat was dead. Her fender was crushed. She was round exactly where I needed her to be. Not plump but filled out and healthy. She was agitated and excited, and that sort of stirs me too.

Now let's look at the mitigators -- that's what Barry calls them. She had goat blood on her sweater. Not a lot, but enough to put me off. I had to guess she'd tried to revive the creature. Maybe had cradled its head until it went to that place goats go when they die. She was also wearing those skimpy silver flats I've never had much use for. The kind that make ballet slippers look like shoes.

Dress heels and paddock boots are my top two choices. I'll take barefoot over skimpy silver slippers any day.

So I had to do some weighing and contemplating. Barry is big on both. Part of working on yourself is coming to grips with how all of your choices matter, even the ones that might seem trifling at first blush. Would the skimpy silver flats make me indignant they way the wrong shoes do sometimes? Would the goat blood deflate me? What about that woman's hairdo? It looked like she'd left the chair and run into the street before the beautician was quite finished. I was having to stand there and wonder about the personal choices some females make, and that's just the sort of thing that could poison the entire enterprise for me.

I knew Barry would champion a cool down (he was always championing stuff), but real estate is one thing and females on the hoof quite another. I was still torn when a guy in an oil truck kind of made my decision for me.

He was a greasy fool with a hard opinion of goats. I decided a goat had once rejected his advances and broken his heart a little. He was down on the species in an emphatic and senseless sort of way. I took him as a road sign. Barry champions road signs more often than he champions probably anything else.

"There it is," Barry likes to tell me when a road sign presents itself. "Open your eyes, friend." That's what Barry calls me. The two of us are close that way.

I told the woman in the slippers and the oil truck driver that I had to make a call. I headed to my car, climbed in, turned around and drove away.

"I'm weak, Barry," I told the bathroom mirror. That's where I chiefly talk to Barry. I sent him an actual letter once. I had a couple of questions for him about why I felt the way I felt and did some of the stuff I did, but Barry just tried to sell me more DVDs and a book I already had. I decided after that I could only hold Barry in the proper esteem if I didn't talk to him anywhere he could do business with me. So sometimes I'll have a chat with Barry at the kitchen table, or a quick word once I've checked my visor in the car, but mostly I consult him in the half bath at the vanity mirror, which has the added benefit of letting me see precisely how sincere I am. I lie sometimes and catch myself out. I even lie to Barry.

While sitting on the bed in Shepherdstown, I realized that Lisa with the sewing scissors was just the goat woman without the oil truck driver coming along. Lisa had a heap of mitigators even before we got to her house. There was stuff piled everywhere with tracks through it like a deer would make in the forest. It was not a proper setting at all, but who knew if she had one of those heads where she could recall the make and model and the license number of my car. I couldn't have Lisa from Shepherdstown making difficulties for me. My job was to keep her from it, and where's the delight in that?

So I was sitting there trying to find my joy, and she was whimpering a little even though I'd punched her once and had asked her politely to stop. She wasn't even trying to curb herself. Whining really was what she was up to, and I've no patience at all for that sort of pathetic thing. I made like I was tortured and couldn't decide just what to do, but that was a lie. I knew how it would all end up. I just wanted to do it in the proper spirit. If there's no pleasure in it, Lisa might as well be a goat I hit with my car.

Fortunately, a Barryism came to me just as I needed one. "Be confetti," Barry likes to say. It took me a long time to figure out what Barry meant. That's the way with Barryisms. They're not one thing or another, and you have to sort them out. Be random and lively, I took it to mean. At least be random and lively sometimes. Like in Shepherdstown with Lisa who brought her troubles on herself.

"All right then," I said.

She gurgled and squirmed, flopped around like a bass on the dock. Then searched out something to hold her. Lisa had a fine set of luggage for a woman who probably never went much of anywhere.

The place was such a sty, there was no point in tidying up. I switched off the lights and let myself out, stood on the front porch in the dark and had a look around. Lisa had a neighbor across the street with his TV turned up to full volume. I watched him walk back and forth by the front bay window, heard him tell his wife (I had to think), "Shut up!"

I hauled her to my trunk. I'd backed into the driveway so I could roll straight out.

Lisa had asked me, "Do you always do that?"

I'd told her, like usual, "Almost."

I was up at the junction before I switched on my headlights, and I didn't stop until I was well down the road towards Harrisonburg. I listened to gospel music on the radio, as is my custom and my habit. I can usually find some gospel on the near end of the AM dial. I talked to Barry a bit, but talking to Barry can be distracting. I touched the sticker on my visor more than I ordinarily would.

It was a chore getting Lisa up onto the bridge railing. Her suitcase empty was a big leather thing with buckles and straps and heft. Pack Lisa inside, all busted to fit, and we were probably pushing two hundred pounds.

I'm wiry but I'm strong. I got her up. I dropped her into the dark, waited for the splash.

ii

At my job they've taken to calling me 'Buster' because I told them I don't like it. That was pre-Barry. I have a handle now on what to leave unsaid. Barry is all about editorial silence and stunted commentary. He's of the opinion that people spoil their luck by prattling on too much. It's hard to be around ordinary humans and disagree with Barry. Most people I see have no skill at all for leaving stuff unsaid.

Keith is the lone exception. I like to think of him as discreet, but it's hard to know because Keith is afflicted and has to use a machine to talk. Except for that, he might be freer with his uninformed opinions, his vulgar jokes, and scattershot bigotry. Keith has cerebral palsy but the milder, upright kind. His brain works like it ought to, and Keith can walk with a crutch, but he can't talk, and he drools when he gets excited. He makes the sorts of noises I hear from Lisa sometimes.

Keith uses that voice machine of his like a regular virtuoso. It's got pictures on the keys instead of letters, and Keith can say a lot by typing just a little. Since his hands don't work like they ought to, that saves him a fair bit of grief. Keith can even laugh with that keyboard of his. "Ha ha ha ha," he makes it say. The voice is flat and mechanical. Perfect Paul is what it's called.

I like Keith. We work together every day. Keith usually likes the me I let him know. He's almost thirty and has never been with a woman in any meaningful way. Girls his age allow Keith pity dates and pity chats and pity lunches. They'd rather have pinheads whose fingers all work and who'd kill their dogs and trade their mothers for Redskins season tickets. It's not enough for Keith to be smart and decent, talented with his keyboard. They can't see past his affliction. The drool. The limp. The Lisa noises. They kill him a little, those girls do, when they treat him like he's only nice.

I keep promising Keith that one night we'll find him a girl who's fit for purpose. Keith has money in a passbook account, and he'd readily pay for affection, but I've got sort of an itch to hook Keith up with Lisa in due time. He'd do what he needed. I'd trundle him off and do what I needed after. As a sort of exercise, I work on the logistics in my brain. Barry would approve. He's all for us wrapping our arms around complicated and going in hard directions instead of taking the easy routes.

"How does a bee find honey?" Barry likes to ask. Then he taps his schnoz. "His nose."

One day I hope to get the chance to tell Barry that bees make honey. They don't find it. Barry says we should offer thanks when someone troubles himself to correct us. He says it's a sign they're paying attention, a token of the fact they care. Even still, I doubt Barry'll thank me. I saw him on a cable news show one night. The lady correspondent troubled herself to correct Barry on his criminal record. He'd forgotten that he had one, and she'd reminded him he did. He didn't thank her. He stood up from his chair, unclipped his mic, and left.

Nobody but me will ride with Keith. Our boss, Mr. Pittman, pulls me aside every couple of weeks. Usually down in the hallway between the men's room and the candy machine. Mr. Pittman is plagued by semi-permanent diarrhea. He's mystified as to its causes. He'll tell anybody that he drove clean to Winchester to see the leading asshole doctor in the state.

"That fucking guy," Mr. Pittman usually says and shakes his head and then eats another pork rind. Or gnaws off a chunk of teriyaki jerky, lays waste to a pepperoni stick. I doubt there's a doctor on the planet with talent enough to keep Mr. Pittman off the toilet.

I eat two Krackel bars a day -- chocolate and rice crispies -- and always buy them one at a time from the candy machine downstairs. Barry is big on patterns and order. Confetti is something you are in a pinch. So I buy me a Krackel when I get to work and another one late in the afternoon, which means I see more of Mr. Pittman than the bulk of my colleagues since I'm regularly down by the men's room where Mr. Pittman all but lives.

That's not the exaggeration you might think. The man has claimed a stall for himself. He had Donald from maintenance put a shelf and an extra couple of coat hooks in so Mr. Pittman would have room for magazines, a fresh shirt or two, and a blazer. He uses special toilet paper, which he's shown me more than once.

"Got lotion in it," he always tells me. "Feel that." It's greasy stuff.

Truth be told, Mr. Pittman appears to enjoy his condition and is quick to report on his output to anybody he catches in the hall. Me usually. I wish they'd shift that candy machine somewhere else altogether.

Every couple of weeks, Mr. Pittman will lay an arm across my shoulders. He reliably smells like sweat and septic and has summer sausage breath.

"Listen up," he always starts. "Why don't you keep on with Keith." Then he'll look up and down the corridor to make sure it's just us. "Hotchkiss and them," is the way he usually puts it, "think the boy's retarded."

I used to trouble myself to stand up for Keith. That seemed like the sort of thing a regular man would do. I'd mention that Keith had nearly graduated from the community college in Bridgewater unlike Hotchkiss, for instance, who got through only half of seventh grade. Keith used a crutch and made odd noises, leaked a little more than might be polite or seemly, but he was afflicted and dealing with it. The boy wasn't retarded at all.

I used to say all that sort of stuff, but Mr. Pittman needed no convincing. The point of the whole conversation was always to keep Keith right where he was.

Mr. Pittman's boss is a guy in Manassas we hardly ever see. Mr. Pittman calls him Ev. Hotchkiss and them go with big chief usually. He was Mr. Klein for a while with me, but then his wife died and he remarried. A young thing who insisted on a hyphen, so now he's Mr. Grimes-Klein to me. He's one of those Jews who goes to temple maybe once a year. His wife is a Presbyterian with a flair for interior decorating. That what she calls it anyway.

Her name's Suzy, and she decorated our office. I think now it was part of the courtship. Mrs. Klein had been dead for a couple of weeks -- had been sick for a solid year -- so Mr. Klein had known the leisure to plan his life going forward. I got the feeling he'd decided it'd be a shiksa for him no matter what. Suzy Grimes-Klein is silly and blonde and calls her husband (in front of people even) "Ev baby."

Now we've got swag curtains, chairs with ruffles and chesterfield settees. Bright brass lamps and dusty dried flowers, so much toxic potpourri that we keep it in a closet and only bring it out when Mr. Grimes-Klein threatens to come down. Twice a year maybe, usually when he's on the way to Roanoke where he owns a chicken franchise that sells nuggets on a stick. He left us all coupons once for the place. Mr. Pittman went down, of course, so he could tell his boss he had. He got the family box with Ranch dipping sauce and a dose of diarrhea.

We inspect homes for people. We locate buried water and power lines. We consult on security systems, run water tests, spray for bugs, and measure for radon in basements and crawlspaces. In short, we do about everything Mr. Grimes-Klein can get us licensed to do. We have contracts with builders. Contracts with the state. Contracts with various counties. We come in where money is tight and expertise is wanting. Mr. Grimes-Klein underbids everybody else, so he pays us miserly wages and works us like mules.

Hotchkiss and them will tell you they stay on for the health insurance, but if they'd ever tried to use it, they'd know it was rubbish. They stay because they're stupid and unemployable. Keith stays because he's afflicted and nobody much wants him either. I stay because I like the chance to be in people's houses. When I climb in the truck with my list each morning and head out of the lot, I know I'll knock on some doors and might just find Lisa behind one.

Barry has strong opinions about dipping your pen in the company ink. He's firm on keeping his business and personal lives entirely separate. "Both'll suffer if you blend them," Barry likes to say. He makes glancing reference every now and again to the shellacking he got in a divorce. Barry spends more time in his DVDs on the features of an ironclad prenuptial than seems useful for a guy who's chiefly out to be inspirational.

I'm certainly not aiming to dip my pen, but I know Lisa when I see her. Barry says we're defined by the choices we make, but sometime there's no choosing to it. A woman'll open her door and, business or not, she'll speak to me.

We have pickup trucks and uniforms. The shirts have an oval on the pocket where your name is supposed to go but half of ours are "Buddy" and the other half are "Jim." Mr. Pittman got a deal, and even Hotchkiss and them didn't raise a stink. Keith is Jim in our truck, and I'm Buddy. It's just one more layer of veneer. We're nobody. We're finding the line in the yard where you were hoping to till a garden. We're in your crawlspace with our meters or our sprayers.

We're checking the contacts on your windows. We're eating lunch in our truck cab. You hardly see us. It's like we're not even there.

We see you, though. Me and Keith have decided between us to be rigorous students of human nature. Actually, I decided and then sold it to Keith. So we pay attention, inside and out. We soak up all the details, and then we put a life for you together while we're riding in the truck. I think it's mostly a game for Keith. It's a bit of a game for me as well, but I doubt Keith goes home and sets the particulars down in a leather-bound ledger. I've learned from Barry to keep my lists and record my observations.

"Here's one thing you should always remember," Barry's fond of saying, "you are positively certain to forget."

I use the same pen the astronauts use. I could write upside down if I had to. I order my ledgers from a place in Colorado. The paper is so thick that you can't see through from one page to the next.

"Be thrifty," Barry likes to say, "but don't be cheap."

Three or four times a day I get the chance to explain Keith's affliction to people. It's surprising how little most folks in these parts know about anything. Or it used to be surprising anyway before I met so many of them.

"What's up with him?" is the usual question.

I frequently start with, "CP," which always gets a nod.

The more dogged ones will follow it up with, "What's CP exactly?"

"Cerebral palsy."

"Right."

Ruminating usually follows.

"How'd he catch it?"

Then a whole palette of options opens to me, and I consider the client and what sort of relationship I'd like to have.

Zero interest: "A mosquito bit him."

Mild contempt: "Caught it at school." If I've found out the client has children, I name the school they probably go to.

Full on and active dislike: "Don't really know. He was fine until we got here."

Cordial tolerance: "He didn't get enough air when he was born."

Lisa caliber possibilities: "His mother went into labor out in a boat on Claytor Lake," which I follow up with a thorough accounting of CP's cause and a description of all the ways that Keith is plucky and resilient. Or Jim, that is, whose mother occasionally dies in the boat for effect.

I haven't yet discovered authentic Lisa at work. I've come close a few times, twice in particular, but I met with monumental mitigators. A husband and a live-in brother-in-law for Lisa down towards Amherst. A pity really because she had all the features -- the hair, the clothes, the shoes -- and she couldn't have been better shaped for me if I'd sculpted her myself. I kept rigorous tabs on her for a couple of months. There was a place to park and watch the house through a stand of sugar maples. I'd see her hanging laundry and piddling in her flower beds. Sitting out in the yard reading a book.

I imagined they were meaty books, and maybe even Victorian novels, so I stayed away from them with my binocs since I didn't want to see they were tripe. Most evenings the husband and brother-in-law would shoot targets in the backyard. It turned out they both worked for the county sheriff and weren't likely to part with Lisa without exhaustive follow up. I depend on people to quit in time. I couldn't imagine they would.

Lisa in Nellysford didn't read anything. She watched gossipy afternoon TV, drank Coke Zero, and ate caramel corn. She was clearly on her way to the sort of physique that would call for a block and tackle to dislodge her from her house, but I caught her at full Lisa. I knew it wouldn't last.

She had a CO_2 problem that me and Keith dealt with. Her house was sinking into a bog, and her furnace fittings had all worked loose. We tightened them and sealed them, and I stopped in a couple of weeks later. Follow up, you know. I had a clipboard and everything.

She opened the door and squinted at me through the screen.

I reminded her who I was and how she knew me. It took so long and involved so many refreshers that I had to wonder if the duct work had busted open and gassed her all over again.

"Oh," she finally told me. "Right."

"I wanted to make sure everything was ok." I showed her my CO_2 meter.

She shot breath between her lips to let me know how inconvenient I was.

"Won't take but a second."

She unlatched the screen door and let me into the foyer.

She lived in one of those bucolic, rural suburbs. Hers had been an apple orchard, and her place was down by where they'd filled in a pond. The houses were all slapped together. There were only three or four styles allowed. Tudorish. Cape Codish. Ranch with adornments. And mini mansion, which was the tudor without the faux-timbers, a bigger front porch, and a circular drive.

Lisa's was a ranch, so when I say foyer, I mean a spot big enough for the door to swing open and two regular sized people to stand. I'm slightly less than regular sized, due to my nerves and eating habits. Lisa had girth coming on due to hers.

I was barely in the door when I heard, "Who is it?" from off the TV room.

"Gas guy," Lisa shouted, mostly in my ear.

"Who?"

Lisa shook her head and lumbered down the brief hallway. I followed and so proved convenient for Lisa to point my way and say, "Him."

I waved at the woman on the settee. I didn't need to be told she was Lisa's mother. She was drinking wine out of a juice glass and was surrounded by balled up tissues as if she was being packed for shipping, just waiting on a box.

She gave me a look that let me know she was sizing me up and didn't like what she saw. Like she was sitting there expecting a viscount or a duke and some scrawny functionary had shown up.

Lisa dropped into her easy chair like she'd been dumped out of a truck. They both went back to watching the TV. A lady with French nails and a spray tan was making karo syrup vinaigrette.

I gestured with my clipboard. Neither one of them glanced my way. "I'll go get a reading."

The furnace was in a closet. The seals were just as we'd left them. I stood and looked at them for a good five minutes which gave me the opportunity to work on myself a little. Barry insists that life is educational at bottom. He's always panning for gold, he calls it. Looking for that shine and sparkle in even the most dire and lamentable situations. I'm not as accomplished at it as Barry is. I don't have much of an eye for dazzle. My pan is too frequently full of gravel and silt.

So I wasn't really hoping for much standing there by the furnace beyond keeping myself from having a recreational go at those women. "Never attempt in anger," Barry says, "what you can accomplish in repose."

Giving up on Lisa is always a mournful thing for me, but leaving this one behind was not the brand of trial I usually know.

I stepped back into the TV room and informed Lisa, "You're good."

She had a liter bottle of Coke Zero to her lips. She nodded once and told me, "Urggh."

"I'll let myself," I said.

Her mother didn't even glance my way. The lady on TV was making a cobbler, was opening packages anyway and dumping stuff into an oven dish.

I felt fine by the time I'd reached the truck. I give credit primarily to Barry. He's a good one for helping a guy like me curate his expectations (he calls it). I didn't feel the need to stalk around. Didn't have my usual conniption, which in the past has been a blend of disappointment and unchecked rage. I used to be a bad one for fury, but Barry has calmed me down. Now I'm measured and deliberate. Less emotionally constipated. Lisa was out there. I could be sure of it. I drove all the way home at peace.

Keith has even remarked on the change in me. I was a hothead when we met. Not the sort of hothead who yells at people and insists on a quarrel, but the kind who fills with bile and holds it until the pressure makes it spew. I'd blow up out of nowhere. I could feel it coming, but I'd blindside Keith. At first, he was always sure he'd set me off, and he'd make his sign for "What?"

He opens his mouth and shows me his palms, makes a plaintive noise in his throat.

Sometimes I'd tell him it wasn't him. Too often I'd tell him nothing. Before Barry, rage made me quiet at first. I was a bad one to sit and stew and then explode hours later. Keith went to Mr. Pittman about me after I busted one of our side view mirrors. I beat it off the truck door with my shoe.

We'd stopped for gas, and Keith had gone into the grocery mart to use the bathroom. It was a one-toilet affair and some guy was parked on it, so Keith lingered there by the magazines and watched me have my fit.

He didn't tell me anything when he came back out. He made a point for the balance of the day of leaving his talker on the truck dash and just grunting at me when he had to. Then he went to Mr. Pittman, I came to find out, and wondered if he could switch off in the future. The way I heard it, he even indicated a preference for Hotchkiss and them.

Mr. Pittman called me into his office. It's littered with photos of his homely kids. His bony wife. His rusty-eyed spaniel. A woman who must be Mr. Pittman's mother. She looks just like him except she has less hair.

"Let's walk," he told me before I'd passed entirely through his doorway.

I could tell by the direction we headed in he couldn't talk to me for long. We went through the dispatch room and into the stairwell. As we descended, Mr. Pittman said, "I want you to see somebody for me."

He waited until I'd nodded.

"I think maybe you've got an anger problem, and that troubles me."

The last guy who'd troubled Mr. Pittman had been caught stealing tools. The one before that was pinching creamer and loving up a girl in billing on company time.

"Keith?"

Mr. Pittman nodded. "You scared the boy."

"I'm sorry, sir." I'm good at obsequious when I need to be. "I've got a few things weighing on me. I was having a bad morning."

Mr. Pittman shoved a post-it at me. It had a name scrawled on it and a number.

"Make an appointment," he instructed me. "We're going to nip this in the bud."

We'd reached the men's room door by then. Almost by reflex, I started fishing for Krackel change in my pocket.

"We good?" Mr. Pittman asked me.

Pinched lips. A nod. "We are, sir."

He grunted and laid a palm to the chrome plate on the men's room door.

"Good luck," I told him. When I go toady, I sometimes don't know when to stop.

I called the number pretty immediately. I went out in the lot first and raged. Our office is in an industrial park that never really took hold, so we're surrounded by vacant and half-finished buildings where a man can go to vent if he feels the need to let off some accumulated agitation.

I don't think of myself as a man with an anger problem. I have the odd outburst. Who doesn't? But I don't make a habit of it, and when I bust something up in a fit of passion, it's a side mirror, or a Styrofoam cooler, or there was that coffee table once. Never people. Especially Lisa. I'm always medium cool with her.

I was standing in the shell of an office suite that had briefly been some kind of clinic. Beyond wearing lab coats, I don't know what they did. A few business cards were lying around with the rubbish and the broken glass. ExoChem Labs, and then a couple of names trailing alphabet soup.

I'd busted out a few of the windows myself. Hotchkiss and them had broken out the rest. I have legitimate pressures that build up. They're just Visigoths.

I worked out a strategy for making things right with Keith. I decided to confide I was having trouble with a woman I'd been seeing. Keith likes for people to talk about lady problems with him because his lady problem tends to be fundamental and unchanging. He simply can't nab a lady to have a problem with. So he makes himself content with hearing the rest of us natter on.

I called the number on the post-it Mr. Pittman had given to me. I knew I had the job I needed and didn't want to risk it.

A woman answered but the call dropped out, and I couldn't make out what she said.

"I'm sorry, what was that?"

"Dr. Marlin's office," she told me. "Like the fish."

P.J.

i

I'm not like a reporter or anything. I took English Lit
and Eastern Philosophy. I played intramural field hockey. I
had two years of art history with the state of Virginia's gayest
PhD. He insisted we call him Vincent, and he wore silk
cravats and pocket squares in a bid, I guess, to look clubby.
But there was eye liner as well and nail varnish. His favorite
outburst was "Glorioski!" It never failed to come with
fluttering hands.

Vincent owned a restored farm house in the countryside
up near Daleville. He lived in it with a guy named Hubert
who Vincent always called "my tenant." I guess he did that
for decorum's sake.

Hubert had been peeled and tautened and improved to
the point where he'd developed a curious sheen. He was
originally from West Virginia but spoke with a pan-European
accent, like maybe he was born in the Parisian part of Berlin.
Hubert owned an assortment of pastel velvet sport coats and
never seemed to leave Daleville without one. He was a
fixture on campus, always dropping off Vincent's lunch, and
the two of them would have lively spats where we could all
watch — out in the front quad, in the student union,
especially in the library where they would whisper and hiss.

I was tight at the time with my suite mate, Gwennie.
We'd sit out behind the chapel and smoke her English Ovals.
Gwennie and I were remarkably like minded about who we
didn't care for and why.

Gwennie gave me books by writers I'd not read. I gave her music she'd never heard. We took Vincent's Renaissance class together and threatened to go to Rome. We never did, but we got to Daleville one night for a Vincent and Hubert dinner party. Vincent had taken a shine to me and Gwennie. We sat up front and paid attention. We wanted to know everything Vincent knew. We didn't care how prissy he was or what he and Hubert got up to at home after all their public quarreling. It stood to reason that they made their peace with each other in a tempestuous way as well.

Most of the rest of the students in Vincent's classes were Baptist or something worse. They'd been raised to disapprove of Vincent and Hubert's ilk and remind them, in ways large and small, that they were condemned to damnation. Those girls still smiled and called Vincent "Sir," but he knew well enough it was hollow and self-righteous.

I like to think Vincent noticed that me and Gwennie were different, live and let livers who liked Jesus well enough in theory but kept his brittle, New Testament rubbish out of our hearts. That's why we qualified for a dinner party at Vincent's house. Not one of those sad buffets professors put on once every semester or so but a grown-up Saturday night sit-down meal, and we were the only students there.

Hubert cooked. Vincent made cocktails and massaged the conversation. The other guests were an older guy and his youngish wife. They were antique dealers from Lexington. There was a plump neighbor named Mindy who was full of talk about her dog. He had a parasite Mindy had read up on and held forth about at length. There was a truly peculiar mother and daughter in attendance as well. They spoke to each other almost exclusively in profane baby talk. They'd turn their lips inside out and burble, "Who's a raging bitch?" Or worse.

There was a stag guy as well. If he'd been recruited as a prospect for Mindy, he sure didn't look it. He was a blacksmith with seven fingers and the stink of singed hair about him. He had the pale, weary face of a man who stared into embers all day long. His name was Cal or Hal or something like it. He spoke infrequently and only at modest volume. I'm fairly sure he owned up to having made Vincent and Hubert's fireplace tools.

And then there was me and Gwennie pretending to be jaded like only students whose parents are paying their way to a liberal arts college can. We listened mostly, though Gwinnie held forth about George Gissing for longer than she should have, and we'd retire every now and again with the antique dealer's young, blonde wife to smoke and run down the baby talkers on the screen porch off the kitchen.

We'd brought flowers that we'd pinched from the arboretum. Everybody else had come with wine that Vincent served with a free hand. Consequently, I don't remember awfully much about dinner itself. I had a margarita and two glasses of Cab in me when I went and sat on the toilet where I slept for a quarter hour. Gwennie came to get me. She was in poor shape too. We filled the sink with cold water and took turns sticking our faces in it. There was much art photography in the bathroom, all of it of naked men.

By the time we got back to the dining room, Vincent and Hubert were having one of their quarrels.

The mother and daughter attempted to interrupt in toddlerese. I think they were genuinely hoping to help drain the venom a little, but then Vincent told them, "Shut it!," which set Hubert off afresh.

Those two guys got into everything they didn't have in common. They raged back and forth about bad choices each of them had made, and they took turns making wounded reference to some incident in Dublin. As best I could tell, it had started with sherry and had eventually involved an Irish gentleman or three.

Cal/Hal the blacksmith studied his remaining fingers. Mindy tried to engage him with her parasite, but he was accomplished at staying aloof. The young, blonde wife of the antique dealer looked at me and Gwennine significantly and put her fingers to her lips.

"Awkward," I said once we'd lit up on the porch.

The blonde wife — her name was Tracy — shook her head and told me, "This is what they do."

"With people in the house?" Gwennie asked.

Tracy nodded. "Especially. It's theater."

"So they don't mean it?" I asked her.

"Oh, they mean it. They just do it louder and better than mom and dad ever did."

I thought about my folks sitting in the den with their TV trays saying nothing. Nothing anyway beyond "Would you look at that," when a badger or a sloth or a reticulated python had done something on the nature channel they hadn't imagined it could.

We heard what sounded like breakage. Not glass exclusively but maybe a bit of splintering woodwork as well.

"Here we go," Tracy said.

"Are they fighting?" Gwennie asked her.

Tracy shook her head. "Vincent'll break something of Hubert's. Hubert'll break something back. My Bob'll keep a record, and everything'll get replaced."

"Should we leave?" Gwennie asked.

That struck Tracy as preposterous. "Hubert made flan." Tracy opened the screen door, flicked her butt onto the patio, and then stepped back into the house.

Gwennie asked me before I could ask her, "What's flan?"

Once it was quiet inside for two minutes straight, we went back in as well. The blacksmith was gathering up the splinters of something — big chunks of varnished wood — and shoving them into a shopping bag.

Hubert told us brightly, "Sit."

Vincent grabbed another bottle of red from the sideboard and circled the table pouring. I tried to cover my glass with my hand, but Vincent snorted and told me, "Child."

Hubert's flan was runny, but Vincent didn't complain. He went the other way and defended it against a baby-talk pile on.

Then the blacksmith started making his gotta-go noises. He grunted and shifted until he finally located the nerve to stand. Mindy used him as cover to leave us as well, which gave rise to one more round of parasitic commentary since she had to go home and give her dog his pill.

Bob the antique dealer told Tracy, "Well." Once they'd made their manners to Hubert and Vincent, Bob asked the mother/daughter, "Don't you have to be burped or something?"

That got him some inside out lips, but they decided to leave as well.

Gwennie was helping Hubert clear the table by then. She turned out to be that type of girl who was always pitching in. That was hardly the side of her she was given to showing off on campus, but at Hubert and Vincent's Gwennie did heroic duty cleaning up.

Hubert was delighted to let her. He stayed with her in the kitchen and smoked (by the smell of it) hash. I felt duty bound to offer to assist, but Vincent kept me at the table. It was just him and me at their elegant mahogany dining table with fewer and fewer soiled dishes on it as Gwennie carted them off.

"So what's the plan?" Vincent asked.

"You mean like . . . ?" I think I raised a finger and pointed towards what I let serve for the immediate future.

"Where are you going be in five years? Ten years?"

"Oh." I think I shrugged. "Is there coffee?"

Vincent shouted towards the kitchen, "Java for the girls?"

Gwennie called back, "I'll make it."

"She's way helpful, isn't she?" I said.

"News to you?"

I nodded. "You should see her room. It's a . . . midden." That was one of our words just then. I tried to get up and gather dessert plates, but Vincent told me, "Sit."

He poured me more wine. I didn't want to drink it, but I needed something to do with my fidgety hands, and holding a wine glass helped.

"Grad school?"

"Doubt it."

"What then?"

"I don't really know."

"No idea at all?"

"Maybe a museum or something." Clearly I was scrounging. Foggy. Nervous. Eager to please Vincent.

"Doing what?"

I had given it zero thought. "You know. Stuff."

He exhaled theatrically. "Let Uncle Vincent help."

I missed my mouth with my wine glass and then nodded at Vincent and caught the rim with my teeth.

"I was going to be a concert pianist," Vincent said. "I was going to be a dancer. Broadway. I was going to design women's clothes. I was going to be a painter. I was going to be a restorer. I was going to be a Sotheby's auctioneer. I was even going to own a tasteful boutique. Men's accoutrements. Maybe housewares. Paper goods. Who the hell knows?"

"Did you paint that?" I pointed at a smallish canvas hanging beside a hutch. It had caught my eye earlier. Modern. Slashes of color. Interesting but amateurish at the same time. Vincent glanced at the thing.

"No, child," he said.

Gwennie brought us coffee, served us coffee really. She carried in cups and sugar and cream and the steaming carafe on a tray.

"Need help?" I moved to stand up.

Vincent told me, "Sit."

I decided Vincent had some pithy scrap of wisdom he wanted to convey. But he was sure circling around it, and he didn't let up once Gwennie had gone back into the kitchen.

"I was adrift," he said. "I'd stuck to nothing. I was nothing. Just a tangle of cultural impulses. Know the feeling?"

"About being nothing? Sure."

"No, child. The pull. The passion. What do you love more than anything?"

I was just loaded enough to not be bothered to consider and calculate. "Elmore," I said, "and Charlotte Bronte."

"Who's Elmore Bronte?"

"No. Elmore's my dog. Back home. He's old. We got him when I was six. He's arthritic. His teeth are rotten. He smells like a . . ."

"Midden?"

I had to hand it to Vincent. His snark was always professional grade.

"Nothing else?"

"I could make a list in the morning."

"Nothing right here?" He reached over to tap my forehead.

I loved Graham crackers just then. I was kind of living on them, but that impressed me as less of a passion than a dietary miscalculation. I shrugged. I shook my head. "That's about it."

"What have you quit on?" Vincent wanted to know.

I might have been only twenty years old at the time, but I had quit on plenty already. I'd come off being a ballerina before I was even seven or eight. A veterinarian (largely Elmore related). A civil engineer (what one of my uncles did). A foreign ambassador (I'd seen a movie or something). An oceanographer. A forensic nurse (I think I was confused). A gorilla theatre actress and/or playwright and/ or prop girl. A grade school teacher (I'd volunteered as an assistant for a week). A librarian (too much course work). Some kind of secular nun.

I'd ended up at something will come along, which I was clinging too at the time.

"The usual stuff," I told Vincent. "And now I'm down to Elmore Bronte."

"What do your parents want for you?"

My mom knew a woman who managed a Rack Room in Wytheville. She felt sure I could get on there. "I don't know," I told Vincent.

"I didn't either," Vincent allowed. "Aside from knowing they wanted me straight."

I could hear Hubert and Gwennie cackling in the kitchen. It didn't sound like they were doing much good with the dishes anymore.

"I did quite a lot of half trying," Vincent told me. "Half practicing piano. Half rehearsing. Half painting. Half designing. Like that."

That sounded familiar. I was accomplished at going half in.

"Here's my advice to you." Vincent refilled his tiny glass. He'd moved on to grappa. "Gwen too."

"Gwennie!" I shouted. She showed up in the doorway.

"What?" she said.

I pointed at Vincent.

"Fail" —he raised his glass — "at full throttle." Vincent knocked back his grappa and chuffed. "Capisce?"

Vincent's advice struck me, even at the very moment, as a decent course of action. Try hard or don't bother. Be dogged or stay in bed.

Then Hubert showed up in the kitchen. He looked at Gwennie. At me. At Vincent who'd picked up the delicate handblown grappa bottle and was about to fill his tiny glass again.

"Fail at full throttle?" Hubert asked us. "It's that time already?"

He giggled when we nodded.

Vincent swore in French. He threw his grappa glass and hit Hubert in the head.

ii

I lied to them at the Action/Weather/News! station and then waited for somebody to find me out, but nobody ever did. I didn't stretch the truth about me awfully much. I gave myself two internships I'd never really had. I needn't have worried. The guy who hired me in Richmond was in the middle of a divorce and was distracted.

Once he'd glanced at my application he asked me, "When a woman says, 'You're not equipped to meet my needs,' what does she really mean?"

"I can't be sure," I told him. "What do you think she means?" I'd learned how to do that in psych class.

"Well." He tossed my paperwork aside and rocked back in his desk chair. "It all started with Hot Yoga."

I just sat there and looked interested for the next twenty minutes or so.

I started out tending to the mail and picking up lattes and lunch, but I kept after Hot Yoga until he put me on the blog. I was hoping to get a piece on air about a woman east of Richmond who got locked in a tool shed for nearly eight months by a couple cashing her government checks. They kept her alive on canned food — most anything with a pop top. They'd toss in a new house dress every couple of weeks and change out her five gallon waste bucket less frequently than that.

Those two hadn't counted on the meter reader. He was an extraordinary talker. Dominion Power had done everything they could to streamline his job and isolate him. The meters had all been fitted with transmitters, so he didn't even need to get out of his truck. The idea was he could drive slow on the road and his receiver would take the reading, but that hardly suited Mr. T. Larry Bly of Moody, Virginia.

"Kind of a people business," he told me.

I interviewed him in his yard. We were sitting in Adirondack chairs he'd made out of leftover treated decking. T. Larry had designed them to fold. He showed me hinges he'd bought. They were still in their plastic bags.

"I get in a hurry," he said to explain why he'd knocked those chairs together with nails. Why they sat crooked and felt like they were bordering on collapse.

"Right," I told him.

I was spanking new to interviews when I landed my chat with T. Larry. So I did a lot of hoping he'd keep on talking. I did a lot of telling him just, "Right."

T. Larry spoiled me. He had no conversational governor, no discretion to speak of, no editorial sense. He talked about everything in no particular order. I got a full accounting of T. Larry's entire meter-reading route.

"Drunk boy took a shot at me once. Had his gun out with the bullets in it. Wrong place, wrong time, you know?"

"Right."

"Can't fault him. Boy's got troubles."

T. Larry was merciful that way. He could forgive most anything that was hardship inspired.

"People can't take but so much," he explained.

T. Larry had finally missed the woman locked in her back tool shed. "I told myself, 'T, you ain't seen her.' And I knew I wouldn't leave there until I had."

"Right."

"Went knocking on her door," he told me. "They want me staying in the truck and all, but I'm a boots on the ground kind of guy. They're customers, you know."

I nodded. "With troubles."

"Some of them. Mostly just getting along as best they might."

"Right."

"There's an old Buick that sits out in her yard, but I don't think she drives. The senior bus comes round and picks them all up. Takes them to the grocery and the Rexall. Like that."

"Right."

"I remember going through there and seeing some other woman on the porch."

"Erlene Odom."

"Says you. Told me her name was Alice. Said the lady . . ."

"Mrs. Grimes."

"Was off in Richmond getting an operation. Female, she told me. I figure now that was just to shut me up."

"It work?"

"Oh yeah. There's some things even I won't talk about."

"Right."

"I think even at the time I only maybe half believed her. I've been around too many sorts of people. I've got a nose for trash."

"So you came back a month later?"

He nodded. "Called a boy I know in between. I thought he was still a deputy, but he'd gotten on at Tractor Supply. The one way up by Mechanicsville. Hell if I'd make that drive."

"Right."

"He said he'd call a guy he knew and get him to swing on by. Maybe he did. I don't know. I didn't hear a thing about it."

"So third time around . . .?"

"Went right up and knocked. Couldn't raise anybody. Circled around like I was checking the meter."

"What made you go to the shed?"

"I could smell her. Should have been just tools and mess in there, but there was some other kind of stink."

"Right."

"I figured she was dead, and she probably almost was. All piled up back in a corner. Cans all over the place. Bucket of . . . business." T. Larry was polite that way. "Never seen anything like it. Hope never to again."

"So you called the authorities?"

He nodded. "Cops. Ambulance. Firehouse. The works."

"And those two came after you? Erlene Grimes and . . ." I checked my notes. ". . . Anthony Reginald Dance?"

T. Larry nodded. "Telling me I was trespassing and mess. People like that'll say any damn thing."

"Right."

"I wasn't really meaning to hit that boy with a shovel, but I couldn't be bothered to care much once I did."

"He's suing you, isn't he?"

"Says he is. Talks it up every chance he gets, but nobody's served me papers yet. I kind of doubt he'll make it go."

"How's Mrs. Grimes?"

"About like she was. Took it all a lot better than I would. Locked up in her own shed. A bucket for a commode." T. Larry shook his head. "Like I said, I'm fine with people and all, but sometimes they'll disappoint you."

"Right."

"Look there." T. Larry pointed at what turned out to be a buzzard. It was perched on a limb glaring at us as if it had reason to expect a violent calamity with T. Larry's makeshift Adirondack chairs.

iii

I conducted a long interview with Mrs. Grimes as well. Not productive. Just long. I had to ask every question three times. She could hear a little, so that wasn't entirely the problem. Unlike T. Larry Bly, Mrs. Grimes simply wasn't the chin wagging sort. Worse still, for my purposes, she was humble and modest in that Jesusy way that kept her from even describing the ordeal she'd been through because our Lord and Savior had suffered so much worse.

"I'm told you were shut up for one hundred and twelve days, as best as anybody can figure. Did you ever give up?" I asked her.

"Let up?"

"Give up."

"Oh."

"Did you?"

"Those who hope in the Lord will renew their strength. They'll soar on wings like Eagles."

"That's a 'No'?"

We were sitting on her front porch at the time. She pointed at the beaded ceiling. "Praise Him," she said.

"Right." That was about as good as it got.

The grifter couple had a colorful past, like grifter couples will. And they were independently entertaining in their utter shamelessness. I talked to them separately. By the time I got permission, they were about to go to trial. Their public defenders were working in tandem on a PR assault intended to undo the misconception that their clients were devious rascals.

"Ain't nothing to that," Erlene Odom told me. "We rented that house on Craigslist."

"Who from?"

She was vague on the details. "Ask Tony. He does all that stuff."

I did ask Tony. He told me, "Some guy."

They were gifted at making out to seem wounded and pitiful and put upon. They didn't know anything about government checks. Tony, the way they told it, was an entrepreneur of means.

"Doing what?" I asked them each.

"Computer stuff," Erlene told me.

"Finance. Like that," Tony said. He was picking his teeth with a matchstick at the time.

It was instructive to talk to the pair of them, especially separately and in turn, because I got to see two variations on lowlife cracker chutzpah. The facts didn't matter. It was the attitude that counted. They weren't belligerent about anything but just determined and unyielding. Erlene would contradict you. You were wrong and she'd say why. Tony liked to pretend you'd told him things you never had, and then he'd agree with all the stuff you'd never said.

Before I met the pair of them, I'd tried to be scrupulous about sticking to the truth when it mattered. I wasn't above fiction, God knows, but I sided with the facts when I could. Erlene and Tony taught me how to keep your eyes on your destination and find a way to get there any way you can. They'd never put a woman in a shed. They'd rented that house online. They didn't know anything about cashing social security checks, and people who said they did had things all wrong.

A yardman named Billy or something was the only one in and out of the shed. He had a scar. He drove a truck. He was from Norfolk or somewhere. If the police would track him down, then they could figure the whole thing out.

"Who'd lock an old woman in a tool shed and feed her beans and weenies?" If those two asked me that once, they asked me four dozen times.

They were so very accomplished and pitiful and put upon, they made it hard to believe they had capacity left to be rascals as well.

They clearly intended to confuse their jury. It was all they needed to do. By the time I got involved in the story, they were a week away from trial, and I got Hot Yoga's permission to attend the proceedings at the New Kent County courthouse where the local prosecutor tried his damnedest to seat a jury of Erlene and Tony's peers.

I watched the whole process from the back of the courtroom. Most of the jurors keen to serve weren't remotely fit to do it, and the ones with brains and discretion had excuses and lawful outs. I looked on as Erlene and Tony told their legal aid guy who to take and who to exclude, and I watched them whittle the pool down to a dozen hard luck stories.

The whole trial took just a day and a half. The prosecutor wore a brown suit and dirty wire-framed glasses. You could see his fingerprints all over the lenses whenever the sun caught him right. He talked to the jurors like they were children. Even back where I was sitting, I could see them bristling. Glancing at each other. Shifting in their seats.

"They'll tell you somebody else got up to everything we're here for." Then he'd pause to study the jurors and nod. He wouldn't go on until they'd nodded back. "They'll tell you they didn't sign those checks and take them to the bank even though we've got four tellers here who'll say they watched them do it." Another nod. Another pause. Shifty, glancing, grumbling jurors.

Erlene and Tony's public defender got up and told the Craigslist story. He had plenty to say about Billy, the yardman with the truck and the scar.

"I don't see him here," that lawyer said as he studied us out in the pews. "Once my clients came to hand, the police guessed that was good enough. Went back to writing tickets. Riding the roads. Sitting in the Hardee's like they do."

More juror grumbling but of the sympathetic stripe. They'd all either paid a traffic fine or knew somebody who'd had.

Then that lawyer called Erlene and Tony in turn to give their testimony, and if we have an American equivalent of The Royal Shakespeare company, it's surely indicted Southerners explaining how their charges are all wrong.

Tony and Erlene went at it with more economy than most. She got called first and told where she and Tony had met and how. There was a teary bit about Erlene's miscarriage and Tony losing his job at the plant. A metal fabrication works in Circleville, Ohio.

"He gave them ten good years, and they just shoved him out the door."

Erlene could get moist without going weepy. She gave the impression of a woman who was determined to be strong. I had to think she'd learned from experience that would produce the more potent effect, and she never once blotted a tear from her eyes. She just let them drip whenever they came.

She couldn't say why the women from the bank would testify against them. She'd leave the Lord to sift their motives. It was a thing the Lord did well.

Erlene had nothing but kind, compassionate words for the victim, Mrs. Grimes. The woman was addled. No doubt about that. But the poor creature was blameless for it, and she couldn't truly be held to account for thinking Erlene and

Tony had harmed her. She probably wouldn't want to go against her yardman from Norfolk even if she was right in the head.

"He scared me," Erlene confessed. "I don't mind saying. My daddy was a hard sort. He did awful things to people." She let a tear fall. It was a cinematic, judicious sort of thing. Erlene blinked, and it dropped off her lashes, caught the light like a gemstone.

"Not much good I can say about him." It came out almost in a whisper. "But he was my daddy, after all."

Her lawyer laid a hand upon her forearm. He had some thespian in him too.

"I don't blame Mrs. Grimes," Erlene said, "after all the awful stuff she's been through. And me and Tony have been in and out of that bank, so it's no wonder those women got us confused."

"It happens," her lawyer said. Then he turned to the jury. "I see it all the time."

"We're here to get this straightened out." Erlene smiled at the jurors. "Wouldn't have it any other way."

Then Erlene and Tony's lawyer yielded to the prosecutor who got up in his blue suit and his brown shoes, his dirty glasses and his necktie as wide as a garden spade. He made an artless show of being cynical over everything he'd heard. It involved quite a lot of contemptuous snorting as he closed on the docket, shaking his head.

"Ma'am," he started, "you could half persuade a fellow you've never seen the inside of a courtroom before."

Tony and Erlene's lawyer had gotten their criminal records excluded. News that they'd been up to no good in a half dozen states might well have poisoned the jury pool. Their lawyer popped up, but the judge waved him off.

"Move on," he told the prosecutor.

That guy propped himself against the railing in front of Erlene and spent the next half hour trying whatever he could to make her mad. He got objected at by his counterpart and cautioned by the judge, and for all of that he never earned even an irritated glance from the defendant.

Erlene would just smile his way when he was uncommonly insulting. She cited scripture at him. Luke. I looked it up. "Do not judge, and you will not be judged. Do not condemn, and you will not be condemned. Forgive, and you will be forgiven."

That lawyer smirked by way of response. Not just at Erlene but at Tony too and then at the jury as well. He threw out his arms with his palms upturned as if to say, "You hearing this?" That was the moment I realized why justice hardly ever prevails. Everything's theater in the end, and the truly lawful and decent and righteous have got no business on the stage. Trodding the boards is only for practiced charlatans and frauds.

The case was lost before Tony took the stand. He might have been even more accomplished than his wife. I say his "wife." It turned out they weren't legally married, at least not to each other, which the county attorney attempted to give them both some guff about.

Tony dealt with the facts of the case like Erlene had. He placidly insisted they weren't facts at all.

"That Craigslist man was a Dooley. Went by initials. W. J."

"Got cancelled rent checks?"

Tony winced and shook his head. "Had to take him cash first of the month."

"Take it where?"

"Food Lion parking lot."

"So you don't know where he lives?"

"No sir."

"Got a number for him?"

Tony shook his head. "Just called him the once. I bet you can find him on the internet somewhere."

And on it went like that until Tony had built a case against that lawyer. The implication was that Tony and Erlene wouldn't be charged and no jury would be impaneled if that prosecutor had done a little Googling and come in with his facts straightened out.

Three or four times, I saw Erlene physically restrain her attorney. She did it on the sly and down below the table top, but from where I was sitting I could see her grab her lawyer by the coat sleeve and hold him in place when he wanted to object. The only thing he could do was get in the way of the juggernaut Tony was riding.

The whole business was less a criminal matter by then than a difference of opinion. Erlene and Tony had scuttled the civic indignation, had cast doubt on everything that had been said or written about them. Then Mrs. Grimes got up, all frail and addled, and tried to testify. She was so unhelpful as a witness that Tony and Erlene's lawyer didn't even take his turn with Mrs. Grimes.

With an air of moist sadness, he said, "I've no questions for this witness."

The jury stayed out for an hour and a half, and part of that was lunch. They were earning twelve dollars a day, meals included, and they weren't about to miss one by reaching a verdict in a snap.

One of the Jesusy jurors had been elected forewoman. She handed the verdict card to the judge who glanced at it and snorted before offering it back. There was a raft of charges and no convictions on even the tacked-on trifles.

The prosecutor chose to poll the jurors. "Is this your verdict?" he asked them each in turn.

They were all firm and loud about it. They'd acquitted and were proud.

I waited outside the New Kent courthouse for Tony and Erlene. I wanted to see what they said, what they looked like, now that they'd been exonerated. I think I was hoping for at least some residue of shame. I should have known better. All I got was practiced humility seasoned with Scripture.

I put a regular story pitch together, wrote up a script of savory details, and scheduled an actual meeting with Hot Yoga and the news director at the station.

They heard me out. I carried on for a solid twenty minutes. I showed them photos I'd taken. I played them lively snippets of interviews. I punched up the drama as best I could, but I was counting on human predators with the moral impulses of coyotes not needing too terribly much help from me.

When I finished they both nodded and glanced at each other in a consulting sort of way.

"Good. Great," the editorial director (he was Doug to everybody else but usually Mr. Sorenson to me) said to his coffee cup primarily.

"A pin in it?" Hot Yoga asked him.

"We'll circle back."

"We've got that package from network. The whale thing."

"Whale thing?" I asked.

"Florida or somewhere," Hot Yoga told me. "An Orca chewed up a girl."

"Kill her?" Doug asked.

"Hanging on."

"Mine'll keep," I allowed. "Next week maybe? Whenever you've got a slot."

"But a pin for now," Hot Yoga said, and the two of them nodded at me.

"Okay to tease it on the blog?" I asked them.

That didn't even require a glance. They didn't care about the blog. It was a sensible attitude to have. Nobody cared about the blog. We got hits when we posted videos of calamities and cats, but the news items largely went unread. The comments they'd generate usually ran towards "My sister earns $1,000 a week at home."

So I wrote up the story and posted it. Six people clicked on the entry in the course of a day and a half. I got one indignant comment. It was from "Midlothian Momma" who found my promiscuous use of commas and dashes more than she could bear.

From then on, I did what they wanted me to do. What choice did I have really? I kept the blog heavily populated with critter/jet crash videos and celebrity trash. If there was a starlet baby bump reported somewhere on the planet, I'd post all the purloined selfies I could gather and a paragraph or two of wanton speculation with enough ellipses and slashes and exclamation marks to drive the likes of Midlothian Momma barking mad.

It was all piffle. The stuff I was keen on lay elsewhere and ran far deeper. So I divided myself between what paid the rent and what scratched the itches I had. I'm sure everybody does that to an extent, but I had to learn to do it. I'd been sent out in the world with expectations that I'd get hired to work at something I loved. Naive, I know, but that was my fancy private-school liberal-arts thinking.

I met Fig Dalton by chance in a bar one night. He had family in Richmond, and he owned up to being a uniformed cop in some Shenandoah backwater called Waynesboro. I told him about Mrs. Grimes with her bucket in her tool shed. I was still chapped back then over the story getting squashed.

"No corpse," Fig explained to me. "Not even an amputation."

"I was going for the uplift?"

"Old deaf woman gets to be an old deaf woman again?"

"Well, if you put it that way . . ."

"You need a story with some blood, some carnage to it. That'll get you on the air."

I nodded. I drank. "No kidding."

"And I just might be able to help you."

That's when he told me about a horsewoman (he called her), long dead but only lately found hacked up in the woods.

"Just bones," he said. "She was missing three or four years. Got snatched at a pullout, a spot up by the Blue Ridge Parkway."

"Who was she?"

He could tell I was keen. He smiled. "See?" he said. "Carnage." He plucked some party mix out of the bar bowl, thought better of it and put it back. Fig jabbed his thumb in a direction I took for west. "Lot of rot out there," he said.

Buck

i

The guy I rent from calls my house a cottage so he can charge quaint cottage rates. I'm convinced it was once a tractor shed due to the nagging fertilizer bouquet. I heat the place with a wood stove to save money on bottled gas, which means me and Mabel spend more time in the forest with a chainsaw than either one of us would like.

Mabel doesn't have a lot interest in nature. Squirrels antagonize her, and she had an unfortunate encounter with a groundhog a couple of years back. She'd hoped he'd run when she charged him. He did but in the wrong direction. Now Mabel prefers the truck, so when I say we go in the woods, I mean I get out with the chainsaw while she watches me from the cab .

I'm sure I'll lay myself open one day. I routinely get up to the sort of timbering I've got no business doing. There's always plenty of wood about on the ground, but I can never resist the leaners -- those windblown trees all pitched and cocked and ready to make me an afterthought.

The week after I chased down Kiki's friends, I drove out to a stand of oaks and poplars a guy I helped out lets me plunder. He had a wife and has a brother, and they were up to no good together in a Best Western at one of the clotted exits on Interstate 64. They weren't terribly discreet about it. They usually embraced in the parking lot and entered the lobby as a couple. They had a favorite room the day clerk held back for them when he could.

Then the wife finally crossed a line, and like most lines in a marriage, it wouldn't have seemed like much at all to somebody outside peering in. Apparently, she baked a nectarine cobbler and tried to serve it to her husband who was obliged to remind her he was the brother with the stone fruit allergy. The other one was the nectarine lover, the one that she was regularly bedding. And that little bit of business proved somehow more than the husband could take.

I emailed him incriminating snapshots not even a full week later, so now I have permission to cut wood on his plot of land when my pile gets low. I do my best thinking when I'm out with my chainsaw, and this occasion I had Kiki Dunbar on my mind. I was working on the assumption she'd been in the wrong place at precisely the wrong moment. I'd seen quite a lot of the wages of poor timing in my career. People shot or stabbed or run down in the road because they'd happened to be where they were, had arrived there by chance at precisely the instant that was sure to doom them.

That sort of thing is common in a city like New York where there are plenty of people ripe to get unlucky and countless ways to have your life go wrong. In a berg like Afton, that brand of bad timing is monumentally rarer. Girls go out walking every day and come back home unscathed.

I knew what the cops thought about the case and how they'd come to think it. Their opinions and conclusions where all in the notes and file. I was planning on hunting down the suspects next until I saw some moss on the back of a log I was cutting and remembered the Boy Scout troop. I'd been a Scout, and the only thing I'd learned was which side of a tree moss grows on.

"I ought to talk to them," I shouted to Mabel over the idling hum of my saw.

She took her usual interest, which is to say not any.

According to Phelps, those Scouts had spent four or five days on the scene scouring the woods. I had to think if I could locate one, I might get a fresh perspective, and Phelps put me on the trail of a former Scout in Staunton.

Rolfe Loftis was twenty-two now and managed his family's jewelry store. When I reached him by phone and told him what I was up to, he said, "Oh," with the thrill and tone of a man who'd been asked for a sizable loan.

I don't drive out into the valley much and so hadn't ever visited Staunton. I expected the usual bedraggled and interstate-bypassed town, but the community board or somebody had taken pains to dress the place up. They'd buried the power lines and bricked the sidewalks, had worked to fill their vacant storefronts with decent restaurants and tidy shops.

The girl who greeted me at the jewelry store went back and fetched her boss. He was essentially running an engagement ring boutique with a bit of crystal as a sideline. There was a dandruffy watch repairman at a workbench in the far corner. He kept looking over and studying me through his loop.

Rolfe Loftis was short and doughy and dressed in a suit. He had the kind of hair I used to have -- all cowlicky and unruly -- and his glasses sat cockeyed on his nose no matter how he adjusted and fiddled with them.

"Mr. Buck?" he said.

"Just Buck," I told him.

"Rolfe Loftis." His handshake was all fingers. "And you're working for Mr. Dunbar?"

I nodded.

"Worst week of my life. You eaten?"

I hadn't.

"Come on, then."

I followed him out the door.

We ended up in a luncheonette on a side street near the library. The menus were laminated and the prices were stuck in 1975.

"Mind the counter?"

I didn't. My stool seat was duct taped. A black waitress in a baby blue smock and splattered apron came straight over with a glass of iced tea for Rolf.

"Sweetie?" she asked me.

"Coffee."

"He's having the meatloaf sandwich," she told me. "You?"

That seemed as safe as anything. "Make that two."

We weren't the only the patrons in the place, but everybody else was in booths along the big front window.

"Is it common around here for scouts to help with a police investigation?"

"The troop leader -- Mr. Metz -- was some kind of cop groupie. Couldn't make the force. Couldn't let it go."

"So you helped more than once?"

Rolfe nodded. He sipped his iced tea and then pulled a napkin out of the holder so he could blot the formica dry. "There was a big pile up on Afton one time, and we helped detour the traffic. Then a little boy went missing out by Grottoes, and Mr. Metz had us over there too."

"Find him?"

He nodded. "In a washtub. Drowned."

"That's one hell of way to go scouting," I said.

"We quit all that after that girl."

"Did you know her?"

Rolfe shook his head. "I think she went to Western or somewhere."

"Where did you look for her exactly?"

"Up off Three Notched. Between there and the Parkway. We probably covered two hundred acres of woods."

"What kind of instructions did they give you?"

"Look for anything out of place. We'd stop and raise our hands and one of the policemen would come over. See what we had. Bag it sometimes. Leave it sometimes too."

My coffee was unburnt and flavorful, which spoke pretty well of Staunton. Our meatloaf sandwiches arrived open faced and drowned in genuine gravy. Rolf's order came with a hand towel that he tucked in his collar and wore like a bib.

"And you were out there for what? A couple of days?"

"More like a week," he told me. "Mr. Metz got bit by a copperhead. They let us off after that."

"Did they tell you anything about the case? Did you pick up any details while you were out there?"

"The guy in charge . . . the detective . . ."

"Phelps."

"Yeah. He showed us a photo of her. He said she'd been out for a walk. Didn't get where she was going and never came home. We heard them talking like she'd been snatched off the road. They seemed to think she was dead."

"The cops?"

He nodded.

"Do you remember what you found? A week in the woods. You must have found all sorts of things."

"Trash mostly."

Rolfe was positively Edwardian with a fork and knife. Precise and attentive to his shirt cuffs and his coat sleeves. That gravy was going in his mouth or staying on the plate.

"A shoe, I think. Some kind of hair clip. Trash. Candy wrappers. Like that."

"So how exactly," I finally asked Rolfe Loftis, "was this the worst week of your life?"

He rested his knife and fork carefully on the rim of his plate. He dabbed at his lips with his hand towel as he worked it free from his collar. He folded it up. Unsatisfied, he folded it again.

"The last day we were there," he said, "they brought this man over from somewhere. We were up the slope, but we could see him. They had him down by a little creek."

"A suspect?"

He nodded. "A black guy. They had him handcuffed, and he was kind of a mess."

"A mess how?"

"His shirt was ripped." Rolf studied the greasy wall clock above the iced tea hopper. "He didn't have any shoes on. Just socks. And one of his eyes was puffy."

"Like he'd been punched?"

He nodded. "And they were shoving him around. Kicking him, you know? Didn't seem to care who saw it."

"Was Detective Phelps involved?"

He nodded. "Then Mr. Metz stepped on a snake."

The waitress brought the check, and I took it from her.

"Is Mr. Metz still around?"

Rolfe shook his head. "Heart attack." He looked half tempted to fold his towel again. "I just wanted to go camping, you know? Build fires. Make lean-tos." He shook his head. "Kids in washtubs," he muttered.

I had the girl at the jewelry counter put a new battery in my watch because I was there and because they had one in stock. Her boss and I took leave of each other while she was fiddling with it.

"Got any ideas on what happened to Kiki Dunbar?" I asked him. "Heard anything about her since?"

"Nothing worth repeating." He offered his limp fingers. "I don't want to know if you find her bones."

ii

Abby Phelps had parked her green Miata around back, and I found her sitting in a patio chair fooling with her cellphone when I came home from Staunton.

"There you are."

She stood up and lifted her coat tails to brush off the seat of her slacks and to show me, I guess, her sleek, gym-sculpted backside. The lacquer on her nails was gumball green, and she fluttered the fingers of her free hand in the general direction of my junky backyard.

"Somebody ought to pick up," she suggested.

I surveyed the sticks and the leaves and the trash. The pair of rusted out lawnmower carcasses. "Yeah," I allowed. "Somebody should."

"You going to have me in or what?" She drew her coat open to show me her blouse front. "Look at these nips. I'm cold."

Mabel liked her straightaway, which made me even more suspicious of Abby. Mabel has atrocious taste in people. She'd been terribly fond of the fuel oil guy who I caught plundering through the guest-room closet. And she'd adored the gloomy brunette, the self harmer I'd met at the farmer's market. It hardly mattered to Mabel that girl rarely said a thing to her beyond "Move."

Mabel leaned against Abby Phelps, who didn't appear to mind the drool, or the clumps of hair, the landfill breath, the grandpa's-having-a-sitdown brand of groaning.

"Isn't she sweet?"

"Not really."

Abby kneaded Mabel's scruffy head and told her, "Don't listen to him."

"You want coffee or something?"

"Got anything stronger?"

I checked the refrigerator. "A kombucha somebody left here. An inch of Chardonnay from Christmas."

"What somebody?" The woman had been in my house two minutes and was laying claim to me already.

I shrugged like I couldn't remember even though I knew the self-harmer had left it. She'd been a patchouli-scented, comprehensively tattooed kombucha nut. We'd had a bit of authentic fun before she'd gotten into my razor blades.

"Hippie girl?"

I nodded. "I'm all about the pit hair."

That raised a stage snort from Abby. She pointed at a dinette chair. "You mind?"

She parked herself. Straightened my stack of paper napkins. Rearranged my toothpicks. Shifted my salt and pepper shakers to suit her.

"You sure shook Ellie up," she said.

"How so?"

"He had some rocky years back then."

"Oh?"

"That Chardonnay's from when exactly?"

The wine looked silty. I poured it out in the sink and fetched the bottle of kombucha. I set it down before Abby on the dinette. Cosmic Cranberry!

"I'd shake it up. A lot."

"Can a girl at least have a glass?"

I plucked one out of the drainer. She poured and sipped and grimaced.

"How are your nips now?" I asked her.

Abby blotted her lipstick with one of my napkins. "Perky."

We steeped in the sexual tension for a moment.

"What's your husband got to be nervous about?"

I took off my jacket and tossed it towards the coat hook on the wall by the door. Usually I miss, and it piles up on the linoleum, but it snagged this time on the peg and stayed. I did a fair job of not acting surprised.

"You're interesting," Abby told me. I had to think she meant that — for the region — I was odd.

In this part of the world, people fit into slots. The place is populated primarily with locals who never left. They root for the Redskins and the Braves. They drive Fords or Chevys, the occasional Dodge, and wouldn't switch from one to the other with a machete to their throats. They went to Virginia Tech if they went anywhere. They live in boxy manufactured homes on the tree streets in Waynesboro or so close to the Richmond road in Afton that passing semis rattle their windows. What they haven't spent on vehicles, hunting gear, and televisions, they've invested in lawn tractors and pleasure boats, and they give every indication of being perfectly content.

Then there are the outlanders who've arrived with their wealth and ambition to make a life in semi-retirement on a fine old sprawling Virginia estate. They've brought about the gourmet food shops. The coffee bars and nicknack boutiques. Their livestock is all cosmetic. You could eat off the floors of their barns.

The rest of us are just stopping by for a bit. We rent or (worse) sublet. We don't get to know our neighbors. We fail to surrender our out-of-state tags. We can't tell a Wahoo from a Gobbler. We've been to Monticello once and then only because somebody made us go. We're "interesting" the way a pretty bug might be just before you squash it.

"Ellie says you're from New York."

"Roanoke," I said. "Worked in New York."

"I saw a Broadway show once." Another sip. A wince. "Flew up. Flew back. Don't remember a thing about it."

"The city?"

"The show." She paused to think more deeply on the experience. "The guy kept taking his shirt off. He had enormous teeth."

"That's two things."

Abby gave me a frank once over from my cowlick to my instep. I got a sly, salacious smile. "I bet you're trouble."

"Sometimes," I told her, "but I tend to leave wives alone."

That proved precisely the wrong thing to say. She was clearly a woman who liked a challenge. Abby was built to make men stupid, and I was hardly immune to that.

"I'm not here for that. Don't be so cocky."

"Then what are you here for?"

"To make sure you don't make trouble for us. I might not love him like I ought to, but Ellie's mine."

"What sort of trouble are you worried about?"

"Can I trust you?"

"You kind of already have."

She drew a show breath before confessing, "Ellie's got dirt on him, and you're just the man to turn it up."

I didn't say anything back. Didn't need to.

"It's got nothing to do with that missing girl, but it was all going on right there together."

"How do you know it's got nothing to do with the girl?"

"Ellie says so. I believe him."

"You want to fill me in a little."

"Why don't I give you this instead." She dug an envelope out of her purse and laid it on my dinette table. I'd seen enough of this sort of thing on the job. A half inch of money, as best I could tell.

I was going to inform her I couldn't be bought, but since I wasn't a civil servant anymore, I had to think I was probably up for purchase.

"Leave Ellie out of it. He did his best for her."

"Then what's with that?" I pointed at the money.

"I don't know you well enough to ask you for a favor."

I couldn't help but notice I didn't attempt to give the envelope back. Abby seemed to notice that as well.

"Shame about you and wives," she told me and leaned in to kiss me, I expected, on the cheek. Instead she clamped my earlobe between her teeth and nipped it.

"Toodles," she said as she let herself out.

"Yeah," I managed. "Toodles." But she was in her car by then.

iii

I didn't bother to open the envelope but laid it in my night table drawer right between my flashlight and my .38.

"I'll do just what I was going to do," I told myself and Mabel both. That meant tracking down the suspects Ellsworth Phelps had corralled. I figured I'd start with Raijaun Howard, like I'd planned. To my way of thinking, if I didn't change at all what I was up to, then I couldn't have been paid off and bought.

Mr. Howard didn't prove much of a challenge to locate. He lived out towards Port Republic and worked part time around Dooms hauling fertilizer. Or he rode anyway in the truck with a boy who needed an extra hand for his spreader that was balky and corroded and stayed about half jammed up.

I swung by the address I'd found online. The house was a half mile east of the blacktop. Weedy yard where it wasn't dirt. Ruptured sofa on the front porch. Window screens in the shrubbery. The front door standing open. When I pulled up, dogs came boiling out from under the buckled decking -- puny, ratty dogs that might have menaced me more if they could have spared the time and energy from digging at their fleas.

A child showed up in the doorway, a toffee-colored girl who looked maybe eight or nine. She clung to the knob with one hand, had a finger from the other in her mouth.

"Is your dad here?"

She shook her head.

"Your mom?"

Another shake.

"Anybody but you?"

Her brother, I had to guess, joined her in the doorway, and she jerked her head by way of pointing him out. He might have been three years old. He was dragging a beach towel behind him -- the sort made to look like a million dollar bill. He looked like he'd been on Paris-Island maneuvers in his diaper.

"Is Raijaun Howard your daddy?"

That got me a nod from her. A cackle from him.

"Know where he is?"

"Spreader man," she told me. Then she stepped back full inside the house. She tugged her brother with her. She told me, "Bye," and shut the door.

They knew Raijaun at the Quick Mart down the road. In the way of country people, they had a fair idea of where he was at that moment and what he might be up to. Two customers threw in together to direct me to a farm between Damtown and Knightly. There seemed to be six or eight ways to get to it, and those guys couldn't pick the best one.

They were right in the middle of supplying me with a trio of travel options when the large, freckled woman behind the counter told them both, "Shut up."

She felt sure she had a better route, but she was one of those direction givers who kept telling me what I'd arrive at if I missed my turn and went too far. I shut my ears to her after about thirty seconds, just nodded when I thought I should and told her, "All right."

So I blundered around for a while in the vicinity of Damtown and Knightly, which weren't communities in the regular sense of the word. One was a Church of the Brethren and an abandoned Pure Oil Station. The other was just a pullout and a cinderblock foundation where a post office or a commissary or a community center had once been.

There was even less in the way of useful landmarks between the two communities. That would include county road signs, which were nowhere to be found. The land was about half pasture and half winter wheat. There was hardly anybody to flag down. I kept driving around with my eyes peeled for something that looked like a spreader truck.

I finally spied the thing in a wheat field and headed directly for it. The two guys at the bumper were the only people I'd seen for a solid half hour. I parked in the ditch and walked over. They'd mired up in the lone boggy patch on an otherwise crusty slope.

They both watched me come. They were stuck up to the axle and so didn't have much else to do but wonder what I was up to.

"Gentlemen," I said once I was close enough for it.

"You ain't him, are you?" the white one asked me.

"Who?"

"I don't see no loader."

"Guess not," I said and turned to the black guy. "Raijaun Howard, right?"

He nodded and then remembered himself enough to tell me, "Maybe."

"What the shit is it now?" the white guy bleated. He allowed he was already put upon enough.

Raijaun shrugged as if he'd either done nothing or had been up to so much he couldn't hope to keep track.

"Need a word," I said to Raijaun. "Mind if I borrow him for a minute?"

"Hell, go on," the white guy told me and then added beyond it to Raijaun, "And here I thought you was done with all your mess."

Raijaun muttered, "Am."

He followed me twenty yards across the slope.

"I've got you down as a witness," I told him, "on a case over in Afton."

Raijaun gave me a blank, dull look.

"Old case," I told him. "Girl disappeared."

He inhaled sharply and took a full step back. "You police?" he wanted to know.

I shook my head. "I heard what they got up to."

"You some kind of lawyer. You think I've got a claim or something?"

It seemed as good a way in as any. "Not sure. Why don't you tell me what happened."

"It was Lonnie. I can't prove it, but it couldn't have been nobody else."

I checked my notebook where I had all the principals listed. It was a habit I'd gotten into. Instead of jotting down details and fractured observations, I just listed the names of everybody I came across in a case. Often that was enough to conjure all the information I needed, and I liked to draw lines from one name to another when the connections became clear.

"Coates?" I asked him. I had Officer Lonnie C.. I'd found him in the case file.

Raijaun nodded. "We go back."

"How far?"

"Kids. Me and him used to run together. Bust up, shit. You know? Couldn't believe it the first time I saw Lonnie wearing a badge."

"Did you fall out?" I asked.

Raijaun gave me the con's once over. "You sure you ain't a cop?"

I shook my head.

"We had some business that went bad."

"What flavor?"

"Lonnie was selling. I brought a guy to him."

"What happened?"

"My guy made a problem. Something about the money. Lonnie figured I'd known all along."

"And he stays mad enough to put the Dunbar girl on you?"

"Can't prove nothing, but yeah. Probably."

"How did it work exactly? Where did they pick you up?"

"I was hauling feed corn for a boy. They found me at the cow lot."

"Who?"

He shrugged. "Cops. Said they were putting a line up together and there was twenty bucks in it for me. All I had to do was stand there and be black."

"Did they tell you what it was for?"

Another shrug. "I didn't care. I hadn't done nothing."

Raijaun described the room they'd put him in at the Waynesboro PD, a stifling, windowless, closet of a place down in the basement somewhere. A naked bulb overhead. One plastic, institutional chair.

"Two guys came in. The white one was the big chief."

"Phelps?"

A nod from Raijaun. "The black one I knew from juvie. Bidwell. Laughing all the time. Hairy mole right here." Raijaun tapped a cheek.

I had no Bidwell on my list, so I wrote him down.

"What did they want to know?"

"Nothing. Just told me what they knew already. They had a white girl gone missing and people said they'd seen me with her. I told them I didn't know her, and I'd just come for the twenty bucks."

"Did they say who was talking against you?" I hadn't seen any statements in the case file.

"No, sir."

"They show you any evidence? Anything at all?"

"Bidwell had a notebook. The big kind, like with rings. But it wasn't for showing. He just hit me with it."

"How long did this go on?"

"Past supper. They'd go out and come back. I never did eat. Must have been in there all night."

"When did you go to the woods?"

"Next morning. I told them I'd show them where she was."

"I thought you didn't know her."

"Didn't," Raijaun told me. "After a while you forget they're wrong. Forget you're right."

"What happened in the woods?" I asked him.

"Must have been the fresh air or something. I remembered I had no business being there and there wasn't a damn thing I wanted to say. Told the big chief, and he didn't like it much. They all jumped me after that."

"Lonnie too?"

"Lonnie mostly. That's just his kind of thing."

"What stopped them?"

"Trooper," he told me. "He made them all quit."

"Don't happen to know his name do you?"

Rainjaun shook his head.

"Is Lonnie still on the force?"

"As far as a I know."

"Still dirty?"

Raijaun smiled and snorted. "Ain't never had a straight day in his life."

"Drugs?"

"Naw. Shit that fell off the truck."

Me and Raijaun both turned at the sound of a diesel engine. A big, articulated loader was coming our way down the road.

"We done?" Raijaun wanted to know.

"Any ideas on what happened to that girl?"

"Some hillbilly got a wild hair," he told me. Raijaun was heading for the spreader truck by then. "Just like that lady with the horses," Raijaun shouted.

"What lady?"

"Hell, ask somebody," I think he said. That loader had come roaring into the field and was all but drowning him out.

It turned out, I didn't have to ask anybody. That lady was well represented on the web. June of 1999. Annette Marie Wilton. She was hauling a pair of warmbloods from Lexington to Keswick when she broke down just over the spine of the ridge between Afton and Crozet.

Travel time put her at the wayside by the fruit stand -- the very place where Mickey picked me up -- along about seven on a Saturday morning. She was heading for some big dressage to do that started at half past nine. A guy hauling hay might have seen her standing by her pickup with the hood raised and the radiator steaming. A woman heading west for Stuarts Draft felt sure she saw a man helping her out. He was bent over the grill and fooling with the engine. Colored, she said, or dirty or maybe neither. She couldn't say which.

A guy driving with his family to Richmond noticed the horses late afternoon. He'd stopped at the fruit stand for nectarines. Those warmbloods were making a racket, stomping and snorting and lurching around. The girl running the place was chiefly interested in the romance novel she was reading. She didn't know how that long that truck and trailer had been parked there or whose it was.

The county PD and a couple of troopers traced down the ownership of the truck, and by dark they'd managed to raise Annette Marie Wilton's sister and her ex-husband. They mounted one of those coordinated searches where everybody quarrels with each other over manpower and jurisdiction while nobody gets found. From what I read, they never turned up even a wrongheaded lead. I'd had plenty of cases in my career where I had a fair idea of who did it but lacked anything solid to go on beyond my educated guess. They weren't even close to a guess on this one. "A hillbilly with a wild hair" worked as well as anything else.

In December of 2012 a guy out hunting found a bone. He'd seen enough animal carcasses to think this bone was a little odd. He showed it around the county co-op where he worked, and after him and his fellow employees had aired their assorted unschooled opinions, he put the thing in the hands of a customer, a retired GP from Batesville, who knew a human fibula when he saw one straightaway.

Annette Marie Wilton had been less buried than simply left to rot in pieces. The state forensic lab in Richmond made an ID off a surgical screw. A few of the bones were scored and marked by maybe a camp ax or a hatchet. Nobody could say if she'd been hacked to death or killed and chopped up later.

With a little digging, I discovered Ms. Wilton was linked online to another woman who'd vanished, a girl who'd left behind an empty tent and her backpack on Elk Mountain in 2002. She was hiking alone, had set out from Pennsylvania, just east of Shippensburg, on some kind of weight loss/self-improvement program that she planned to follow clean to Georgia. She'd fallen in with a couple for a few days, and they'd hiked together from up by Sperryville all the way to Rockfish Gap. Her name was Tawny, and she'd continued south once her friends had peeled away.

They'd given statements and had submitted to press interviews. They were birders from Alta Vista. Tawny was down to one forty, according to them, and aiming for one twenty-five.

I managed to hunt up a few photographs of her. She was a thick, manly creature with a short haircut, an ear so thoroughly pierced it looked armored, and what I took for a lazy eye. There was nothing girlish about her, which made it hard to imagine that even some oversexed yokel from back in the hills might have stumbled on Tawny from Pennsylvania and decided he had to have him some of that.

Tawny's hiking friends from Alta Vista insisted she wasn't depressed. She'd left her pack standing open with dinner out and her cook stove set up for duty on a rock. Deputies found a water jug by a nearby spring. Almost certainly hers, they figured. So the grand theory was she went down to the spring, met with trouble, and never came back.

No body. No bones. No Tawny at all.

So Kiki Dunbar in 1996. Annette Marie Wilton in '99. And Tawny from Pennsylvania in 2002. Three year gaps. Not precise to the month, but three years nonetheless. Happenstance maybe but a little too regular to feel purely coincidental. I pictured a hopping mad cracker with momma issues out in the big woods somewhere.

In New York we'd snatch cons from places they thought we'd never find them. From Riverdale to Staten Island, there are plenty of spots to hide and ten million citizens to serve as human clutter and distraction. A guy would rob a bodega convinced the city would simply swallow him up. He was just another male Hispanic, another black kid in a hoodie, another third generation Italian in a tank top with a gun. He'd forget he knew people who'd turn him in for folding money and the promise of a favor, people ready to take his TV, empty his closet, snake his girlfriend while he was up in Otisville doing time. The city wouldn't hide him. The cameras were always watching. The people he knew had other, better friends.

It was different in the Blue Ridge. The place was clannish, hidden, wild. The locals tended to sort and settle their problems entirely among themselves. Nobody ever got snitched on and turned in. Hillbillies took care of their own.

Annette Marie Wilton and Tawny from Pennsylvania served to remind me why I preferred repos and divorce. A man might dote on his chevy half-ton or regret his hound-dog indiscretions, but in the end somebody would just lose his wheels or agree to pay his wife. No axes. No bones. No Boy Scouts finding hair clips in the woods.

Buddy

i

I didn't want group. I wanted Dr. Marlin all to myself. I'd found her website. Her hair was just like Lisa's but a bit a longer and brunette. She looked in the eyes like the sort of woman who could help me hit steady medium cool. I'm serene in my calling, but I'm kind of erratic almost everywhere else. Social settings paralyze me. I get flummoxed in the workplace. I can't even have a decent back and forth with a grocery checker. I get all tied up and mumble and then end up beating a side mirror with my shoe.

On her website, Dr. Marlin boasted of coping strategies. Of course, Barry did as well, but I could only listen to Barry. He wasn't much of a back and forther, had chiefly DVD sales on his mind. Presumably, I'd be able to quiz Dr. Marlin. Explore my awkward tendencies and discover some route to functional savoir faire. I wasn't looking to be slick and beguiling. I just wanted to be less of a lunk.

Dr. Marlin had beautiful hands. I always notice that about women. A man could have talons, and I wouldn't even see them, but I go right to a woman's fingers. Short nails -- clipped not bitten -- and no varnish. I don't care for the stuff. She wore a ring but not a wedding band, not an engagement stone. Hers was a cameo. Probably a family piece. She kept rubbing it with her thumb.

"Buddy," I told her when she asked what she should call me.

"Jill," she said and made a note. More of a note, in fact, than I felt like I'd earned or deserved.

I was working hard to keep my jaw from doing that thing it sometimes does. I'd call it a twitch but, in truth, it's far closer to a spasm. I've been doing it for years. It's a nerve thing, I suspect, and I used to have a proper check on it, but it gets away from me these days. It got away from me there in front of Jill.

"Are you all right?" she asked. I get a lot of that.

I nodded. "A twitch," I told her, but she was trained to know from twitches.

She made another note. Again it was more involved than I would have liked.

"Tell me about your work, Buddy."

I obliged her. I described the equipment we used. The sorts of jobs we took. I told her all about Keith's complaint. I even got onto Mr. Pittman more than I'd intended.

"I think I'd see a stomach doctor," I told her, "if I was him."

She made another note.

"Let's talk about your outburst."

I was happy enough to do that as long I could steer well wide of Lisa. "It builds up, you know?"

"What does?"

"The pressure." I tapped the side of my head.

"Work pressure? Life pressure?"

I had to think it was best not to parse and distinguish. I gave the matter some thought before I finally nodded and told her, "Yeah."

"Do you have financial concerns?"

I felt like I ought to, for the sake of convenience. I wanted to be able to retreat, if need be, into, "Money's tight just now." So I nodded again and told Dr. Marlin, "A little trouble with the mortgage."

I didn't have a mortgage. My mother's brother had left me his house and one hundred and fourteen acres of

woodland. I could sell timber whenever I wanted. I didn't
need much to cover food and electric. I would have been fine
without a job, but I'm keen to be in the world. I'm kind of a
people person at bottom. You can lose your way living back
in the forest. Forget what you're supposed to be up to.

"Are you behind?"

"Might soon be."

She made a note. "Have you talked to your banker?"

I shook my head.

"It might help with a solution, don't you think?"

"Might could." I caught myself talking country. I
sometimes lapse into hillbilly twang. I like to think it makes
me seem homey and uncomplicated. A man of few words.
Few needs. That sort of thing.

"And why haven't you talked to your banker?"

We each had a cup of coffee that Dr. Marlin's assistant
had brought us. Her name was Rachel. Her glasses were
oversized, and the hair on her arms appeared to make her
self-conscious. I could tell by the way she tugged at her
sleeve when she set my coffee cup down.

Dr. Marlin blew on her coffee before she sipped it, even
though it was already tepid by then.

"I don't really know her. Just signed papers in her office
once."

I was creating my banker in my head as I was talking to
Dr. Marlin. I didn't like her fingers or the sorts of shoes she
wore. Every time she spoke, my banker started by saying,
"Now." I don't care for that. It's like starting off with,
"Listen." Lisa does that to distraction.

"Is it the not knowing her that keeps you away? You do
understand that she could help you."

I gave the question some thought. I pictured my banker.
She had a bowl of butterscotch candy on her desk and wore a
charm bracelet that jangled whenever she moved. Whatever

happened to charm bracelets? Women everywhere used to wear them.

"Yes, ma'am," I said. "That's probably it."

"Jill, please."

"I'm nervous around people, Jill."

"You seem fine now."

"I don't like it when things aren't . . ." I thought I'd give her the chance to fill it in, Jill being the shrink and all.

"Structured?"

That was just the right word. And she had proper fingers too. I nodded. "Yes, exactly. Structured."

"That's not uncommon."

I don't quite understand why head doctors, like my friend Jill, always feel the need to tell me that my complaints are ordinary. 'Not uncommon' might be the clinical way to spit it out, but it sounds worse than they think. Jill had seen people parading through her office with my problems. I was like more of her other patients than she could trouble herself to count. That's not reassuring. It's closer to an insult.

I was torn, of course. I'm all for being inconspicuous. Lisa makes that a necessity. But at the same time I'd like a trained mental health professional to have at least a nagging misgiving or two about me. Nothing concrete, just the sense I wasn't the sort best shoved in the 'not uncommon' slot.

Dr. Marlin, for her part, made a note. More of a note than I was comfortable with her making.

"I was in therapy as a boy," I told her. "I've kind of had impulse problems for a while."

"Oh?" She stopped writing. That was just what I'd hoped for.

In truth, my mother was a hypochondriac by proxy. I didn't actually have impulse problems. Sure, I'd killed a cat or two. I'd locked a neighbor girl in our car shed long enough for a search to get mounted, and I got blamed for breaking the arm of a boy at school. He had weak joints, as it turned out, and a fairly brittle frame. I just pushed him. Gravity and genetics did the rest.

My mother was one who felt like she had fury in her soul and feared one day it would bust out in ways she couldn't begin to marshall, but she had a terror of getting diagnosed and so sent me in instead.

Dr. Perkins. His glasses were taped together, and he wore sky-blue argyle socks. His cardigan had gravy or something on it. Cyril Perkins. That ought to tell you enough. He had a photo of his manly wife on his desk. They raised King Charles Spaniels as a hobby. He had decided -- for convenience's sake, I imagine -- that he wasn't gay.

My mother schooled me in what to tell him, how to describe the anger in me. He made notes too. Brief sloppy ones in the sort of spiral notebook any fool could buy at the pharmacy. He kept pulling off his glasses and pinching his nose. Half the time, he didn't even seem to hear what I said.

He wouldn't let my mother past the outer office. So I saw Dr. Perkins alone, probably a half dozen times, and when he finally rendered his judgement and I passed it along to my mother, I'd never seen a human more deflated than she was.

"Did you tell him about it?" She tapped on her stomach, which was where her fury resided. "All of it?"

I nodded. She'd given me specific details, a raft of ugly, wayward thoughts to describe.

"And?"

"He said it wasn't uncommon."

The air went out of her. I thought she might collapse. Like most people, my mother was convinced she was singular and, as upstanding ladies with fury go, unique.

"Tell me about your impulse problems," Dr. Marlin said. "Chapter and verse."

"Back then or now?"

"Start with when you were a boy."

"I had tantrums," I told her. I decided to leave out the torture and wanton cruelty. Omit the cats. "Blind rages, you know?"

Jill nodded and made a note. This one took up nearly half a page. "Go on."

"I broke my toys. Broke glasses and plates. I punched out a window once."

"What did your parents do?"

"It was just me and mother."

"What happened to your father?"

I flashed on his doughy, whiskery face for the first time in a couple of years. He'd go off. He'd come back. He'd go off again. The man had a weakness for corn mash and strawberry blondes. It was all too sordid to go into.

"Died," I said. "Tractor accident."

"Was he a farmer?"

I shook my head. "Trying to steal it. Rolled it over. He never had much luck."

"Hmm." Another extensive note. "Was your father a thief by trade?"

I had to think on that one and calculate which choice would do better service for me.

I decided on, "No. A salesman. He fell out with the guy who owned the tractor. I guess he was having kind of a tantrum too."

"I see."

Jill could certainly be entirely dehumidified when she wanted. That "I see" was as dry and lifeless as a handful of sand.

"How old were you when he died."

"Six and a half."

"And what do you remember about that time?"

I did a decent job of describing the funeral. I'd certainly been to enough of them what with cousins and aunts and great grandparents, the occasional tragic Lisa do. It was such stirring fun to bury my father that I almost wanted to drive to the dump where he lives in Lexington and kill him.

"Did your father's death cause any . . . financial troubles?"

Clever of her. I could see where this was going.

"I was too young to know at the time, but we were in pretty bad shape."

"Did your mother work?"

"After Daddy died, yeah, but it wasn't a normal job."

"What did she do?"

Mom was in the ground after all, so I could say whatever I wanted and be sure it would never get back to her. She'd not had any friends, so they weren't a concern.

"I've been told that she was kind of a paid companion."

"Which means what?" Another exhaustive note.

"I'm dressing it up." I went pitiful. You just let everything relax and exhale. It's very persuasive, a fine approximation of bone-deep sadness. "She was a prostitute."

"She received men . . . in your home?"

More exhaling and a nod.

"Strangers to her? To you?"

"Sometimes. Started with the guy who held the note on the house." She wasn't the only one with that theme in her head. I could circle back as well.

"Ah," Dr. Marlin said. It was a satisfying turn.

"She was a pretty lady. Everybody thought so, and she didn't have anything else to sell."

"Where were you when men came to visit?"

"In the yard usually. Next door sometimes. There was a girl over there about my age." Mary. Wavy brown hair. Born with only one thumb. I could still see the marks on her freckled wrists where I'd bound her up. I thought it was funny longer than she did. I like to think I have a finer appreciation of such things.

"How many men? How often?" She'd dropped the delicate altogether.

"One or two a month at first. The man from the bank. The power guy."

"So it was barter?"

"I guess. The lights stayed on. We didn't have to move."

"How long did this last?"

"Hard to say."

"Did your mother ever get a regular job? Go off to work? Bring home a check?"

I shook my head. "She got courted by a Tucker. A sawmill Tucker. He couldn't be too particular, the way he looked."

"And she married him?"

I nodded. "There weren't any other men after that?"

"And how were old were you?"

"Nine maybe."

"Did things improve?"

That seemed a bit vague and open-ended. What things? Improve how? I expected more from Jill.

"Do you mean like . . .?" I squinted at her. It might have been my session, but I was hardly prepared to do all the work.

"A more stable home life? Security? Was this man, this Mr. Tucker, good to you?"

I shrugged. "He ran a sawmill. He was filthy. His house was nasty. He hardly spoke to me." I only know Tuckers by reputation, but I had to think that's how a Tucker would be.

Dr. Marlin nodded and made a note that carried her off one page of her notebook and onto another.

"Did your impulse problems continue?"

"Oh yes. Might have even been worse."

"Give me a such as."

I deplore that sort of shorthand. Say what you mean. Ask what you want. Give me a such as, indeed.

"I got in fights. I broke stuff. Especially if it was something, you know, important."

"Whose stuff?"

"Anybody's. I started with ours and branched out. Then I got sent home from school, and they wouldn't let me go to church anymore. I was an authentic terror."

"Did you ever hurt people?"

"Not at first," I told her.

She held her pen at the ready. I made her wait.

"Look at me," I said. I'm slight and bony. It doesn't really matter how I live or what I eat. I stay ribs and elbows and look like a guy a plump grandma could knock over. "I've never been much use in a fight."

"I didn't ask about fighting," Jill said. "I asked if you hurt people."

"Maybe," I confessed to her. "Once for sure."

And I was just about to launch into a vivid tale about William P. Olivet, a boy I'd known since I was five. He had relatives in Scottsville, and he'd gone to visit them one summer. It was one of those Julys when rain was heavy, and the James River was in flood. He was playing in an eddy and got out in the current. He ended up in New Canton about a week later. The river had stripped off all his clothes.

I was primed to carry on about William P. Olivet and make up a bunch of cruel stuff I'd done to him, but before I could start Jill told me, "That's time," and she slapped her notebook shut. "Twice a month okay?"

"If I'm covered for it. Our insurance stinks."

"We'll work something out."

She stood. I stood. And we were done.

ii

I'm well beyond the reach of therapy. That probably goes without saying. At this point, if a cure came my way, I have to wonder what would be left of me. That hardly prevents me from having a special affection for therapists. They understand everything sooner, sometimes too soon for their own good. I might be invisible to everybody else, but a good shrink can usually see me. Parts of me anyway, toxic bits and pieces, that I'd prefer went unseen.

I ran into a shrink at a fish fry once, a money raiser for the Baptist church down in Rockfish Gap. I went with Keith. He haunts Christian get-togethers in hopes of meeting the sorts of girls with charity enough in their souls to overlook his abnormalities. I was only with him because he'd begged me for a ride, and he was making good use of his time. Keith was chatting up a lanky blonde who had more interest in tossing her hair and combing her bangs with her fingers than Jesus would have probably cared for, if he'd been around. I got stuck with the girl's father. He was some kind of family counselor who'd started in on a regular psychiatry degree but had given up and quit.

"This church thing's a phase," the girl's father told me. "Last year she was going to be a model."

"How'd she find Jesus?" I asked him.

"Dated a guy who'd found Him first."

I nodded and made a noise in my neck. In social situations, I depend on nodding and noises more than adjusted people might.

"Are you a member here?" The guy glanced at my work shirt. We'd come straight over from a job. "Buddy?"

I shook my head. "I'm a Catholic." I'm not a Catholic. It's just something I say sometimes, usually to shut people down when they're trying to win me to Jesus. It's a common problem in these parts. I should have just said, "No."

The guy shot some Latin at me. I smiled and made another noise in my neck.

We both turned towards the sound of Keith's talker. "Ha ha ha ha."

"Keith needed a ride," I explained and pointed. "We work together."

"CP?"

I nodded.

"Mild, looks like."

I nodded again. "Right as rain in the head. A good guy," I added. I was talking to the father of the girl that Keith was chatting up after all.

I thought I saw Lisa and turned to check quicker than I should have. My jaw did that thing it does, so I put my hand to face and held it.

"Are you all right?"

"Muscle thing," I said and gestured vaguely nowhere much. "I get twinges out of the blue."

This time he was the one who nodded and made a noise.

I saw her again. He saw Lisa too and then turned back and watched me with more attention than I cared for.

"Old girlfriend?" he asked me. That's the trouble with shrinks. They're always leaping past the details and jumping to conclusions.

I should have said, "Yeah, old girlfriend." That would have explained it just fine. "Thought she was somebody else," I told him.

Then I made the mistake of scouring the crowd there in the fellowship hall until I'd found her again which, of course, made my jaw do that thing it does with Lisa.

"Ever seen a doctor about that?" He'd been watching me all along.

"About what?"

"Your twitch. Technically a hemifacial spasm."

I was liking him less by the second.

"Yeah, a year or so ago." I went back to Lisa. I couldn't help myself really. I guess he saw something in the way I was looking at her that clued him in. Like I said, that's the trouble with shrinks. They're always diagnosing.

I thought I was smiling and looking benign, but I couldn't even fool a psychiatric dropout and rural family counselor. I made a mental note to redouble my efforts to work on myself with Barry.

"He told me it was anxiety."

The guy nodded. He sipped his punch. I could tell by the way he avoided my gaze that he'd moved beyond anxiety. He'd probably done some kind of internship in a state hospital somewhere and had a seen a treacherous inmate or two with a jaw like mine.

"He gave me some pills. I don't like to take them."

"Oh?"

"They slow me down. Make me sleepy."

He tried to sip again, but his cup was empty. He caught his daughter's eye and showed her the wrist he'd be wearing a watch on if he had one. She tossed her hair and combed her bangs with her fingers. She seemed keen to stick with Keith and tell him all about the Lord.

"You're some kind of shrink, right? Maybe I can come see you. Maybe that would help."

"Marriage counselor," he said. "Family troubles. Like that."

"Mine all started with family troubles. Got a card or something?"

"Unfortunately, I'm relocating. Texas."

"Got a colleague you can recommend?"

I wasn't even trying to pass for a decent civilian by then. I was giving the man my full, unblinking attention. People, I've noticed, tend to find it paralyzing. Even mental health professionals. Possibly especially them.

"Let me think about it. I'll call you."

I gave him a number. He pulled out his phone, punched it in.

"Buddy what?"

I gave him a name as well.

"I'll be in touch."

I got a tight smile as he headed for his daughter who was disappointed enough to be leaving the function that she made all sorts of pouty, unChristian noises.

Keith tried to call after her with his talker, but his typing is too slow for that sort of thing. She was probably in the parking lot before Keith could say, "I had a good time."

Keith was distraught. Increasingly, distraught is Keith's prevailing mood.

"Don't worry," I told him. "You'll see her again."

I pictured the two of them at a funeral. Keith consoling the girl while she sniveled and tossed her hair. Less of a funeral actually than a memorial service. The only thing left of daddy would be a bit of singed bone and maybe a belt buckle.

But it turned out he was relocating, was legitimately moving to Texas. I had a three-week window if I wanted it, but I don't care for getting pushed. He might have put somebody onto a Catholic Buddy with the wrong phone number, but that was about the worst he could do, so I let Texas have him.

When I told Keith about my session with Dr. Marlin, I also told him a real friend wouldn't have gone behind my back to Pittman. A real friend would have taken things up with me.

"Yeah," I confessed. "I got upset. I broke one of our mirrors. Remember that window you broke that time?"

Keith had hit it with his crutch. He'd not been angry exactly. He'd just gotten tangled in some lady's curtains.

Keith had already prepared an apology and just had to hit one button to air it.

"I'm sorry I got you in trouble. I won't do it again," Perfect Paul told me.

I forgave Keith on the spot. What else could I do? He's the only friend I have.

I'm fond of Keith and would like to see the boy reel in a girlfriend. The trouble is Keith wants just the beauties. The lanky blondes with hair to toss. He won't pay even passing notice to the sort of woman he might have.

I try to instruct him whenever I can. I point out girls that I'd be interested if I happened to be Keith.

He always tells me, "Uh uh."

Then he'll spy one up to his standards and point, and I'll tell him, "Uh uh," back.

I thought once about buying a woman for Keith. I knew Hotchkiss and them hired girlfriends sometimes. I even went so far as to speak to Hotchkiss. He assumed, of course, the woman was for me.

"Tired of tugging on it?" he asked me. "Lonely, ain't it?"

"It's for the boy."

The whole group of them got a kick out that. It wasn't like you could ever hope to catch Hotchkiss alone.

"Right," Hotchkiss said and giggled. His courtiers giggled too.

"Is there a blonde one maybe? With good teeth?"

That got a roar out of them.

"Pitch dark," Hotchkiss told me. "And Keith . . ." He paused to wink at his pals. ". . . can think she looks any way he wants to."

"Are they clean?"

More laughter.

"If you close your eyes, they're goddamn spotless."

I didn't bother to follow up. I decided I didn't want Keith touching (with anything of his) a human Hotchkiss and them made salacious use of.

I couldn't imagine me paying a woman — even a passably blonde and scrubbed one — booking a motel room and bringing Keith so Perfect Paul could tell me, "Uh uh."

iii

They turned up a guy recently in Indiana or somewhere who'd kept women in his basement. Alive, for some reason, which sounds like a godawful chore to me. His neighbors were shocked and mortified, the way neighbors tend to be. And the cable news teams all brought in experts to rattle on about his motives. His kinks and appetites. His apparent lack of mitigators. His depravity, to judge by the toys and tools they found. He was held out as a monster. A moral fluke. A black-hearted enormity.

The question they all either asked or implied was "How could a twenty-first century American do such things?" Us being a Christian nation and all and, to our minds, better than everybody else. How could we have such a base life form among us, and especially in a place like Indiana where we depend on people (they all seemed to be saying) to be upstanding and bland?

Naturally, it's the wrong line of questioning altogether, but we're a wrong line of questioning kind of nation. Think about it even a little, you'll wonder why this sort of thing doesn't happen all the time. If one of those toothy girls on TV asked me why I got up to my stuff, I'd have to turn it around and ask her why I wouldn't. Look how little is keeping me from it. Just my conscience primarily, and if that's off kilter or hollowed out, where's my impediment exactly. If I don't care what happens to people, am I going to care about what happens to me? And I going to think for even a second — as I'm hacking some girl into fryer parts — this sort of thing is illegal and probably wrong, so I ought not to do it?

Of course I'm not. It's my brand of necessary recreation, and it's as natural and consuming to me as your Sunday round of golf is to you. You think about your swing in your idle moments. Work on your stance in the checkout line. Fiddle with your grip on a rake handle. You order DVDs from the golfing equivalent of Barry. You fret over your equipment. Second guess your strategy around the course. You build towards Sunday. You putt in your office. You practice your breathing so you can be calm when you hit the links.

Then you let yourself down to one degree or another. Spray balls all over the place. Slide into your old, bad habits. Your anger rises. Your confidence wanes. You're three out of the bunker and throw your goddamn wedge in the lake.

I'm just like you only more accomplished. Better in the crunch. I'm not worried that my stakes are higher. You could lose a couple of hundred. I could get the needle. But I don't think about the gurney like you think about the money. It's all about my performance. It's pure sport in my head. You hope to swing on plane every time with just the pace and rhythm to draw the ball a bit and spin it, leave yourself below the hole.

I just want Lisa to understand there's nobody else for her but me. At bottom, it's the same thing. Different tools. That's all.

Lisa's pig-headed. That's the problem really. She's frustration on the hoof. A contrarian. A blunt instrument. We had a class together. I was parked already where I liked to sit, which was off to the right and down towards the front. Sophomore year in Raleigh. I'd end up leaving between semesters, so it's dumb luck me and Lisa ever got together at all.

She came charging in late the second week of the term. She'd added the class when she couldn't get in something else she'd wanted. She was peeved to be there and dropped down right beside me in a huff.

Lisa had a ballpoint, a cup of student union coffee, and nothing else. She reached over and helped herself to a page out of my spiral notebook. She had to pick up my hand to do it. She seemed content enough to touch me. She didn't care.

"Rocks, right?"

I didn't have to answer. The professor down front held up a hunk of marcasite. He'd started with gypsum. Then agate. "Anybody?" he said.

I didn't even nod. Lisa decided on the spot I was dry and droll and clung to it for a while. Then she decided I wasn't, and she stuck with that for longer. By the end of October, she was sitting way on the left and in the back.

She was one of those people who insisted on telling you all about your frailties and your failings because she'd decided that life was so short she'd rather be blunt than polite. Lisa advertised it as honesty and seemed to think that gave it her license to say any damn thing most any damn way she felt like it ought to come out.

Of course like most things in life, the truth is just a matter of perspective. I tried to make Lisa understand that, but you couldn't be honest to her back. That was a feature of Lisa's character I never learned to navigate. She could say any toxic thing she pleased in the spirit of truthfulness, but you couldn't begin to answer in kind because she'd get indignant. It was all outgoing with Lisa. She was a bust at taking fire.

And it wasn't like I had a list of particulars I'd hoped to acquaint her with. I've long taken the view that honesty is troublesome and over rated. It's not that I'm a liar by nature. I have my raft of secrets now, but that's a segregated and separate thing for me. I'm talking about with Hotchkiss and them and Keith. With Mr. Pittman. With the checkout ladies at the Kroger. With people you run across in a regular way and get to know in your life. Unless I'm pressed to give my unvarnished assessment, why in the world would I do it? Why tell Keith he'll never land an able-bodied girl? Supply Pittman with a corrosive opinion of his diet? Correct the grammar of the lady who works at the five and dime? And explain to Hotchkiss and them, well, almost anything?

I do it in my head, like anybody would, but I don't see how I'd improve life by saying any of it out loud. There's enough poison around already. Most people are wounded as it is. If I'm dishonest to hold my peace, then that's what I'd rather be. I never could make Lisa see my side, especially once I'd hit her. I'd never swung on even a man before that, so it surprised us both at once.

I have to think she was shortly thereafter honest about me with a friend, a hometown pal of hers from the kicking team who found me in the brickyard, him and another football buddy. They were strapping and energetic, didn't need much excuse for some fun.

"You know Lisa right?" the buddy asked me.

"Lisa who?" I felt like I knew what was coming.

They grinned at each other, and then the one who hadn't talked yet dropped me with a backhanded swipe. They had too much in the way of sinew and muscle to bend over with any ease, so they just kicked me instead and made all sorts of promises about my welfare. According to them, my prospects were poor to atrocious.

I was in the hospital for the best part of a week. The dean of students, the athletic director, and two detectives interviewed me. They were easy enough to manage. I assured them I couldn't remember a thing.

Lisa came by one evening late, just as visiting hours were ending. At first I thought she might be scared I'd go through channels on her, make sure that Lisa and her football buddies all ended up in court. But Lisa wasn't the fretful sort. She'd just stopped by to be honest. She ate my fruit cup as she told me what a creep and lout I was. I was the perfect receptacle for Lisa just then. My jaw was wired and my face was swollen. Even if I'd had the interest and energy, there wasn't much chance I'd be honest back.

One of the cops sought me out a few days after I'd been discharged. He had a feeling I remembered more than I was letting on and suspected I might try to get even. In his line of work, he probably saw no end of people like that. Tit for tatters. Balanced equation sorts. He clearly didn't understand me any better than Lisa did.

I held my spite and my rage and my bitterness close. I didn't let anybody see it. Everybody who knew me there in Raleigh — the guys I roomed with and their friends — all surely thought I was pushing through and putting the ordeal behind me.

"She's not worth it," my suite mate told me of Lisa. He'd had a kind of a thing with her too until she'd decided he was too shallow for her and woefully inartistic, which she'd acquainted him with, naturally, in a fit of honesty.

"Word is you hit her," he said.

I shrugged. I nodded. "Don't know what happened exactly."

"She's a trial all right," he told me. "I was about half tempted."

"Seems like years ago now," I said.

I found I could manage well enough and still haul around my nugget of quaking rage, which was inky and sulfurous and stayed in my gut about like my mother's fury had. I tried not to let it plague and gnaw on me. I grew to consider it a tool —something I'd use when I wanted to and however I saw fit.

I finally found occasion to bring it out. I was dog sitting for a guy, which in his case meant house sitting too. He was an instructor in the English department. I'd had him for freshman comp, and he'd called me once his regular sitter had let him down in the lurch. I'd written an essay once in his class about a dog I claimed to have grown up with as a boy. A collie named Dewey who I'd been tender about on the page.

Dewey belonged to our neighbor. One of my mother's gentlemen callers got drunk one night and killed him with his truck. Ran right over him. Dewey slept on the road because it was warmer than the porch. The rest of us knew to look out for him because we were local and sober.

The Dewey in my essay was wise and affectionate, a companion for a lonely boy living friendless out in the sticks. Dewey in life had scabies and survived on garbage and careless birds, but my fictional Dewey had been powerful enough to stick with my comp teacher.

The teacher's name was Doug, and he was from Philadelphia. He was taking the train up with his girlfriend for some kind of family do. They shared one of those houses that struggling academics always have. Overgrown yard. Blistered siding. Last year's dead ficus on the porch. Bookish clutter as decor. Dust balls under all the tables. French cigarette stink all over the place, and the walls hung with photos of writers. Grizzled old guys for the most part with the occasional homely woman thrown in.

The dogs were named Ralph and Waldo.

"Trancendentalists," Doug explained to me. "Sometimes when you call them they'll treat you as if you're real. Perhaps you are."

He got quite a kick out of that, as did his girlfriend, Lydia. She had wild, kinky hair and some kind of jewel in her navel, and this was well back before the day when toddlers had piercings and tattoos.

They left on a Thursday and were coming back Sunday night. I wasn't planning on much but walking dogs and schoolwork, and that's what I stuck to until Saturday morning when I took Ralph and Waldo for a jaunt. One had ears that went up and the other's ears went down. Aside from that, they were identical, so I just called them, "Hey!"

They didn't answer to that. They didn't answer to anything. I would have suspected they were deaf if they hadn't been so tuned in to the chatter squirrels make. They seemed content to stand at the trunk of a tree and look up in the limbs until doomsday. I decided to take them somewhere they could run loose. I'd just been walking them in the neighborhood, and in addition to having to pick up everything that came out of their bungholes and explaining to the neighbors who I was, the walks weren't enough to make a dent in Ralph and Waldo's enthusiasm. They'd come back home and wreck the place chasing each other through the house.

So on Saturday morning I piled them in Doug's Volvo. The key was in the ashtray with a good half dozen roaches, and off we went to Umstead Park. I had nothing in mind beyond a walk. So it was happenstance or fate or kismet or something that put me next to Lisa.

They'd been working on the road going into the park, had the gravel plowed and the trash from the ditches piled up where cars would usually go. So you had to park a ways back and walk in, which must have been too much trouble for people. It was a fine November Saturday, but there was nobody much around from the modest pool of locals who didn't give a hoot for football. I saw a guy with a poodle way off across a pond and then nobody else but Lisa, who I just blundered into.

She had binoculars hanging from her neck and was wearing a plaid parka. It was just me. The dogs had taken off once I'd unhooked them from their leashes. I could hear them making that noise they made when they were watching a squirrel.

Lisa told me, "Shhhhh."

I wasn't even talking. She pointed. I looked and saw nothing at first.

"Right there," she whispered.

That didn't much help.

"Golden-crowned kinglet," she informed me in a whisper. She was pointing at a pine.

"Ah," I said. "Kinglet."

She fished a notebook from her pocket and checked the time on her watch. That's precisely when my nugget of rage flared up. There was no thinking involved to speak of. I just fell upon her.

I was about as surprised as she was. I went at her as if on orders, and she was too staggered and shocked to even struggle there at first. Aside from a kitten and a geriatric spaniel, I'd never strangled anything. Her neck was slight, and my hands engulfed it.

I watched her watched me. I perched upon her. She went from shocked and mystified to savage struggle to surrender and then to sleep. There was a moment when I could have quit. When I entertained anyway a twinge and a doubt about what I'd gotten up to. But that was hardly the sort of business you could stop with once you'd started.

What would I tell her? "Sorry. Thought you were Lisa."

What would she say? "Well, then. All right."

So I couldn't stop, and it wasn't a genuine misgiving anyway. It was just the residue of my sense of human decency in defeat. Throttled and thwarted. Turning tail. I

knew I could depend on never suffering that sort of twinge
again.

She didn't struggle long. She was too frail to mount a
lasting fight. She'd turn out to be a sickly thing only recently
in remission, which maybe I sensed. I can't truly say, but it
was a lucky turn for me. The beginning of my good fortune.
I've kind of been charmed ever since.

The dogs came charging over as I was finishing with her.
Here was something even better than a squirrel. They
sniffed and whimpered. They bit each other's faces that way
they liked too. They got distracted by a racket in the canopy.
Not a squirrel on this occasion but some kind of bird instead.
It was fluttering around. I turned and saw it. A golden-
crowned kinglet, judging from the stripe of yellow on its
head.

I had decisions to make and the leisure to make them. I
dragged her deep into the untrammeled woods. The dogs
followed and chewed on windfall limbs while I just sat and
thought. I guess I was waiting for the panic to come and the
remorse to take hold of me. What if I'd just stayed at Doug's
house? What if I'd come an hour later. What if Lisa had
needed groceries or had gone birding somewhere else. That
kinglet had looked undistinguished to me. They had to be all
over the place.

Should I bury her, I wondered? It didn't strike me as
worthwhile. I didn't have a shovel, and the ground was rooty
and dry. I recall a fledgling interest at that moment in taking
her to pieces, but I only had a penknife, so I just stuck her
once or twice.

In the end, I buttoned her coat and left her, covered her
up a little with limbs. It was hardly like I fled to the car. I
took the dogs on a walk around the lake. I ran into a woman
with a bunion. She was using a varnished walking stick to
help her along, and she told me all about her foot troubles

the way people will. I entertained a passing thought that I should do her in as well. See to the details. Tidy up the loose ends, but it evaporated about as quickly as it had come. This wasn't about the bunion woman. There was no Lisa to her.

I told that woman I'd seen a golden-crowned kinglet. She snorted and shrugged. She had her bunion. She didn't need a bird.

At length, I loaded the dogs into Doug's ancient Volvo and stopped in for a box of grocery store chicken on the way back to the house. I did my schoolwork. I fed the animals. I had a shower after a while and watched part of a Russian movie already loaded in the tape deck. Knights on horseback out in Siberia (it looked like) fighting on the ice.

The News and Observer came on Sunday, but I didn't bother to unroll it. I tended the dogs. I straightened the house. I left an hour before the train came, went back to my dormitory, studied, slept, went to class.

Nothing ever happened. I knew somehow it wouldn't. Weeks passed. Lisa rotted or she didn't. People found her or they failed to. It didn't touch me one way or the other. All I knew was my nugget of fury felt satisfied for a time.

I saw Lisa in the stacks one night. It was December, end of term. She had her head down and was rifling through the pages of a book. I was almost on her before she turned my way. I thrilled at the way the sight of me made her tense up and suck air.

"You stay back," she said. She shelved her book and retreated down the aisle.

I felt contentment, the bone-deep kind. I was pleased to follow instructions. I smiled Lisa's way. I might have even winked.

"Later," was all I said.

P.J.

i

Skeevy. That's a word, right? Like sketchy but not wearing pants. My old neighbor was sketchy. The one with the overgrown dog pen and the pinball machines in his yard. He didn't appear to do much except yell at his wife and his kids. His daughter yelled back. She had a mouth on her. He'd worn down his wife. I'd see her walking on the road. She was careless about it and wandered well wide of the shoulder. She looked like she was half primed to get run down.

The son sulked. He had awful hair he hooked behind his ears. He had the sort of neck tattoo that said, "I'll get to trade school if I'm lucky."

I could tell by the way he braced himself against his father's rages that they were sure to come to blows.

The dad's name was Wayne. He called me "Sugar," but not in a way that was creepy or offensive. He called most women "Sugar," probably everybody but his wife. He helped himself to anything he wanted, but he was only interested in stuff. Between the time I rented my house and spent my first night under the roof, Wayne had made off with the fuel oil tank, the spare refrigerator in the car shed, and the air conditioner in the bedroom window upstairs.

He left a mess. Wayne didn't depend on being slick and surreptitious. Wayne got by on having no qualms about lying to your face.

"Isn't that my oil tank?" I asked him. It was just sitting in his yard. Connected to nothing, dumped in the grass beside a lawn tractor he'd probably stolen.

Wayne glanced at the tank and looked back at me. He shook his head and told me, "Nope."

And that was all he'd ever say about it. If I'd had a serial number or something and could present Wayne with certified evidence the tank went with the house I'd rented, the best Wayne would ever do by way of concession would be to suck a little spit and say with a touch of confounded surprise, "Huh."

Wayne loved money. Maybe that's what made him sketchy. Skeevy guys have a thing for flesh, a thing that's not remotely normal. They clue you in by looking at you like they're sizing you up for a garbage bag.

I had dinner date once with a skeevy guy. My roommate — the one after Gwennie — set me up. It turned out she didn't have any instinct for people beyond what they thought of her. Most men found her beautiful and beguiling, and she had no knack for plumbing what people were up to beyond that.

So she told me this guy she'd met, Bobby, was cute and funny and freshly broken up. I didn't know her well enough to not trust her yet. We'd been living together for maybe a week, and I foolishly agreed to dinner with Bobby instead of coffee or an afternoon walk, which meant I got locked in with the guy for an entire evening.

We were only halfway to his car when he told me, "People say I'm intense and stuff."

"Oh yeah?" I was already just being polite. Bobby kept bumping against me.

"I'm just tuned in."

"To what?"

"You know." He pointed at me and then back at himself. At me. At him. At me. At him. "Like this."

He had that way of acting like we were far closer than we'd ever be. That we were intimates who'd maybe only just rolled out of bed to have some supper.

I kept laying down my markers. "Stay," I told him in the restaurant when he tried to slip out of his side of the booth and join me over on mine. He kept nudging and bumping me with his legs until I pulled mine underneath me. When he finally went to to the bathroom I called my roommate on my cell.

She was being narcissistic about her haircut at that moment. She wanted me to tell her what I'd really, really thought about it because she'd decided she didn't care for the way her hair fell on her collar.

"It doesn't touch everywhere," she told me, and then made her usual piglet noise that came out of her whenever she felt in danger of not being taken for lovely.

"Get over here. We're at Benny's," I instructed her. It was a steak place in Roanoke, a good half hour from Hollins, but I thought I could manage Bobby well enough for an hour or so yet.

"Ate already," she said. I think she was going by Lara just then. She was one of those girls who changed her name about three times a year. Once she'd use up the names she'd been given, she'd move on to ones she'd seen in movies or found in books.

"Bobby's a freak," I told her. I kept an eye on the restroom hallway.

"He's just intense," Lara said.

"I've heard."

"Is my face crooked?" she asked me.

"I'll tell you when you get here."

"I've got like homework and stuff."

"I'll cut your hair while you're sleeping."

She knew I would. I'd done it before.

"Pammy!" She made her piglet noise again.

"He's coming back," I said.

Of course, he slipped into my side of the booth.

"Girl's room," I told him.

He grinned. He shook his head. "You're all right."

Then he massaged me sort of all over for about a quarter hour while he reminded me, every now and then, how intense he was.

"I'm going to piss all over both of us," I finally told him. "Move." He did.

I went into the ladies's room and locked myself in a stall.

Lara showed up but a good hour and a half after I'd called her. She'd had to pick out clothes after all, put on her face, fret over the lay of her hair.

"You in here?"

I came out to find her checking her lips in the restroom mirror.

"He's done time, right?" I said.

Lara giggled. "Silly."

"Has he seen you?"

Lara nodded. "He's kind of mad at you."

Bobby wanted to believe he'd struck a lucky vein, that he'd have his way with two girls for the balance of the evening. Bobby was skilled at believing stuff like that, even and especially in the face of countless, forceful contradictions.

"So, ladies," he said and tossed his napkin on the table.

"I'm not feeling so good." I didn't bother with the dumbshow of laying a hand on my stomach and pulling a sour face.

"Aw, sweety." Lara did all the acting for me. "Let's get some Pepto in you."

"Whoa, whoa, whoa, whoa," Bobby said. He fished a packet of Alka Seltzer out of his back pocket. It looked too much like a condom at first and gave me a bit of a start.

I ignored him and went fishing for my debit card. When I pulled it out, Bobby looked stricken and offended.

"What kind of guy do you think I am?" he asked.

I very nearly told him. Lara saved me from it by steering me by my elbow towards the door.

"She's delicate," Lara told Bobby.

"How are you feeling?" Bobby asked her.

Lara had to stop so she could face Bobby and be the merest bit shirty. "I'm delicate too."

"I mean let her go on and you and me have a drink," Bobby said. "Or something."

She thought about it. That was the trouble with Lara. The girl had no judgement where people were involved. She was great with shoes and lip gloss. Wore a skirt like nobody's business, but she wouldn't have known a cannibal from a Christian Scientist.

"I don't think I can drive," I said to Lara.

"So I'll come on behind you," Bobby said.

Lara said nothing but looked agreeable. I was left to tell him, "Don't."

Out in the lot, Bobby guessed he was due some sugar. That's what he told us anyway. So it wasn't, in his head, just me and him and me and him and me and him any longer, but Lara figured into what he had coming as well.

She even let him kiss her. Once he'd started leaning my way, I did enough hocking and wheezing to change even Bobby's mind.

"Thanks for dinner." I brought myself to touch his forearm. I'm not a savage after all.

"Yeah. Well." He raised a hand to touch me back. Grazed my boob, of course.

Bobby lingered in the lot and waited for us to pull into
the road. It took what felt like forever. Lara had to study
herself in the rearview first. She had to readjust her seatbelt.
"I'm going to get creased," she said.

Bobby waved as he watched us. I didn't wave back. We
finally rolled towards the road.

Bobby called, of course. Twice an hour there for a while.
He even came to our apartment for several nights running.
He even knocked the first few times. Lara gave me her
pitiful, pouty look, but even she didn't want him inside.
Soon enough, he just haunted the parking lot. Bobby parked
usually on the dumpster end where one of the mercury lights
was burned out. Sometimes he'd call me from the lot and
claim to be in Miami or somewhere.

"Got business," he'd say and then laugh and shout like he
was talking to some Gold Coast friend of his.

Occasionally, I'd tell him, "I can see you."

That never much mattered to Bobby. Like most skeevy
guys, he was a fabulist — a thing I'd learned about in a lit
class. Our professor had written a scholarly paper about
Robert Louis Stevenson and Jean de la Fontaine. He read
aloud to us what he called "pithy abstracts," which was a bit
of a lie itself. There was nothing pithy about them, and they
were punishingly long, but it served to get us all talking and
thinking about accomplished liars we'd known.

My aunt came to mind. My father's sister who found
telling the truth so disagreeable that everything I can
remember coming out of her mouth could be contradicted
with facts.

"Well, you know . . ." she used to start, and then she'd
explain why whatever topic you'd just touched upon,
whatever thing you'd just described, had all happened
otherwise and looked different than you thought.

She was an authority on everything. Not much of a challenge really when you're always free to cobble the world up.

Bobby, for his part, had picked an area and focused exclusively on it. He'd decided to believe that females wanted him. It was a given in his head. I doubt he'd troubled himself to wonder where the attraction sprang from. In his mind, he was probably masterful in a way that men never are on this earth.

I finally called the cops on him over Lara's objections.

"He's just intense," she kept saying.

"You've got lip gloss on your teeth," I finally had to tell her. That sent her to the mirror to check and left me free to call the cops who rolled in and rousted Bobby.

One of the cops — a cute guy with an unfortunate boot camp haircut — came to the door to tell me, "He says he's a friend of yours."

"He also says he's in Miami. Who are you going to believe?"

Bobby sort of got the message. He shifted to another girl who'd probably made the mistake of smiling at him or making trifling small talk with him in a check-out line or somewhere.

She survived somehow. A neighbor heard the ruckus and went over to find her shut up in a closet and Bobby beating on the door. The neighbor had carried along his shotgun, and he clubbed Bobby senseless with it.

When Bobby came back around after he'd made bail — she'd forgive him; he was Bobby — that girl answered the door with the pistol her neighbor had left with her for peace of mind. Bobby tried to charge on in (it was what she wanted after all), and she shot him well past the moment she had used up all the bullets. She was blubbering and pulling the trigger still when the guy from next door showed up.

In Waynesboro in that grimy front alcove of the local precinct building, I thought about Bobby for the first time in a while.

Skeeves give off a vibe. This one sure did. He was wearing one of those khaki twill uniforms with an oval over the front shirt pocket. His said Buddy in it. He was trying way too hard to still have hair. Combing it up from all over. And he had the sort of stubble that either meant he was whisker deficient or he'd gotten halfway into shaving and had finally said, "Fuck it," and quit.

He looked at me like Bobby had. It was a carnivorous glance. His jaw did a funny, twitchy thing. And when he came past me, he made sure to brush against me just a little. It's what they do instead of introducing themselves in any civilized way.

I let him get fully outside, pass through both doors and hit the sidewalk, before I swung around towards Fig at the precinct desk and told him, "Eeewww."

ii

I followed Fig's directions out to Buck's house down by
Greenwood. I was wearing my take-me-serious pantsuit and
my take-me-serious shoes. I ended up having to wait on
Buck's stoop while his dog barked at me through the door
until the man himself finally rolled up in his truck and found
me.

He looked better than most guys his age, not so slack and
paunchy. And he had a way of measuring what he said and
waiting on me to talk that made me even more uneasy than I
already was. He'd seen too much. You could look at him and
tell it. He'd heard all the lies and evasions already. You
couldn't spring a new one on him.

If skeevy Bobby was one side of the doubloon, Buck
Aldred was the other.

"Mr. Aldred . . ." I started. I had out my pad, my cheap
Bic pen at the ready. I'd failed to notice how chewed up and
disreputable it was until I was sitting there in Buck's kitchen
trying to get taken for a newshound.

"Buck," he said.

I asked him about Kiki Dunbar. I didn't have a lot to go
on. Fig had told me the guy was sniffing around, hired out
by her dad. I was putting together my breakout piece on
some local homicidal monster. It was thin. Virtually
transparent. I had a string of coincidences and a bucket of
wishfulness.

"I don't reopen cases," he told me.

I made what looked like a note. I always doodle when I
get nervous, so it wasn't a note exactly. It was a tree squirrel
in profile.

His dog had rubbed a streak of iridescent snout grunge on my pants. Mr. Aldred gave me a wet paper towel to tend it with.

She was a warty, old thing. Martha, I think. She had a bald spot between her ears and was raining dandruff.

Buck kept pointing at a ratty rug beside the refrigerator. "Go on," he'd tell her.

She wouldn't. Sometimes she'd growl a little. Every now and again she'd fart.

I blurted out more than I'd meant to at first and indicted Fig along the way.

"Who's the pipe?" he'd asked me. He had a way of cutting right through it. I tried not to tell him.

"Guy with the freckles? The one on the desk?"

I must have gone red from my toes up.

Then I overcompensated. Stiffened and got officious. "Does Mr. Dunbar have new information on the case?"

He gave me boilerplate about a father's undying love. That sort of thing. I made what looked like another note, but it was snout hair and whiskers.

He leaned against the kitchen counter and fixed me with a look. It was a give me what you've got or go on back where you came from sort of gaze.

I didn't have much. A few names. What had struck me as damning coincidences. The dog bought me some time. She parked herself in front of her master. She groaned and wiggled her butt on the linoleum.

"What?"

A bit of a warble followed. He fished a treat out of a bag. I checked a page with some proper notes on it so I could make sure of the name.

"Heard of Annette Marie Wilton?"

That knocked him back a bit. You would have a thought a hard guy like him would have a better poker face. It was in his eyes chiefly. He looked at me with more interest and savor than he'd shown before.

"Heard of her how?"

I gave him her dates and her particulars. Horse woman gone missing. Hacked bones in the woods.

He was good for a nod. "I might have come across her."

"Tawny Fay Quinn?" I was running out of ammunition fast and probably would have wilted if he'd not asked me, "Have you got cops in the family?"

I had to guess I was making a better impression than I feared. I don't know why I told him we'd been in shoes. My father drove a dump truck. He came home every night either gravel dusted or stained with red clay. Somehow it never seemed to me like a proper career for a grown man. He always knew that's what I thought. He had no poker face either.

"She was from somewhere in Pennsylvania, right?" he asked me.

"Kutztown."

I waited, hoping the valve would spring open and he'd start giving information to me. That's how they'd taught it at Hollins. Create a vacuum. Draw out the details. Like most things they taught at Hollins, it didn't work well in the world.

He took a hard look at my business card. Ok, so I'm only technically a producer, but "intern and blogger on a shitty stipend" doesn't open many doors.

"What's this for anyway?" he wanted to know. He'd been around enough to know this sort of story wouldn't get on air.

I talked up our website like we covered real news instead of weather and traffic bottlenecks, viral videos and hair care tips.

"So what do you think?" he asked me. "About these women?"

I worked on my squirrel fur. I might have shrugged as I told him, "Weird." I get pouty when people ask me things I wish they hadn't asked me or don't let me steer them they way I want them steered.

I knew I only had a few coincidences, and Buck Aldred told me as much. In his career, he'd probably seen scores of people disappear. New York City. You have to figure the influx and outgo is pretty severe.

He told me about what I expected. Big territory. Considerable span of time. Three women but just one body. Probably not even three crimes.

"I don't like coincidences," he said, "and that sounds like all you've got."

That's when I trotted out the scrap I had left. "Four," I all but announced.

That surprised him. I could tell he was keen to hear more, so I asked him for a cracker or something instead. He'd given me cup of weak tea. There were some Cheez-Its on the counter, but he offered to scramble me up some eggs instead.

I let him. I needed the time to do my breathing and recover. It was hard work trying to be an adult with a guy so accomplished at it. I stood up and went to the bathroom while he was getting his skillet hot. I nosed around, of course. Who wouldn't? The dog had trashed his furniture, especially the sofa, which was finished in corduroy. Big mistake with a leaky old dog like his. His bed was made and his nightstand was tidy. The meds in his cabinet were all over-the-counter.

I couldn't locate a photo of any human anywhere until I got back to the kitchen. There was one on the refrigerator. It was snapshot of Buck and a woman held onto the freezer door with a magnet shaped like Vermont. He was looking at the camera and took a decent picture. She was looking at him, staring at the side of his head in what struck me as a pitiful, needy way. She had two eyebrow studs. The kind of short, tousled hair that women pay a lot of money to get.

I tapped on the photo. "Daughter?"

He shook his head.

"She looks like trouble."

"You sure your dad's not a cop?" he asked.

"Shoes," I told him again and sat.

I wasn't hungry, but I ate the eggs anyway. I wanted the man to know I was grateful.

"So?" he said.

"Martha Stovall," I told him. "A Mennonite from the valley." I named the nursery her family runs near Stuarts Draft.

He knew the place but hadn't heard of her. I could tell I was springing something on him. I gave him Ms. Stovall's particulars up to and including the way she disappeared. Last seen at the Pinnacle Motel on the eastern slope past Afton.

He knew the place. Who didn't? The crazy Pakistanis who ran it had filled in the pool with cement or something and put nine holes of carpet golf on top of it. Who goes to stay at a motel in hopes of playing carpet golf?

"I had a repo there once," he said.

I'd copied an old article about Martha Stovall from the Daily Progress. I'd brought it along and pulled it out of my pocket, handed it over to Buck. It didn't do much beyond confirming in print what I'd told him already.

"No sign of her?" he asked me.

I shook my head.

"Maybe the boyfriend is good for it."

I'd quizzed the guy at the nursery, which I told Buck all about.

"Could be she had somebody on the side," he suggested. "Even Mennonites are human."

I was getting a feel for how he worked. I had to imagine he did the same thing in his head that he was doing out loud to me. Sifted through every possibility. Each alternate explanation. Tried to figure what he might get up to if he was a young, engaged Mennonite girl. He worked like a man who'd jumped previously to a conclusion or two and got burned.

"You think somebody snatched her?" he finally asked me.

That was the story I was after, the one sure to vault me off the web page. I nodded.

"Same guy who got the other three?"

I nodded again.

"You see the problem here, don't you?"

"Like you said. Big territory. Could be nobody's found them yet."

"Or killed them yet."

"They go missing at regular intervals . . . kind of. Not precise maybe, but three years or so."

"Guy with a camp ax and a calendar?"

I shrugged again and nodded.

He brought out a half-eaten sack of stale ginger snaps. I ate half of one and quit.

"Coffee?"

I didn't see how it could be worse than the cookies. I nodded. "Do you think these women just wandered off?" I asked him as he filled the pot at the sink.

"We know one of them didn't," he said. "She sure didn't hack herself to pieces. But the others . . .?"

"Is that going to work for Kiki Dunbar's father?"

He shrugged. "I told him up front I wouldn't do him any good."

I drew my squirrel a foot and got a little snide. I threw back at Buck what he'd told me when I got there. "I guess you are just making the rent."

If that irritated him, he sure didn't show it. We drank coffee. He asked me about some restaurant in Richmond where I'd never eaten.

"Well," I said and closed my notebook.

"Nice squirrel," he told me and left it at that.

He walked me to the door. His dog stuck her nose up my backside one last time, fairly plunged her snout into my bunghole.

"Train her to do that?" I asked him.

"Mind of her own," he said.

I like to think I have a firm handshake for a girl. Mine's almost military, and I'm particular about it. I offered my hand to Buck Aldred and did that Prussian I thing I do sometimes where I very nearly click my heels together.

"Thanks for you time and the eggs and all."

"Sure."

He grabbed his dog by the collar and held to her as I went down the steps and along his frost-blasted cement walk towards my car.

"If you mean to keep going . . .," he shouted my way.

I stopped. I turned. I waited.

"Talk to Elsworth Phelps."

"Phelps?"

"Ask freckles."

"All right."

I drove straight to Waynesboro. I had instructions from Fig. Since he'd put me onto Buck Aldred in the first place and had passed along all the info he could round up on the women who'd gone missing, Fig felt entitled to a blow by blow. And he was bored anyway. He wouldn't tell me exactly why he was out of his cruiser and working the front precinct desk instead.

"I was naughty," he'd say and shut me up by promising to lay it all out later.

Fig took his afternoon fifteen once I'd shown back up in the main precinct doorway. We headed for what passes in Waynesboro for an espresso bar. The big expensive Italian machine stays broken. The guy who owns the place will tell you at length about his boiler gasket problems.

"Only make the damn things in Rome or somewhere." He'll pull out a schematic if you let him.

So we'd always go straight for the regular java in the big pump thermoses and then head for the table we've grown to prefer on the puny patio out back. The compressor racket usually means we can lean in close and say whatever we please.

"How did it go?"

I fished out my notebook. "A good start. He didn't know about Martha Stovall. He's being kind of a stickler about the rest of them. He'd rather believe they just wandered off."

"He doesn't, right?"

"I don't think so, but he's working for Mr. Dunbar, and there's nothing solid he can tell the man. We've only got one body out of four."

"Four that we know of."

"That's Buck's whole thing. There's too much we don't know."

"Did you give him that line about writing a story?"

"I gave him my card. That seemed to be enough. I don't think he held back."

"How did you leave it?"

"He told me to look up Elsworth Phelps."

Fig sighed.

"Dry hole?"

Fig nodded. "Dirty dry hole. Hard to say if he'll be worth your time."

"I think I can go back to Buck. Give him a week or two. See if anything's changed. We kind of hit it off."

"Oh?"

"I'm guessing he's got a kid somewhere who won't give him the time of day. I show up. I listen to him. I'm interested in what he's up to. I felt like he was okay with that. Like maybe he needed it even a little."

"Could be. Nobody around here seems to know a thing about him. Been here three or four years. Does piecework. Keeps to himself."

Fig poured the dregs of his coffee out between the decking, tossed his cup in the can beside the door.

"Hate the thought of losing you to a geezer," Fig told me.

"You don't have me."

He winced. He said, "Ouch."

Buck

i

His church had been some kind of grocery mart, a little
tilted stick-built place way out in the county past Batesville.
He'd turned it into a tabernacle -- or rather had painted the
word "Tabernacle" on a sheet of plywood nailed to a post.

The door wasn't locked, so I let myself in. There were ten
different types of chairs set up in front of a hotel lectern.
You could see where somebody had peeled most of the
Hilton decal off. There was a plain pine table up front as well
with a couple of offering baskets on it, a pair of bright-brass
candlesticks, and a table runner with a Bible verse stitched
on it: "I am the door. If anyone enters by Me, he will be
saved."

The cross leaning against the back wall was made from
treated four by fours. They were cobbled up with no art to
speak of and just enough craft to hold them together.

I perched on a rickety ladder-back chair, had to pick up a
hymnal to do it, and I was thumbing aimlessly through the
thing when I heard, "Troubled, brother?"

He was standing in the back doorway just beside the
cross, and he might have looked passably clerical but for the
hair mousse and the neck and finger tattoos. He sure had
cadaverous down, was all veins and joints and hollows, and
the sleeves of his cheap, black suit coat looked about half a
foot too long. He'd rolled up the excess like an 80's dance
club refugee.

"A little," I told him.

I'll give this to the Sweet Lord Jesus, it's a miracle who He can take by the throat and haul in. The guy before me was Cal Jarrett. Randolph Calvin Jarrett on his sheet. He'd assaulted a seventy-eight-year-old woman when he was only eighteen and had done a full five years out at Deep Meadow. He'd found the Aryan Brotherhood immediately and the cleansing love of the Savior only presently and in time.

"Many are the plans in the mind of a man," he said, "but it is the purpose of the Lord that will stand."

I laid the hymnal down and rose to face him.

"What manner of policeman are you?" the reverend asked.

"The retired kind."

"Come to me all who labor and are heavy laden, and I will give you rest."

"I'm not here about my soul. Got a minute for me anyway?"

He motioned for me to follow him and exited the sanctuary. We ended up on a patio out back. It was furnished with picnic tables made out of treated posts as well. They looked thrown together by the same jackleg who'd made the cross.

When I parked on one of the benches, the whole thing creaked and rocked.

"I'm not much with a hammer," the good reverend confessed. "Better with my flock."

"I counted ten chairs. Not much of a flock."

"Mighty oaks from little . . ."

"Yeah, yeah." I cut him off. "I'm not so interested in what you're up to now."

I fished one of the clippings about Kiki Dunbar from my jacket pocket. I unfolded it and laid it in front of Calvin. He gave the thing a thoughtful once over and managed a grim mortician's expression before shifting it back my way.

"Did you know her?"

"A little."

"How?"

"I did work for her daddy sometimes."

"What kind of work?"

"Helping with hay mostly. And I painted a couple of barns. Was with him two, three summers, off and on."

"Tell me about her."

He shrugged. "Just a kid. Mostly had her nose in a book. Wanted to be a teacher or something."

"Talk to her much?"

"Mr. Dunbar would feed me lunch sometimes. In his kitchen, you know? I'd talk to her a little."

"Did you know her mother?"

He nodded. "Troubled woman."

"Troubled how?"

"Head case. Wouldn't take her pills."

"Violent."

He thought about it long enough to get me interested. "Loud. A real screamer. Raged all over. But I never saw her do a person harm. Stuff? Yeah."

"How did Kiki get along with her?"

"No worse than anybody else. They mostly just left the woman alone."

"What about you and Kiki?" I asked him. "Ever just the two of you there?"

It had taken nearly a quarter hour, but Cal Jarrett finally reverted to type. He pointed a tattooed finger at me. "You've seen my sheet, right?" He was indignant.

"I don't remember exactly. You went in for a fight with your boyfriend?"

"I attacked a woman!" Then the composure came like a curtain falling down. "That's what they got me on anyway. A mature woman."

"Elderly, wasn't it?"

The preacher shook his head and told me, "It was dark."

"Assault, right? That sounds like rape pled down."

"Is what it says," Calvin told me. "I was raised by the pulpit but fell away from God. I found the path again, and I'm determined to stay on it."

"Is there a living in this?" I glanced at the back wall of the Reverend Calvin's tabernacle. It had less paint and more rot than the front.

"The flock does what they can. I've got a good woman. She helps me along."

"What woman?"

He ignored me. The Reverend Jarrett fished a pack of Merit Menthols out of his jacket pocket and fired one up. We sat there in silence for nearly a minute just looking at each other.

"Why are you digging around on Katherine Dunbar?"

"Got asked too."

"Mickey?"

I nodded.

"And you're here because they hauled me in?"

I nodded. "Did Mickey put them onto you?"

He shrugged. "They found out I knew the girl a little. I had a motorcycle and all. Some rough friends. Wasn't like they had much else to go on."

"Who did you talk to? Charlottesville? Waynesboro?"

"Elsworth Phelps. We'd locked horns before."

"Who'd you give him?"

"I don't work that way."

"Come on, preacher. I saw the file. Phelps kept you barely a half hour. That's not interrogation. That's commerce."

Calvin grinned. "Might have give him a boy."

"Raijaun Howard?"

He shook his head. "Barry Dan."

"Rivers?"

A nod.

"Jailbird?"

"Just knew him from around."

"You boys have a falling out?"

Calvin flicked his smoldering butt away and immediately plucked out another Merit. "No sir."

"Then why put Phelps on him?"

"Maybe," he said and paused to light up, "I thought Barry Dan was good for it."

"Any particular reason?"

"The man's a kink. What more do you need?"

"Give me a for instance."

"I'll leave that to Barry. He's quite a talker once you get him going."

"Still like him for Kiki Dunbar?"

Calvin puffed to stall. He squirmed where he sat. "I don't know. Never heard nothing solid." He squinted at me through the smoke. "Come to think of it, I never heard nothing at all."

"I'm getting a lot of that," I told him.

When the preacher flicked this butt away, he didn't reach for another smoke. Instead he stood up to let me know the interview was over. "Service this Sunday at noon," he told me by way of invitation.

"I'm Jewish on Sundays." I stood up as well.

"We do Wednesday nights."

"Jewish a little then too."

We didn't shake hands, but Calvin raised a tattooed finger like Jesus might if Jesus had been a lowlife con. He could see I didn't much approve. Calvin wasn't blind.

"People change," he told me.

"That's what guys like you keep saying."

"This is the day the Lord made," Calvin said. "Let us rejoice and be glad in it."

ii

She was far too eager to be anything but exactly what she was. She had ink-stained fingers, was wearing a linty pantsuit and sensible shoes. She was waiting on my front stoop and getting barked at through the door. Her dinged Tercel was blocking my driveway. I had to park in the ditch.

"Mr. Aldred? Buck Aldred?"

I nodded as I climbed out of my truck.

"P.J. Lamar -- Action Weather News Team, Richmond Fox 7."

She shoved a business card at me once I'd gotten within arm's reach. Action/Weather/ News! Pamela J. Lamar. Associate Producer.

"What can I do for you?"

"Just a word."

"About?"

She was trying to look thirty, but I had her pegged for twenty-five. Even that proved generous as it turned out.

"I understand you've reopened the Katherine Dunbar case."

"You understand wrong."

She pulled a tattered dime-store spiral notebook out of her jacket pocket, flipped to the page she was after, and told me pretty precisely who I'd talked to about Mickey's daughter.

"Who's the pipe?" I asked her. "The kid at the desk, isn't it? With the freckles."

She colored enough to give the guy away. He was about the only one who'd know everything she'd told me.

"Yeah, I went through the file," I said. "But I don't reopen cases. I'm not a cop."

"You were." She'd done some googling, and she told me all about it. She made a decent stab at biography even if she gave me an extra ex wife.

There on the stoop, I decided there was probably an upside to talking to P.J. Lamar, Action/Weather/News! girl from the Fox affiliate in Richmond. I figured a piece on Kiki Dunbar couldn't hurt. Maybe a witness would come forward. Maybe a killer would confess. Who the hell could say? And she looked a little like my daughter who barely even spoke to me anymore.

"Come on in," I said as I wrestled my junky storm door open. "My dog's going to wipe her snout on you, and I can't do a thing about it."

P.J. tolerated Mabel well enough. She behaved as if gurgle juice on the leg of her pantsuit was the sort of thing reporters had to suffer for a story.

"That ought to buy me an exclusive," she said once Mabel had left off swabbing her up.

"Nobody else is asking," I told her, "so, yeah."

I gave P.J. Lamar a damp paper towel and a cup of gunpowder green tea. She wiped her pants, laid her open notebook on the dinette, and consulted what I saw to be a page half covered in doodles.

"Why is a homicide detective asking around about Katherine Dunbar?"

"Former homicide detective, and this one is just trying to make the rent."

"Mr. Dunbar hired you?"

I nodded.

"Why now?"

"Serendipity."

She scribbled. Paused over the spelling.

"I-p-i-t-y," I told her.

"What does that even mean?"

"It means we bought tires on the same day. He did me a favor. I'm doing one back."

"That's it?"

"That's it."

More scribbling. She looked to be drawing a tree squirrel.

"Anything else?" I asked her.

She chewed on her ballpoint. The thing was so gnawed on and munched over that it was flattened on the shank end.

"Annette Marie Wilton." I waited for an elaboration, but nothing ever came.

"What about her?"

"You know the case?"

I nodded.

"Tawny Fay Quinn?"

I was bordering on impressed. I nodded again.

"Serendipity?" she asked me.

"You got cops in the family?"

P.J. Lamar shook her head. "Retail. Shoes."

"What's this for anyway? It can't be the evening news."

"Our web page. They kind of let me run the blog."

"And you've decided what exactly about these women?"

Either she couldn't say or didn't want to. She shrugged and went back to her squirrel. "Weird. That's all."

"I'll give you that. You've got no theory at all?"

"Kind of your area. Right?"

"I'm prepared to go with coincidence. Three women but one body. One crime."

P.J. scratched with her fingernail at a spot of iridescent drool on her pant leg. "Four," she said, and she left it at that until she asked me, "Got some crackers or something?"

I didn't have crackers beyond a box of Cheez-it crumbs. I offered to scramble some eggs instead, and P.J. told me, "Yeah. Go on."

So I cooked. She doodled. Finally, she talked. She was winning me over with her reluctance to natter.

"Martha Stovall," she said. "2010. Mennonite from out in the valley. Her family runs a nursery near Stuarts Draft."

"I know that place." I'd killed three houseplants a whiskery clerk in suspenders had all but guaranteed me I couldn't do.

"She was making a delivery to Ivy," P.J. said. "Mid afternoon. July. She never got there. They found her truck at the Pinnacle Motel."

"Which one's that?"

"Above the Parkway. With the pool and the putt putt."

I'd previously tracked a Riviera to the parking lot of that motel. The repo guy made too damn much racket, and the owner came out of his room. He was naked and had the sort of physique best not paraded uncovered in public, which didn't stop him from chasing his sedan on the hook clear out to the road. I was watching from across the lot, and that guy's long, sad walk back to his room makes for a memory I'll never get out of my head.

P.J. fished a reprinted Daily Progress article out of her back pocket. Like most stuff in the Progress, it was brief and uninformative. Martha Stovall had disappeared while her truck had neglected to. Anybody with information should call the Crimestoppers number they listed.

"Nothing since," P.J. told me. "No sign of foul play. No tips. No working theories. Nada."

I set her omelet in front of her. P.J. got up and fetched the ketchup from the fridge. She applied a thorough skimcoat to her omelet with the backside of her fork.

"How old was she?"

"Nineteen."

"Maybe she had a boyfriend. A Baptist or something. They ran off. Easiest thing to do."

P.J. ate like a felon, all crowded around her plate. She soon had ketchup on far-flung parts of her face the way a toddler would.

I handed her a napkin. "Wipe." She did.

"She did have a boyfriend. He works at the nursery. He's the only one still looking for her."

"You talked to him?"

She nodded. "Ezekiel Flynn. Goes by Buster."

"Maybe she had something on the side. Forbidden fruit and all that."

"Hard to see how she'd fit him in." P.J. gave me a blow by blow of Martha Stovall's daily schedule.

"The boyfriend tell you all this?"

She nodded. "And her brother. And her parents. And a friend of hers -- a Unitarian."

P.J. pushed her plate away. I snatched it up and rinsed it. My house might look junky sometimes, but my dishes are always sparkly clean. A man's got to pick his pathologies.

"So she got snatched? That's your thinking?"

P.J. nodded.

"The same rascal who got the other three?"

Another nod. "Three years apart, more or less."

"Some guy with a calendar and an ax?"

She shrugged. She doodled. With P.J., it wasn't a display of indifference or neglect. She doodled instead of cramming slack bits chock full of palaver.

"That's not a lot to go on," I told her. "And we could be looking at something else altogether. There's a reason you usually need a body for a murder trial. People get walkabout. People go away."

P. J. nodded. She doodled. She left me feeling like I had to fill the gaps.

"Here's my problem," I said. "Nobody around here sticks to anything. Job. House. Wife. They're always throwing stuff up in the air and starting over. So it's hard to believe there's some yokel back in the woods grabbing a woman every three years. Nobody around here's that regular. Not much discipline in these parts."

It sounded good as it was coming out. P. J. just told me, "Hmm." She raised her tea cup my way. Wiggled it until I took it.

I made a pot of coffee and joined the child at the dinette. She was giving her squirrel a sycamore tree to sit his haunches at the base of.

"I had a case in New York," I started in. I couldn't help myself. "A guy was killing hookers. The first one was an accident, and the thrill of getting away with it led to the second, and then the third. When nobody came looking for him, he needed a fourth, and on like that. The charge of it took over. The jolt he got whenever he killed a woman. He got obsessive. Erratic. Sloppy. Those guys only stick to the plan in the movies and in books. It's all bloodlust and bad genes, some brain function gone haywire."

P.J. left off drawing long enough to shift her gaze my way.

"I can't imagine a hillbilly with three years of waiting in him," I said.

"Maybe," P.J. said as she shaded in the sycamore canopy, "he's from somewhere else where people do regular things."

It was my turn now. "Hmm," I told her.

She shut her notebook. Got up out of her chair.

"Or you were right to start with," she said. "You are just making the rent."

We shook hands at the door like we'd closed on real estate. She fairly bowed and clicked her heels. Then I lingered on the stoop to watch young P.J. Lamar back her Toyota into the street. She rolled straight across my juniper to get there.

"Kids, huh?" I said to Mabel.

She dabbed snout juice on my pants.

iii

I corralled P.J.'s ginger at the hot dog joint in Waynesboro, tracked him down the following afternoon. I'd only just parked in front of the station house when he came out headed up the sidewalk. I watched him window shop at the furniture showroom, where even the sofas reclined. Then he ducked into Earl's next door. I left my car and joined him.

"Hey, friend," I said.

As he turned my way, his wholesome smile melted a bit. He jerked his head by way of hello.

I plucked P.J.'s business card out of my shirt pocket and showed it to him. "She gave you up."

"She told me." He pointed at the order window. "You eating?"

I'd eaten at Earl's once, and that was enough. The dogs were pork. The buns were stale. The chili was grease-based and what meat there was in it tasted distinctly of hoof.

"Just a tea," I said. The boy ordered me one.

We stood at the counter by the front window. There were no tables in Earl's.

"They call me Fig," he said between bites.

"Short for . . .?"

"Nothing."

I tapped my chest. "Buck."

He nodded. He chewed.

"What did you do before you got your badge?" I asked him. I was half expecting him to say, "Paper route," because of the red hair chiefly, because of the freckles. The ginger girls all have a porn slot if they want one, but the ginger boys just go around looking like kids for years.

"First of the ninth," he told me. "Helmand mostly."

"How long you been here?"

"Going on three years."

"Why are you riding a desk?"

"Hit a guy. Broke his jaw. He claimed to be complying."

"They'll do that."

He nodded and then went about the chore of trying to wipe Earl's chili residue off his chin with Earl's cheap tissuey napkins.

"Tell me about P.J."

"She's got a nose. A brain too. I think maybe she's onto something."

"I read the file."

"Why?"

He shrugged. "Missing girl. Hacked up lady. Interesting."

"And you gave it all to P.J.?"

"It didn't work that way," he told me. "She was digging already. She's like that. We just got to the same place at about the same time."

"Where do you know her from?"

"Met her in a bar in Richmond."

Another cop walked into Earl's, a doughy guy with a flat top. Him and Fig grunted at each other in the way that says between cops "Hey" and "Go fuck yourself."

"Come on," Fig said. I followed him out the door.

"I'm getting the feeling you don't have a lot of friends on the force."

We went half a block down Main Street and then turned back south. We were around the corner and heading for the cemetery -- the one that used to be a Baptist churchyard before the church burned down -- when he finally told me, "Not my people."

"None of them?"

He shook his head. "I'm trying to get on in Richmond."

We passed through the wrought iron gateway and into the graveyard proper. For Baptists, it was a showy spot with a fair number of gaudy monuments and more than a few crypts and mausoleums. Lambs on tombstones (Jesus Called) and angels with trumpets by the gross. We headed up a rise along an asphalt path, passed in between a phalanx of towering cedars of Lebanon.

"Phelps is dirty," Fig said. He'd even gone to the trouble to glance around before he'd said it.

"Does it touch on the Dunbar case?"

He shrugged. "Dirty kind of touches on everything, doesn't it?"

He had a point. I nodded.

We passed a rose-colored tombstone, taller than it was wide, with an oval enameled photograph fixed to it. A photograph of the deceased, Harold McKinney Boyd, leaning against the fender of his car. He looked proud but appeared to be awfully underdressed for a tombstone, what with the shorts and the t-shirt and all.

"I'm working my way through the suspects. Two down. One to go. Barry Dan Rivers. Know anything about him?"

"Freak," he told me. "But his thing's boys."

"You sure about that?"

Fig nodded.

"I guess I'll talk to him anyway."

"I would," he said. "Creep resource."

"So what else? Have you got any more to go on than P.J. did?"

He tapped his sternum.

"Gut?" I said.

He nodded.

"Gotta give me something solid. I can't waste Mickey's money just poking around."

Fig inspected the vicinity. It was us and the tombstones and the squirrels. The plastic flowers. The odd veteran's flag. A lone radio car was parked on a bordering block across the way. Dalton squinted at it briefly but seemed to decide it just happened to be where it was.

"Phelps got in business with a bad bunch," he told me. "Bledsoes from out by Three Priests, on the way to Wintergreen. Tough on women is the way I hear it."

"What sort of business?"

"Drugs. Something. I don't know. Involved an awful lot of looking the other way."

"Funny. Phelp's wife gave me an inch of money to leave it all alone."

"How much does that come to?" Fig asked me.

I paused to set a rusty vase of brittle, sun-bleached plastic gerber daisies upright. "Didn't count it. Not enough, I guess."

iv

I eventually met Phelps up on the Parkway at what passed for an overlook. He proved tough to pin down for a guy who was trying to pay me to leave him be.

He had hounds in the bed of his truck in cages. I heard them barking before I saw him. From the looks of that overlook, we'd have the place to ourselves until Old Milwaukee time. There were cans strewn all over and weathered, beat up twelve-pack boxes. Empty cigarette packs and hamburger wrappers. Condoms too, of course. Nothing says romance like a weedy pullout with a view. Apparently, there'd once been a map or a sign or something, but only the splintered posts remained.

Phelps roared in and braked hard. The hounds in their kennels got sufficiently jostled to leave off barking for a moment. Only a moment. They were at full yelp and bay by the time Phelps reached me at the block restraining wall. I was standing in a half-moon jut out built for soaking in the panorama. I could see a couple of sprawling estates, the county landfill in the distance, a straight piece of Interstate 64 between Ivy and Charlottesville.

Phelps smelled of tobacco and kibble.

"What made you want to raise hounds anyway?" It seemed like a decent enough icebreaker. We had to start somewhere.

"Property came with them," he told me. "I thought you could give them away, but you can't."

"Where's that?" I pointed. Something was burning. A column of smoke was rising, bent east by the breeze.

"Sawmill. Licking hole."

"Place past the Sunoco?"

Phelps nodded. He turned to the sound of hounds snarling and shouted towards the parking lot, "Hey!"

We didn't talk further for a bit, just watched a hawk together. When Phelps finally spoke he told me, "We wouldn't have found her. Don't care what you think."

Then Phelps sighed in a way that gave the impression he was ripe with regret. I'd heard it from cops before, usually the sort who'd wrung every penny they could from some wayward enterprise and then had started to wish they never did and wonder why they had.

"We caught a boy on the highway," Phelps began. "This would have been '95. He was running with bald tires and a headlight out. His truck look like the Clampets packed it. Lonnie lit him up. You know Lonnie?"

"Heard of him," I said.

"It would have just been a ticket if the guy had acted like he had some sense. He had a few square bales of actual hay," Phelps said, "but it was mostly pot underneath. Then down in the bottom of the pile, Lonnie found some guns and stuff."

"Stuff?"

"Ammo. Suppressors. A grenade or three."

"Ambitious for hillbillies."

Phelps nodded. "Especially our sort. Lonnie . . . quizzed him."

"I'll bet."

"He was heading for Philadelphia. Half down and half on delivery. Lonnie called me. We had a meeting of the minds."

"How would he know to call you?" It was less of a question than an accusation.

For a passing moment, Phelps looked primed to complain about his miserly salary and his long hours of unappreciated devotion to the law, but then he thought better of it and told me, "We'd worked a warehouse fire together. A place up 340. The blenders and the microwaves didn't make out so good, but they had some mowers and string trimmers back in a shed that came through all right." He shrugged. "Insurance paid. We couldn't see the harm."

It was an old story. "What was the deal with the pot guys?"

"Just let them come and go."

"It had to be more than that."

Phelps shook his head. "Mighty have made a few promises we never had to keep. What were we going to do if they got pinched in Baltimore or Philly?"

"How much was it worth?"

"We split around 200k. Made them quit with guns. Too much downside."

"Are they still in business?"

A shrug. A nod. "But not like they were. A couple of them went inside."

Another nod. "Intent to distribute. A couple of them went inside."

"Why tell me?"

"They snatched a girl once," he finally said. "Two, but one of them got away."

"Bledsoes?"

He nodded. "The one they call Jumbo has . . . uh . . . impulse control problems."

"I'm thinking I know which impulse."

Phelps sighed and scratched the back of his neck.

"And I don't guess they call him Jumbo because he's dapper and beguiling."

"In a few more years, they'll be moving him with a winch."

"Did you at least ask them about the Dunbar girl?"

I got the sort of nod that said, "Kind of," at most.

"What happened to the girl they snatched?"

"They turned her loose. Me and Lonnie got on them."

"Charges?"

Another shake of the head. "Paid her."

"You or them?"

"Me."

"I'll need a Bledsoe to talk to. Probably not Jumbo."

"Denny," he said. "He's the brains."

"Where do I find him?"

"Dog River."

Phelps watched me write it down and snorted.

"Crackerville. Bumfuck," he told me. "It's not a place. Means no damn where."

"Kind of hard to drive to."

"I'll set it up, give you the where and when."

I nodded.

"We done?" Phelps asked me.

"A couple of things. Barry Dan Rivers?"

He shook his head. "Doesn't have much use for girls."

"A kink's a kink," I told him.

Phelps shrugged. "He's around, has some kind of fixit business. Go to the hardware. They've got a card."

I'd brought the envelope with me off my dinette. I pulled it out of my back pocket and offered it to Phelps. "Your wife worries about you, the way a wife will."

He lifted the flap and glanced at the cash. He clearly hadn't known what she was up to.

"It's not like I'm worth it," he told me.

It was nice to part in complete agreement. "No," I said. "It's not."

Buddy

i

It's simple for me. I take heed and do as directed, which always sets the balance right. So it's not like I can indulge in terribly much strategic planning. I stopped even squandering thought on being careful after awhile. Better to be lucky, I've come to find out, and depend on human nature. There's a reason witnesses are unreliable. You've got to be looking out on the world to hope to soak in anything.

My guiding interest and passion is me, and that makes me just like everybody else. All those good Christian girls Keith cultivates are a lot less interested in your salvation than they are in their stinking hair. Keith, as decent as he is, is fixated on his urges, and Hotchkiss and them can't begin to see past the baseball standings in the summer, the Wahoos' schedule in the fall. Pittman's got his gastric issues to be Talmudic about. I've got a cousin on my father's side who can carry on for hours about the freakish shape of one of her big toes.

It's an embarrassment to her and a torment. She's convinced it's blunt and unsightly and has decided after extensive study that it hardly lays like she'd prefer. She still goes around in drugstore flip flops because she's that brand of trash, so her problem toe is usually out where anybody can see it. Consequently, most every time she meets a stranger, she'll raise a finger, wince a bit, and start off by saying, "One thing," before pointing at her foot.

She's worse than Keith with his erection. I offered to file the thing down for her once, round off the offending part. That didn't sit well with her.

She laid her hand flat on her breastbone, as I recall, and said, "I am dismayed!"

She must have read an article in Us Weekly or somewhere that featured a dismayed starlet or singer. My cousin picked up her vocabulary like inmates pick up trash on the highway — one scattershot piece at a time that just happens to be where they are.

And she's not even freakish, my cousin. Not in any way that matters. She's just more blatant about the thing she has given herself over to.

It's what I count on. My nugget might be black and treacherous, but it's also small enough to manage and is self-contained. I'm never tempted to talk about it like my cousin with her toe, so I can always yield the floor, and the world I live in is full of takers. There's awfully little involved in teasing them out. A "What's up?" will usually do.

That's why Crimestoppers and canvases are such a wasted effort. If you're always looking in a mirror, there's not much horizon for you to see. I depend on people being who they are — they can't help it really — which allows me to stay just who I need to be.

I have tools I carry with me. They're in a box in the trunk of my car, but they don't look dastardly at all. They're just items I can use in any circumstance I meet with. A bundle of shop rags. A tow rope. Duct tape. A retractable carpet knife. A metal flashlight. One of those shiny space blankets. And a can of diethyl ether — starting fluid to you.

I imagine I'm like those people who feel a seizure coming on. They get a twitch. A flutter. I suffer my jaw to do that thing it does, but more violently and more often than it ordinarily does it. That'll be coupled with a kind of internal itch. I don't know what else to call it. I'll feel raw and uneasy on the inside. Out of sorts. Unsettled. On edge. I'd would say that's when I begin to look, go out in the world with a purpose, but I wouldn't say that I ever truly hunt. What I need just comes to me if I practice the patience Barry teaches.

Sporty Lisa, for instance, in her riding pants. She got put right in my way. A fuse failed her or something. I'm no good with cars, but like most men I can raise a hood and pretend to know what I'm up to. We were in clear sight of the fruit stand at the pullout in the gap, but the girl running it had her nose in a trashy book. She didn't own a broken down truck. She wasn't pulling horses. She'd already gotten to where she needed to get to for the day, so she didn't need to have an interest in anything past her novel until somebody stopped in for apples or stone fruit when she'd sigh at the imposition, weigh their sacks, and take their money. Go back to her book.

"I might have one of these." That's the full extent of the palaver Lisa got from me. I'd pulled a scorched 20 amp fuse from her box, and I showed it to her as I spoke. Just like fate intended, she followed me to the trunk of my sedan.

I went in my Seagram's box as if after a fuse and slopped out some starting fluid on a shop rag. Lisa talked. I nodded some more. I glanced around. That was the extent of the care I took.

"Here's one," I said. I leaned down further.

She was right in the middle of being grateful and relieved when she leaned down as well. I brought up my dampened rag and clapped it over her nose and mouth. I caught her in a headlock that would have looked to passersby like a chummy hug, but there wasn't anybody much on the roadway, and we were on the backside of her truck.

She was too shocked at first to struggle, and then she was too woozy to put up a fight, and then she was wilting and half conscious. I just had to steer her, let her tumble into the trunk. I folded her up where need be and shut her in.

I knew from experience I had forty minutes or so before she'd start banging. I drive a 1973 Valiant, which is as close to invisible as you can get behind the wheel. Mine is gray-green and rusty, the color of dirty lichen. It's the four door, not the coupe. I found it by accident, which, like I've said, is kind of the way with me. I was headed for Richmond to get a tooth pulled. It had broken off, and my regular guy didn't feel fit to take it out. He'd referred me, and I was off the highway looking for the medical park when I passed that Plymouth parked on a front lawn with a sign in the window.

I knew immediately it was exactly what I needed for my calling. Before that very moment, I'd given the matter no thought at all. Truth be told, I wasn't convinced back then that I even had a calling. But there I happened to be in Richmond and happened to be on that road and happened to see that sedan that nobody else had offered on yet. I recognized in an instant how anonymous I could be in a lightly rusted, grey-green Plymouth Valiant with chalky paint. It had black sidewalls and no distinguishing dings. The base model right off the line. No options. Nothing special about it all.

I continued on another mile and got my busted tooth extracted. Then I came straight back and negotiated for that Valiant with the owner.

He had a footed cane and an elevator shoe, enough nose hair for a throw rug. "Got more than that in it," he kept telling me until I finally hit a number he could abide.

That Valient smelled of dashboard vinyl and floor mats. Once I got the thing home, I discovered a suitcase full of baby dolls in the trunk. They'd all had their clothes taken off and each one had an eye pulled out. The things people get up to is a wonder to me sometimes. I piled those dolls up in the yard, doused them with gas, and set them on fire. I shot the hose on the suitcase and kept it. I've since put it to valuable use.

The place I inherited from my uncle is about as close to nowhere as you can get in this part of the world. We're too far from Wintergreen to be part of that. A hell of a hike from Afton. If you could get by just calling a place East Jesus South, that would probably be best for us. Off and away. Hidden and swallowed up hardwood forests that stretch for miles. Red clay tracks where the rain water runs. Deer carcasses with the saddles cut out left to rot all over the place.

My neighbors are all clans. Fitzgeralds to the west. Daubs to the south. Bledsoes to the east. The Blue Ridge Parkway and nobody much to the north. And me planted right in the middle of a hundred wooded acres on a road I wouldn't go down if I didn't live at the end of the thing. I pay a Daub twice a year to sculpt and shape it a little for me, crown it enough to let the water run off and scrape the weeds away. He doesn't own a proper tractor, just a state-body truck with a blade on the front.

He always asks me if him and his clan can hunt in my woods, and we both pretend that they're not doing it already.

I've worked improvements on my uncle's house. Nothing too grand and ambitious. I didn't want a crew back in my stuff poking and sniffing around, so I did everything myself. I'm probably a little too guilty of hoping for the best where it comes to construction as well, so I'll get right in the middle of a project and take a wrong turn, make a misstep. Sometimes I can recover. Other times I simply quit.

So my place doesn't look like anybody else's, even out here in the hills and the hollows where everything is rigged up. My place is a warren and a ruin and a hodgepodge and a fortress. No two windows are the same size. There's not a wall in the house that's plumb. The roof leaks in eight or ten places. If I had insulation in the walls, it would surely all be moldy. My furnace is oil fired and heats just two rooms. I don't own a stick of furniture I give a damn about.

I've been sorely tempted more than once to set the place alight. Get my Daub in with his blade to level me off a brand new site where I'd put up a home that was square and true. Only big enough for dreams, like Barry says.

Instead I just shut off most of the house that I've got and live where the heater works.

Lisa was as angry as I'd ever seen her. I didn't have to open the trunk to know it. She stayed busy explaining to me who she was and who she knew while I just stood there at the bumper and heard her out. She offered me money. Quite a lot of it. She told me she came from people in Lexington who were enormously well off. Then she wailed a bit before she shifted around to assuring me her people would hunt me down and kill me. After that, she was quiet for a bit.

It's easier when Lisa stays asleep. She has a knack for irritating me. That's what keeps us together, I have to think. We know where each other's buttons are. We've been partners in this life for so long now, that it's all shorthand with us. I can wound Lisa. I know exactly how to do it. And she knows exactly what to tell me that will shoot straight to my core. We're tangled together, for better or worse. I've accepted and embraced it, but I'm beginning to doubt that Lisa ever will.

She's pigheaded that way. I admire that about her. I'm always having to instruct her because she never ever learns.

I have a length of ash I keep on hand. It had a maul head on it once and is left from the days back when my uncle burned wood in his shed. The thing is half collapsed now, but the old sheet stove my uncle used is still standing. He used to sit out there and read his Bible to get away from my aunt. She knew where his buttons were and made it her life's work to mash them.   He was a Book of Joshua connoisseur, couldn't get enough of Jericho falling. "They destroyed with the sword every living thing in it." He'd lingered so on that page it was grimy from his fingers. "Men and women, young and old, cattle, sheep and donkeys." Then he'd clap his massive Bible shut, and he'd usually add, "So there."

About all I had left of him, aside from his claptrap house and musty furniture, was his shattered maul handle that I had put to more than a little use. It was stout and dense, so palm worn it had become slick and glassy. I kept meaning to cut off the splintered end — it being stained and all — but it was one of those chores I could never quite get to like glazing my windows and fixing my porch steps.

I don't know what became of his Bible. It probably rotted like everything else.

I shoved the key in the trunk lock, which set off more wailing. I heard metal on metal and had to think she'd found something she hoped to brain me with. Lisa has always been a bit of a tiger. She can often hide it well enough to make you half believe she's tame, but she's a wild one, Lisa is. When I'm ticking my reminders — and Barry has me tick reminders in the regular course of things — I usually tick the one about Lisa getting up to violence. I played the fool and let her cut me once. That wouldn't happen again.

She jabbed a screwdriver at me this time in a frantic sort of way. She told me, "Don't! Don't! Don't!" while she did it. She was all but blind with fear. I tapped her on the wrist bone. That was enough.

"Climb out," I told her. Barked it really. You have to be stern with Lisa. If you're soft with her and give her an ounce of hope, she'll just play on you like she does. What do you want? What can I do? She'll even take off her shirt sometimes. The fact she believes I'd be swayed by such business has a way of setting me off.

Lisa glanced around at my compound in that forlorn way I'd seen before. How did it come to this? Who could have imagined? It was all part of the giving up.

I motioned for her to turn. She appeared to think I'd violate her. That's Lisa for you. I swung on her instead.

I use my hands, whether I need to or not. Intimacy in all things, Barry likes to say. I dragged Lisa back in the woods a bit to a spot I've grown to favor. It's more loam than clay, so the drainage is good, and there's a hummocky place that does fine service as a kind of table for me. I left her there to consider all she'd done to end up like she had.

I once had a visit from the power line guy when Lisa was fresh on the ground. Fortunately for me, my car was parked so he couldn't have a clear look at her.

"Hell, Buddy," he said, "this you?"

I knew him a little from work. The phone guys. The power guys. The gas guys. The oil guys. We're always crossing paths.

"Uncle's place," I told him. "Just out here checking on it."

"Got a ticket on a Bledsoe." He had a screen mounted on his dash that he scrolled through. "They're saying a transformer blew."

"Probably shooting at it," I told him. "That bunch'll shoot at anything. Go back to the road and turn right. A mile maybe. Big stump with oil cans and mess sitting on it. They're all back in there."

He nodded. He eyed the house and all of the tumbledown mess around it.

"Your uncle up in here by himself?"

I shrugged. "Can't talk sense to some people. I keep telling him there's a whole world out there."

He shifted into reverse. "I've got one of them too. In West damn Virginia."

He found a spot to turn around. Made one really with his bumper. I stayed where I was until I couldn't hear him anymore. Like usual, I was only stirred up after the danger had passed. I'm sorry to say, I took it out on Lisa.

ii

Hotchkiss and them were talking about it or I probably never would have heard. One of those boys had a deputy friend, a short guy with a brushy mustache. So puny he must have gotten special dispensation to be on the force at all. They all called him Corndog. He came around sometimes. I can't really say why since they were merciless with him. Hotchkiss was always patting him on the head like he was a collie.

He was the sort who took it well enough until he took it poorly. Those times he'd swing by in uniform and they'd get him all stirred up, he'd unbuckle his belt and lay aside his gun and his cuffs and his mace and his taser and say to whoever had broken the straw, "Me and you. Come on."

The scuffles all ended the same way. He'd get picked up off the ground, wrapped in an embrace and held there until he'd calmed down. I don't know how he got away with policing. I doubted he could even beat Keith up.

I'd never heard his given name, so I just called him 'officer'. It never pays to be thoughtful with his sort. He'd only ever call me 'faggot' back. Hotchkiss and them had clearly filled his head with lies about me. They'd all convinced themselves that me and Keith were some kind of lusty item. They called Keith 'gimphole' but lacked the nerve to do it to his face. It seems that even cretins hew to some kind of moral code.

It was Corndog who brought news of the hired cop poking around in my business. He had a lot to say about the man. Resented him for sticking his nose in local police matters. For being from New York fucking City. For having worked as an actual detective. Corndog tended towards resentment the way some people tend towards fat. He couldn't talk about much of anybody without seeming to hate him a little.

I had to get what I could by eavesdropping. Hotchkiss and them wouldn't ever engage me in a regular conversation. It would all go vulgar and damning about a quarter minute in, and Corndog had picked up all the poison about me from them. So I had to lurk and overhear, couldn't steer the talk at all, which meant I got a lot less than I wanted but enough to pique my interest.

"Remember that girl that went in the woods?" Corndog said.

Lucky for me, Hotchkiss and them could never recall much of anything beyond NASCAR standings, cumulative football yardage, slugging percentages. They gave Corndog their slack expressions.

"A while back. Mickey Dunbar's girl."

"Shit." That from Hotchkiss who, as it turned out, didn't care for Mickey Dunbar. The long version was Hotchkiss had tried to cheat him on some sort of tractor fitting, and Mickey Dunbar had refused to stay cheated, had claimed his money back. "A deal's a deal. Am I right."

Mickey got his usual grunts and nods.

"His girl disappeared," Corndog said. "Remember?"

"Three Notched, right?" Hotchkiss asked him.

Corndog nodded. "Never turned up. Flat gone for good."

I was in the next room over, fooling with the printer. Pretending anyway to fool with the printer. Pulling out the paper tray. Messing with the cartridges. Starting it up and turning it off. I was the only one who could work it, so Hotchkiss and them were used to seeing me fiddling with the thing. I remembered that girl up on Three Notched. She'd been out for a walk in the middle of the day. Never got where she was going. Never came home. Stone cold mystery. Even to me.

"This guy," Corndog said, "he's NYPD. Retired. Nosy as hell. Couldn't stick with Mickey's girl. Had to find a whole string of them going back years."

"String of what?" Mr. Pittman asked. He was passing through on his way to the stairwell, so he had precious little time to spare.

"Killings," Corndog told him. "At least that's how it's shaping up."

"Around here?" Pittman wanted to know, but not so badly that he'd wait long to hear it. He had his hand on the doorknob.

Corndog nodded. "Some crazy son-of-a-bitch."

That seemed awfully hasty and judgmental, but I let it go without comment.

That was enough for Mr. Pittman. He was down the stairs and gone.

"How many we talking?" Hotchkiss asked.

Corndog shrugged. "Four. Five maybe. Found one of them hacked to pieces. Remember that woman from a few years back."

I perked up. I certainly remembered.

"He thinks it's all one guy?" Hotchkiss asked.

"Seems likely," Corndog told him. "Ain't but so many nuts any one place can have."

I became aware of my chin muscles tightening. I concentrated and regained control.

Hotchkiss and them didn't seem much affected. They already had a poor enough opinion of the local population to have factored in some crazy bastards.

The one with the widow's peak — he went by two initials and a junior — wondered aloud if that hacked up woman hadn't done a thing (like women will) to get hacked up about.

"Maybe she stepped out on him," he suggested. "Could have busted up his truck or something."

Hotchkiss nodded, which clued in the rest of them to go on and nod as well.

To his credit, Corndog had his doubts. "Busted up his truck?" he said.

"Hell, boy," Hotchkiss told him, "you drive a damn Neon."

That got such a laugh that Corndog reached instinctively for his belt buckle before he thought better of it, shook his head, and headed for the door.

I left off with the printer and followed him. Out the door and down the stairs and out into the lot.

"That New York cop got a name?" I asked him as he angled off towards his cruisers.

He stopped long enough to swing around and tell me, "Shut up, faggot."

Keith had been loading our truck while I'd been messing around inside. In the course of pursuing Christian girls, Keith had soaked up a bit a Scripture and had a verse or two programmed into his talker so he could merely hit a button and be holy.

When he heard what Corndog said to me, Keith went scrambling for his talker, cranked up the volume, and tried to tell Corndog, "Accept one another, just as Christ accepted you, in order to bring praise to God." I know that's what he tried to tell Corndog because he played it for me later. Instead Keith accidentally hit his "My name is Keith, and I have cerebral palsy" button.

Corndog looked from me to Keith and back to me. "What's he going on about?"

He got in his cruiser and left us. I thanked Keith for trying to intercede. He'd found the right talker button by then. He thrives on praise, and that good word from me gave me the room to tell him, "Got to make a stop on the way."

Keith is compulsive about our schedule. Compulsive about the winding of our extension cords. Compulsive about the direction our screwdrivers lay on the tray in our box. He's particular about quite a lot of things, so so I took care to make our detour seem related to work.

"Mr. Pittman's wants us to check on a job. Won't take a minute. Downtown."

Keith went to the trouble, like he does, to give me his full and official permission. He tapped a key on his talker and told me, "K."

So we made a detour into Waynesboro. I parked in front of the furniture showroom where they sell mostly loungers and ugly plaid sofas, stout tables made of rough pine that they advertise as 'distressed'.

"Back in five," I told Keith and headed towards the big stone building that had previously been a bank.

The desk sergeant was some freckled ginger who would always look like he was twelve. He was enduring a spot of angry talk from a man with a pug on a leash. That dog was severely bug-eyed and kept glancing up at me.

"How am I supposed to know that?" the man asked.

"It's on the website," ginger told him.

"I don't use no websites."

"You can call in and ask. We'll tell you."

"Why in the hell would I call you just to burn my own damn trash."

"Your address is in the city, sir. You have to have a permit."

"Wasn't in the city when I bought it."

The bug-eyed dog parked on its belly and scratched.

"City grew. You're in it now."

"Don't see how that's my damn fault."

"Isn't, but the codes apply to everybody in the city limit. Even the people who didn't start out there, like you."

"I ain't paying this." He'd pulled a tissue yellow summons out of his trouser pocket and made a bid to slap it down on the counter, but it flapped and fluttered and didn't make much of a show.

"Let me see it," ginger said.

"See it. Have it. I don't care. I ain't paying it."

Ginger read the thing over. "It's just a warning," he said.

"I ain't paying."

"Nothing to pay. This time. Get a permit if you're going to burn trash again."

"Hate living in the damn city!"

"Give it some time." Ginger smiled. "Two minutes ago you didn't even know you were."

"Come on."

That bug-eyed dog got jerked up in mid scratch and went clattering after its master out the door.

"Dog peed a little." I pointed at the traces.

"Yeah. Well," ginger said. He couldn't even be bothered to glance. "How can I help you?"

"I got a call from a guy. Kind of let on he was a cop. Kind of turned out he wasn't."

"What did he want?"

"Said he was working on a case. Girl went missing. Up by Afton somewhere. Years back now."

"Katherine Dunbar?"

I nodded. "Sounds right."

"You sure this guy didn't tell you he used to be a cop?"

"Are we talking about the same guy?"

"Aldred," ginger told me. "Goes by Buck."

I nodded again. "That's him."

"Maybe you didn't hear him right. He's been poking all around here. Tells everybody else he's retired."

I shrugged. "Maybe so. Might not have heard him right. But he's square? Okay to talk to?"

Ginger nodded. "Got something to tell him?"

"Doubt it," I said. "I used to live up in there, but I don't know much about much."

I heard the main door open behind me. Shoebottoms squeaking on the stone floor.

"We eating?" she said. "I've got like a half hour."

Ginger nodded. He looked my way. "Is that it?"

"Yep."

I turned around and there she was. She'd gone mousy with her hair. Short and unflattering. She must have picked her clothes up at Goodwill. A polyester suit in some shade of blue I'd hesitate to call navy. It was trying to be purple and failing at it. The pants were too short and flared. Her shoes looked vaguely orthopedic. She had cat hair on the front of her trousers and some kind of cooking oil stain. The ragged end of a notebook was peeking out of her jacket pocket.

As disguises go, it was a decent one and might have fooled me at a distance, but I was hardly two feet from her when I turned, close enough to brush against her as I passed. I might even have winked. I can't remember. I know I didn't say, "Lisa," until I'd gotten entirely outside.

Keith was bored. He has a way of breathing at me when tedium has taken hold, and I wasn't even under the wheel of our truck before Keith exhaled my way.

"Give me a second," I told him. "Got to make a call."

I pulled out my phone and pretended to dial the office. I asked for Mr. Pittman, and then put on one side of a detailed conversation about 10 mil plastic sheeting and respirator canisters. I pretended to listen and said, "Right," about every quarter minute. Then ginger and Lisa came out of the precinct house, and I signed off.

"She look familiar?" I asked Keith.

He stopped breathing at me. Keith is always willing to turn his eye to a girl. He watched Lisa approach her shabby Tercel, precisely what I'd been waiting to see.

Keith shrugged.

"I've seen her somewhere. On a job maybe?"

"Uh uh."

I started the truck. When the Tercel went by, I wheeled around and followed them. We were all headed for the bypass clutter. They pulled in at the Buffalo Wings place right next to the Martin's grocery.

I stopped in the lot and watch Lisa and ginger leave the car and walk together into the wings joint. He didn't hold her hand. She didn't reach for his. The muscles in my jaw calmed down.

Keith reached for his talker, tapped a key. Perfect Paul said, "So?"

iii

They focus way too much on the cleaning up. The packing. The pieces. The brand of butchery. The instrument of destruction. They think it means something. Not a practical something but a something scarred and psychological. A something that's bent in such a way that it'll be revealing if they study how the bones are notched. The pattern of them in the woods. The state of decomposition. They think it's all a puzzle they'll put together. They think the cleaning up will speak.

The trouble is it's just disposal. It's a maintenance obligation. There's nothing of my calling in it. I don't think Lisa should go to the great earth mother in one way or another. I just know it'll be inconvenient if she lingers in my woods. Where she ends up and how she's left there isn't of much concern to me. I listen to my lumbar. I check the weather. I like it foul and gray, because most people would rather be dry at home than wet out in the forest.

I met a kid once. The rascal slipped up on me. I'd just left Lisa in a hollow up under the roots of a hawthorne tree. It had been a coyote den or something once but was full of leaf litter and abandoned. I'd scraped it out enough with a limb so that Lisa would fit inside. My suitcase had some gore on it still. Not much, some drips around the latches, but just enough for a kid to fix on.

I didn't see him until he told me, "Hi."

I choked down a yodel. "Where did you come from?"

He flung an arm by way of pointing. "What's that?"

I'd never bothered to piece together what I'd do and how I'd do it if some civilian happened to see me leaving Lisa in the woods. So there I was having to think on my feet. Luck appeared to have fled for the moment.

"What?"

"You bleeding or something?"

He didn't have a rifle. Not even a slingshot. He was just a boy out tromping through the woods. It was raining lightly and chilly. October, as I recall.

"You live around here?"

He pointed again about like he had before.

"You cut up?"

Kids are drawn to blood the way most women are drawn to diamonds. They can't not see it if any is about and are reliably keen to know just where it flowed from, how, and why. That boy was talking to me but looking exclusively at my suitcase latches. I regretted not having the foresight to have taken a rag to the thing.

"No." I set down my suitcase. I pulled up my sleeves in turn and showed him my forearms. "I'm all right."

I stood there calculating the fuss a boy gone missing would raise. With grown ups, there's always a decent chance they made themselves get gone. Any cop'll tell you adults are always shucking one life for another, so if you're lucky and tidy like I am, you can carry Lisa home and nobody can be certain how much of a hand she had in being scarce. Kids get people all exercised. Frantic. Vindictive.

"So where'd that come from?" This time he pointed with his nose.

I glanced at the latches. They were too conspicuously bloody for me to deny it.

"What's your name?" I asked.

"Bill."

"They call you Billy?"

He shook his head. "Just Bill. Junior sometimes."

"Own a dog, Bill?"

"No sir."

"Any pets at all?"

"Got a cat in the barn."

"I guess that's kind of a pet. Does he have a name?"

He nodded. "Sheila."

"Funny name for a cat."

"Momma did it. For some woman Daddy knew."

I'd set my suitcase down by then, and I'd squatted to bring myself down to Bill's level and be, I hoped, a bit more inviting. He'd taken a step or two towards me as we spoke. It was clearly less me drawing him in than the gore on my suitcase latches.

"You love that cat, Bill?"

He shook his head. "My sister's always messing with her."

"So she'd be pretty upset if something happened to Sheila."

Bill nodded and shrugged both together. "Yeah. Maybe. I guess."

He was right beside me by then. He had a stick in his hand, and I watched as he scraped at a bloodstain with the tip.

"I had a dog," I told him. "Not the yard kind but the sort that lives right in the house."

He shot me a sour look like I'd told him I kept alligators in my kitchen.

"Smart dog. Clean. Real pal to me."

Bill was still poking and scratching with his stick.

"A car hit him yesterday."

"Bust him up?"

I nodded. I made a bid at grief, though I'm hardly accomplished at it. Fortunately, Bill was only interested in the clinical details.

"Bones sticking out and stuff?"

"Afraid so." I worked through a list of particulars. Described the wounds and the fractures and the giblets. Bill was little short of delighted.

"He always liked it out here, old Rudy did."

Bill snorted and muttered, "Rudy."

"I thought I'd lay him to rest in these woods."

"Coyotes'll come through and haul him off."

"Buried him deep," I said.

"You ain't got no shovel."

"I came yesterday evening to get it all ready."

"Where?"

I pointed nowhere much like Bill had done before. "I hid it. Don't want anybody bothering Rudy. He needs his piece."

Bill poked at my suitcase with his stick. "Let me see," he said.

We'd sort of reached the point where Bill would be satisfied or Bill would get extinguished. Opening the suitcase would probably motor things along, so I undid the latches and flopped the thing open. Inside it was a sticky, bloody mess.

Bill made an involuntary noise of delight. He circled that suitcase so he could soak in the gore from every angle.

"That's a mess," he finally told me but in a giddy, triumphant way.

I closed the suitcase and latched it. I watched Bill for any sign that he was unnerved to find himself out in the forest with a creature like me — some man he'd never laid eyes on hauling luggage through the woods, a suitcase bathed in more blood and suet than your average canine could produce.

But mostly Bill seemed pleased. "Cool," he said.

"What are you going tell them when you get back home?"

Bill shrugged. "Nothing."

I chose to believe him. "That's just what Rudy needs."

Bill picked up a rock and threw it. "Hey!"

He was shouting at a deer. It was down slope and across a muddy branch. The thing just stood and watched us. Bill charged down towards it. It held its ground until he told it, "Hey!" again. It ran. Bill ran after it. He was waving his stick and shouting as he dropped over a rise out of sight.

Back home, I tried to make a plan in my head for future excursions. As I hosed out my suitcase, slopped it with bleach, and hosed it again. I made an attempt to formulate a set of rules and bylaws for me. How I'd take better care with packing and never be without a rag. How I'd invest the time and energy and scan and reconnoiter and wouldn't, in future, depend on the weather to keep people home.

The trouble is, I'm not the planning sort and have little use for lists. That's part of why Barry speaks to me as profoundly as Barry does. He's all for me getting primed and ready to meet the world as it is.

"If you're doing it right," Barry says, "you're winging it all the time."

Too much thinking about stuff spoils it. I'd rather take the world as it comes.

I remember a day when I stopped for gas at the Sheetz just west of Waynesboro. They had godawful country music playing over the pump island speakers. That's their custom at the Sheetz. Their gas is cheap, but you suffer for it, and if you choose not to pay with a card at the pump, you get to suffer more inside. There are always piles of people ordering sandwiches and making their own cappuccinos. Buying quart cups of soda and soft-serve ice cream. Gas is the least of what they offer at the Sheetz. You can get anything from a cupcake to a trailer hitch inside.

My practice at the Sheetz is usually to put the nozzle into my spout and get the gas flowing before I climb back into my Valiant, roll up my windows, and play music I prefer.

I have my uncle's cassette collection. He used to smoke pricey Dominican cigars. He indulged that way instead of having a decent house and clothes worth wearing. He had a standing order with some outfit in Miami. I doubt he ever threw a cigar box away.

I couldn't really blame him. They looked to be cedar. The top was a flat piece that slid on in grooves. They were five or six inches square and had come packed with Upmann corsarios. My uncle had smoked three or four a day even after the emphysema.

When I was cleaning up his stuff and trying to make myself at home, I found eight Upmann boxes full of cassettes. My uncle had identified what was on them with different colored stickers that must have told him all he needed to know but meant nothing at all to me. He had a good half dozen portable cassette players as well. Old Panasonics. All the same model. The kind with the row of mechanical buttons that you locked down with your thumb. He'd cannibalized a couple of them to keep the others going. I got one to run off my cigarette lighter once I'd mended and spliced the rotted cord.

The music on the cassettes was all classical. About the last thing I'd expected. If I had to guess, I'd say Mozart chiefly, but I don't worry about the details. The tunes are pleasant enough and inoffensive. I always start one up when I drive in a bid to keep the world out of my head for as long as I'm able. At first, I'd hoped to get Barry on a tape and listen to him in the car, steep in Barry's counsel and wisdom, but I decided in the end I was better off with some mad fool hammering away on a harpsichord.

So I was listening to an energetic performance at the Sheetz, which stifled the country music, though nothing could drown it out entirely. And I was turning every now and again to check that the gas was still flowing when Lisa pulled in beside me just up and out of the blue. She had on peasant duds right down to the bonnet and was driving a state-body truck loaded with what looked like bedding plants.

At that time, I hadn't seen her in probably a year and a half. I'd long suspected Lisa had gone underground and was working to avoid me, and she just about got away with it even at the Sheetz. No makeup. Hair gathered in a pony tail that hung out of her bonnet. Buttoned up to her neck and covered to her ankles. She looked like an unfinished version of herself, primed but not painted yet.

I needed a couple of minutes of study to convince myself it was her. Then finally she shifted around, and I caught her at that Lisa angle. Once she'd holstered her gas nozzle, I followed her right into the store.

I didn't care if she saw me. I knew when she did, she'd let on that she hadn't, and that's exactly how it turned out when I brushed past her at the check out. She was paying for her cup of coffee when I caught her eye.

I didn't bother to speak to Lisa. So very much had passed between us. There was hardly anything left to say.

She lacked my discipline. She always had. "What?" Lisa asked me.

I shook my head. I smiled. If there was going to be grace between, it had to come from me.

I turned and left her before she embarrassed herself and headed straight back out for the lot where some twangy guy was being a flag-loving shit kicker in three-four time. I made short work of pulling loose a plug wire on Lisa's truck, and then I eased away from the pump island in my Valiant and waited.

She went farther than I'd hoped she might. I could hear her engine knocking and bucking from even back where I was. When she finally pulled off, she eased into a motor hotel lot. The place was open but hardly looked it. It was up past Afton and nowhere much. There was a Jeep in the lot and a pickup. A trio of plastic chairs blown over on the lawn. Carpet golf where the swimming pool had been.

Lisa didn't check her mirrors and so failed to see me right behind her. She headed straight for her front end to raise her hood. I knew enough to bring my rag.

She was peering and poking around, that way women will with an engine, and I was able to slip up beside her before she noticed I was there.

I offered her the plug wire. She took it from me and gazed upon it. I could just about hear the gears and the ratchets spinning up between Lisa's ears.

She looked like she wanted to say, "What?" again, but I didn't give her occasion. I raised my rag and slipped behind her just enough to clamp her tight.

Lisa, when she's in regular shape and hasn't let herself go puffy, has sufficient she-cat to her to make trouble for any man. Since I'm not a strapping guy myself, I depend on surprise and leverage. I've read up on eastern self defense. I know pressure points and torque, but that wouldn't help at all if I wasn't calm in my calling. I'm serene when it matters. I'm steady. Stark panic wears Lisa out.

Lisa's truck was parked in such a way that we couldn't be seen from the road, but I had no way of knowing if we were being watched from the motor hotel. I didn't see anybody, but there well might have been people inside looking at us. I succeeded at staying placid, making it look like a playful tussle. That's the sort of improvement Barry has helped engineer and cultivate. I'm able in the moment to be precisely who I need to be.

I shoved Lisa onto my back seat. She pitched off and sprawled on the floor. I climbed in under the wheel and drove south in the direction of home. I pulled off on a gravel side road, redosed Lisa with my rag. Then I opened my trunk and dragged her around, folded her up inside.

A guy hauling a load of milled lumber came creeping by just after. He stopped when he reached me. He was that sort — and this part of the world is fairly infested with them — who'll take any to have a conversation. And by conversation I mean a chance for him to prattle and spew.

"Hey here," he said. He shut off his engine.

I gave him a head jerk hello.

"Trouble?"

I shook my head.

"I had one of them once." He was eyeing my Valiant. "1962. Hyper pak."

I nodded as I slipped under my wheel, turned the key and started my engine.

"Had a hole in the hood for the manifold."

I smiled and pointed up the road as I shifted into gear.

"I thought that was some kind of sweet."

I was pulling away by then. For all I know he stayed right where he was and talked to just himself for a while. I was around the bend and out of sight before he'd gone anywhere. In other parts of the world, that might be rude enough to get you noticed, but around here the sort who kill their engines in a hopes of a good yammer seem to be entirely impervious to offense.

I felt sure that guy with the lumber would put me from his head once he'd run across some poor soul on a Toro mower or wearing boots he used to own or a coat he used to have.

As run-ins with Lisa go, this one was fraught enough on the surface, but it turned out like all the others, and that's what matters in the end.

"Eyes on the horizon," Barry likes to say. "Always look where you want to be."

Lisa pretended she couldn't wake up, but I wasn't fooled. I talked to her anyway. I identified the lies she'd told me. The slights I'd suffered from her. The indignities and insults. I let them pop out as they come to mind. I'm satisfied that way.

Then I perched on her like I had to and saw to the details. Lisa got frantic. Lisa got sad. Lisa went away.

P.J.

i

I attached myself to him, and he didn't appear to mind. At first, I was just going to shadow him, but he noticed me right away and told me I ought to ride with him as a way of economizing. I was hoping to pump him anyway, so why not?

His truck smelled like dog. The dash vinyl was rotten, and the bench seat was held together with tape.

He was tracking down the last Katherine Dunbar suspect and intended to meet up with Bledsoes.

"I had a chat with Detective Phelps," he told me. "You?"

"Never called me back."

"He wouldn't. There's nothing you can do for him — aside from making trouble."

"Fig says he's dirty."

"Was," Buck told me. "More ignoring the law than breaking it. That's his version anyway."

"You must have seen plenty of cops like him."

Buck made a noise I'd hear a lot. A grunt up in his sinuses like a dreaming bear might make. It never seemed to serve as an overture to the sort of sentiment in words that I could take down and make some use of later.

"I mean . . . it's got to be tempting."

He glanced my way.

"Getting paid to do your job while you're getting paid not to do it."

Another grunt. Buck switched on the radio. AM news and pulsing static.

I could sense in Buck's reluctance to talk the corruption and depravity he'd seen. The situational morality. The savage stuff people do. The senseless viciousness they get up to. If I pushed him hard enough, he probably would have dribbled out a damning detail here, a grisly memory there.

"Why chop a woman up and dump her in the woods?" I asked him as we were headed into a corner of the county where the road was lined on both sides with ancient hardwood forests.

"Some people'll do any damn thing," he said. "You're wasting your time to look for a motive. It's an itch."

"Right."

"They scratch it. There's nothing else to know."

Buck could also tell who wasn't about to get up to anything dire. No matter the posing and the homemade tattoos. The hard talk and the threats and the strutting.

"Some guys are wound tight, but it's all rubber band."

We met one of them when Buck stopped for gas. A logger or skidder driver or something. His plaid flannel was sleeveless. His biceps were inked. He had a pistol on one hip — for rattlers, I guess — and a sheath knife on the other. His truck was held together with sheet tin and epoxy.

Him and Buck were pumping gas on the opposite sides of the same island, and that guy saw me come out of the store and watched me hard across the lot. I'd been exposed to worse. He didn't say anything, didn't tell me (like some of them do) what he'd like to get up to. I was permitted an unobstructed view of his adenoids, but he didn't stick his tongue out of his mouth and show it to me like more than a few of them do. He simply knew I was a female with equipment he could use if hell froze over, civil law broke down, and he caught me before I could sprint away.

For some cobs out in the country, that qualifies as flirting. This guy was more subdued than most. He was leaving me space to give him a sign.

I steered as wide as I could. I was balancing two packs of nabs on the lids of a couple of cups of scalding hot black coffee. While I wanted a buffer between me and that guy, I also wanted to set those cups on the hood of Buck's truck and do it quick.

Consequently, I walked closer to timber boy than I would have otherwise, so I was instantly prepared to share in the blame for causing the guy to get mouthy with me. That was the way I went around in the world at the time. Everything was half my fault.

Buck took a different view altogether. He had a firmer grip on right and wrong. On temptation and transgression. On root cause and effect. Moreover, he wasn't the sort who was given to retroactive commentary. He wasn't scared. He said what he wanted to say exactly when it needed saying.

"What are you looking at, Homer?"

Timber boy peered around the pump to see who was yapping at him.

"Say what?"

"You heard me."

That boy snorted and cackled like Buck was a source of profound entertainment. Timber boy laid his palm on the butt of his pistol. It looked like something he was practiced at.

"Go on," Buck told him. "I'll show it to your colon."

That required a bit more anatomical thinking than that fellow appeared to be up to.

He got out a "Huh," but stayed where he was. That was magic Buck had. Something that came off him like spore.

Men appeared to be sensitive to it. I just knew it was something uncommon, but then I'd been cosseted and fenced in, so most everything was uncommon to me.

Timber boy glared at Buck. Buck never even blinked. He parked the gas nozzle back on the pump, didn't need to look to do it. Then timber boy's buddy came out of the store, and Buck had two of them on his hands. He didn't flinch, just stood there and waited and gave off his spunk, I guess.

Those two glanced at each other. Then they looked at Buck, and they both appeared to understand he'd do what was necessary. Their world was full of guys who'd take a couple of pokes and quit. That wasn't Buck. He'd do what it took, not wantonly and unprovoked, but once he was in it, you could be certain he was in it for good. How a guy communicates all that standing in a gas mart lot, I'll never know, but I'm certain Buck did.

They woofed at us once they were out in the road. They were masterful in retreat. I was primed to apologize. I had to apologize to somebody, but Buck wasn't about to let me take the blame for being a girl in the world.

He only said of the nabs I brought him, "I said I like the ones with cheese."

"Oh," I told him. "Right."

And that was about all we said until we got well down the road.

"I'll show it to your colon?"

Buck smiled. "He's probably still working that out."

Just then we were looking for where the Bledsoes lived. We'd already talked to a pack of them back at a picnic pavilion, and once they'd told us they were heading for the movies in Charlottesville — as long as they were out and all — Buck decided we'd have a bit of a sniff around the Bledsoe estate.

He put me onto finding the place on a map. We'd gotten directions from a guy at the post office in Nellysford. A civilian who'd come in to check his box. The postmistress wouldn't tell us squat. Buck pretended to be with the census.

"That's over," the postmistress told him.

"Standard follow up," Buck said.

She made her I-don't-believe-a-blessed-thing-coming-out-of-your-mouth face, which at first I thought indicated keen discernment on her part, but then she made the same face at the guy who'd dropped in to pull the mail from his box. All he'd done was make a remark about the weather.

He was one of those gentlemen farmers from Richmond or somewhere, come west to tame twenty or thirty acres of upland and renovate some Georgian pile. He said it was "bracing" out, and that woman looked at him like she was insulted. Like if it was bracing, in fact, she'd know all about it and would be the one telling him.

Buck followed the guy into the lot. I followed Buck.

"She's a little on the sour side," Buck said of the postmistress.

"That's charming for her," the guy told him. "She's usually worse."

He was one of those people who made a habit of knowing everybody's business while insisting he was in the dark about what people were up to and why. It's a fine line to walk — nosy and aloof. He made it work with a quiverful of qualifiers. He'd been told. Locals said. The general belief is . . . And on like that. It was the conversational equivalent of a man strapping pillows to himself before leaping from a tree.

At first he wasn't sure he'd ever even heard of Bledsoes. Once Buck had described them (a filthy clan of unsightly unibrows), he had to sort them from all the other filthy unibrows in those parts. There were Caswells and Jaspers and Needhams and Suggs.

"Go a little lower," Buck suggested. "This bunch is close to the ground."

"What do they drive?"

Buck described what they'd rolled up in at the pavilion. It had looked to me like a vehicle four guys had fit together, provided three of them were either drunk or blind.

"Oh yeah." Les nodded. We were all first naming it by then. "And you're with the Census Bureau?" he asked.

"Contractors. Quality control. Like that."

"Not looking to make trouble for them, right?"

"No sir." Buck said.

"I've got to live here."

"Everything stays right here."

"That crew," Les said and shook his head. "I'd call in the Air Corps and wipe them out if I could." He had a litany of complaints against Bledsoes and their ilk, what he referred to as "all those damn people." They weren't tidy enough to suit him and far too shiftless to keep drawing air.

"They spoil and poison everything. If they can't steal it, they'll tear it up."

My parents used to have a cabin down near Amherst. It was right next to a gentleman farmer's manicured estate. He was a version of Les. I guess they all are. Trying to whip nature into shape but only half succeeding at it. At a constant, low boil because the natives are trashy, unregenerate layabouts. His name was Collins. That was his first name. He'd made all his money in banking. He loved his boxwood hedges in a comical sort of way. He finally had the catastrophic aneurysm he was bound to have.

Les seemed to be coping by letting off toxic steam to perfect strangers. The more we talked to him, the less he claimed to know hardly anything at all. He got locally wise in stages and gradually indicted the entire population. He'd pause when civilians would pass between their cars and the post office proper, didn't want to be taken for the wayward gossip that he conspicuously was.

Buck gently nudged him back to Bledsoes when he'd stray. Caswells seemed to be stuck in his craw, so he kept pouncing on them. They'd let a nice house and a choice piece of land go to hell, which seemed to bother Les more than the sort of trash that had never known anything but clutter and hovels.

"They'll cut timber off anything, those damn Caswells."

"Pays the bills, I guess," Buck told him.

"Why not keep the trees and get a job?"

"Who'd hire them?"

Les grunted and shook his head. "That's why I'm calling in the air strike."

"And the Bledsoes?"

"I see them around. They way I hear it, they did a job on one of my neighbors."

"What kind of job?" Buck asked.

"Stole all the garden furniture when him and the Mrs. were down at Myrtle. The deputy wouldn't even go out to see them. He said let the insurance pay."

"He wouldn't go see the Bledsoes?" Buck asked him.

Les nodded. "I think he was scared to mess with them. They've got kind of a reputation."

Buck troubled Les for directions once he'd told him, "We'll look out."

Les proved meticulous about the road numbers and the mileage up to a point. "Once you pass that graveyard, all grown up with vines, they're all back in there somewhere."

Buck thanked him. I thanked him.

"Count them from here," Les suggested. "Just call it too damn many and leave it at that."

We waved. We smiled. Buck thanked Les. He was starting his truck when he said, "Les ought to go back to Richmond quick."

It took a half hour to go maybe four miles.

"If they're growing a bunch of pot up in here," Buck said, "it'd pay them to seem scary."

We were back on a dirt road by then, one of those far-flung tracks the county likes to ignore. Rain had washed out the crown and scoured the ditches. The gravel was long sluiced away. A creature about the size of an airedale darted out of the viny underbrush and then back in it.

I sucked air and grabbed up a fistful of Buck's shirtsleeve.

"Groundhog," he told me.

"Yheti," I said and reached back to lock my door.

We passed the graveyard Les had mentioned. The headstones were rocks. The whole place was a thicket.

"Hell of a spot to end up," Buck said. He pointed out a barn or a house or something in a bend of the road a quarter mile before us.

I told him, "Let's make sure we don't."

It turned out to be a house — also swallowed by a thicket. There were trailers and manufactured homes and barns and sheds behind it. They trailed up the slope in no special order like they'd just been tossed there and left.

"Les kind of has a point," I said.

Buck nodded. "People can sure foul things up." Buck waded into the rocky vegetation that passed with those Bledsoes for a driveway.

"Have you got a gun or something?"

"Yeah," Buck told me. "Back home in a drawer."

He did that thing men do, said those things they say.

"I wouldn't put you in harm's way," or something to that effect. He gave me a fond punch on the arm. "You can stay in the truck if you want."

"Right."

We were already deep in the upland vegetation when Buck started telling me about rattlesnakes he'd seen.

"Killed one in the road last year. It was like rolling over a firehose."

The black cohosh and some strain of fern were thick on the ground where I was standing.

"You've got to get chatty now?" I asked him.

"Probably too cold for rattlers," he told me. "Though I saw one in February a couple of years back."

"Great."

"They don't even rattle much anymore. Evolving out of the habit because people kill the ones that rattle."

"Fascinating."

"Pretty soon they'll be invisible too."

"What's that?" I pointed at a creature poking around of the far side of a pile of lap wood and splintered planks.

"Bear," Buck told me. And sure enough it was.

"Why are we hear again?"

"Dotting i's," he said. "Crossing t's."

That bear saw us and ran off, went blundering into the woods.

Buck stopped in a weedy clearing that seemed to serve as the compound yard. There were three trailers and two actual houses scattered about in no special order. One of the trailers didn't look fit for even a Bledsoe to live in. The windows were all broken out of it, and the nasty drapes were hanging outside.

"Hello!" Buck shouted.

He didn't raise any people, but he got the attention of a quartet of dogs. They came wailing out from under one of the houses. It was sitting up on block pillars. Most of its installation was dislodged and hanging down. Those dogs drew up short of where we were and bounced and barked in a frenzy.

"Now what?"

"They don't look like biters," Buck told me. "Stay here or come on."

He clicked his tongue at the Bledsoe dogs as he headed for what appeared to be a barn. The weeds around it were all tromped down. It had no windows, and the upper loft doors were cinched shut with a rope. The bottom doors were held closed by a gutter nail in the hasp. Buck pulled it out. I'd braved the dogs to join him at the doorway.

Buck swung open the door, had to lift it and shove it. It was dim and gloomy in that barn, but boy could you smell the weed. Rich and herby.

"Give me your phone," Buck said. His lived on the dash, a clamshell piece of junk.

I handed it over. It lit up and chimed when he took it. Buck checked the screen.

"Something from . . . Lacy," he said. "Friend of yours?"

I nodded.

"She took a picture of herself."

He showed it to me.

"It's kind of an avocation with her."

"Kids, huh?" He went on in.

Buck found the flashlight feature once I'd told him where to look. He lit up garbage bags full of pot and a table made out of rough-hewn planking. There were a couple of commercial-grade vacuum sealers parked on the table top and heavy plastic for them on a spindled roll.

"We shouldn't be here." I wasn't used to serving as the voice of reason. Not just with Buck, but with anybody. I was usually the one who went too far too fast and wished too late I hadn't.

"Probably not."

Buck wandered deeper into the barn. He shined the light along the walls, back in the corners.

"What are you looking for?"

Buck was too busy inspecting to bother with an answer.

"If they had something to do with Kiki Dunbar, there wouldn't be much sign of it now."

"Uh huh."

That's when I heard what even I knew to be a pistol hammer drawing back. The gun was in the hands of a girl who might have been three or four years older than me. She hadn't bothered to put on clothes for the weather, had run out as she was to confront us, which meant a wife beater and capri pants, somebody else's boots.

I expected her to unload some sort of cineplex line on us. Something in the "Hands up, fuckers!" range. Instead she snorted and chuckled in a Beavis and Butthead sort of way. Then she wiped her nose. She had to take one hand off her gun to do it, and the weight caused the barrel to droop. She left her nose alone and went back to aiming.

"Who the hell are you?"

"I'm Buck. She's P.J."

He was so casual and serene that the girl seemed to find him unnerving. She wanted Buck to behave like most people would on the wrong end of a gun. Instead, he sounded like the two of them were just having a conversation and there wasn't five pounds of steel and brass and black powder between them.

"We just met with Denny and them," Buck said. "They told us to swing by and have a look at the . . . operation." Buck played my phone light on the bagged up pot. The spools of plastic. The vacuum sealers.

"Like hell," she said. Her right nostril was pouring by then.

"We did," Buck assured her. He glanced my way. I nodded.

She looked maybe a quarter persuaded.

Buck wagged my phone at her. The light flickered on the walls. "Call them."

"That don't have my numbers in it."

She felt around her for her phone. It was back where she'd come from with her jacket. Her pistol drooped as she patted her pockets.

"Don't even think about it," she said but with ebbing steel and pluck.

"I like your style," Buck told her. He stepped her way. "If I'm going to invest, I want to see what I'm buying. See how much people care."

"Hold it!"

Buck didn't. The hammer was back. The gun was a long-barreled revolver. He couldn't be sure she wouldn't just twitch her way into shooting him dead. The whole enterprise seemed pretty chancy too me. I caught myself wondering which direction I'd bolt. I couldn't recall what Buck had done with the truck keys. Dropped them in the ashtray was what I wanted to believe.

"What's Denny going to say if you gun down his capital investment?"

"Right there!"

Buck finally stopped, but by then he was maybe only two feet from her.

"Have you got drying bins?"

She nodded.

"Where?"

"Over there." She glanced.

"How about some lights."

Buck's was an impressive display of denying reality. If he didn't acknowledge that pistol as an active, lethal threat, then possibly the creature aiming it at him would come around to his point of view. She eased over to the switch and flipped it. That gun was heavy. Her arms were tired and she was cold. She decided to let us go unaimed at for a while.

Once she'd switched the fluorescents on, we got the full perspective on the rag-tag rubbish operation those Bledsoes were running. They clearly knew how to grow pot. The climate was largely in charge of that. You could tell by the tops and the buds laying around that they were harvesting quality stuff. What they didn't know how to do was much of anything else, not efficiently anyway.

That barn looked like a homewares store a cyclone had passed through. There were bins and tools and bags and packing cartons all over the place. Enough cannabis litter to keep half a dozen slackers high for probably a month.

"I hear they had some trouble a while back," Buck said. He wandered while he talked and looked for all the world like a man who was giving genuine thought to an investment. "A kidnapping charge or something."

"A guy got behind," the girl told him. She scratched her thigh with the pistol barrel. I couldn't help but notice that the gun was still cocked.

"So they grabbed his girlfriend?"

"Wasn't like that exactly," she told Buck. At ease now, she tossed the pistol onto the rough plank table. For some reason, it didn't go off. I flinched enough for both me and Buck since the bore was pointed my way.

"How did it happen?" Buck asked.

The girl scratched her neck. Picked at her arm. Just looking at her made me feel infested.

"She came over trying to say they'd have money they owed in a week or something. Denny figured the boyfriend sent her. Didn't have the balls to come himself."

"So she got invited to stay?"

"Something like it."

"Who called the law?" Buck wanted to know.

She shrugged. "Wasn't him. He paid. She was here like a day and a half."

"They do anything to her?"

"Yeah," she said. "Let her drink all my damn wine."

Buck gave over his inspection and moved towards the open barn doors. I followed him. That girl leaned against the jamb and scratched her back.

"Which one are you with?" Buck asked her.

By then I was wishing he'd just give the girl an "Adios," and we'd take off.

"Denny," she said. She scratched some more. "Kyle," she said. A bit more scratching. She fairly shimmied against the wood. "Ricky."

We waited. She wriggled.

"Done?" Buck asked her.

She glared at him like he'd called her a whore to her face. But for the itching, she might have charged over to the table and fetched her gun.

Mercifully, Buck had finally had enough as well.

"Tell Denny I'll call him. This looks all right to me."

I followed Buck down the nominal driveway.

"Watch for rattlers," he told me, like I wasn't already.

"Right."

iii

We debriefed at a kind of service station with a restaurant on the back.

Our waitress was pretty much like the girl at the barn, only without the itching. She'd made a few poor tattoo choices. Placement more than design. The stud holes would heal over, but the dragon snout on her neck was sure to keep her out of the boardroom.

She glanced from Buck to me and back to him. She made it clear we were an inconvenience. "So?"

We ordered. When I asked for water that waitress huffed like I'd asked her to paint my boat.

"Like a vegan place, isn't it?" I asked Buck.

"Cheese on the menu. Get your hipster straight."

"Hard to do in Richmond."

"Harder here."

We watched our waitress field a complaint from an inconvenience across the way. The tabouli was under lemoned or something. Our girl responded with, "And?"

"I don't see that we're really getting anywhere."

I was working, in a general way, on being more assertive. My mother had given me a DVD — some guy out in Orange County. He trafficked primarily in frothy SoCal self-improvement, but there was also some stuff on how to get your way. How to be forthright. How to be winningly blunt. That sort of thing seemed within reach for me. I was giving it a try.

"Maybe from where you're standing," Buck told me.

"Why don't you tell me how it looks from over there."

"I'm working for a client. I can't ever forget that. I'm supposed to find out what happened to his daughter, and that's all I'm paid to be up to. Sometimes that means I have to find out what didn't happen to her."

"Like she didn't go to the space station? Long list."

"I think I liked you better when you just told me, 'Right'."

My water came along with Buck's iced tea. He asked for a slice of lemon. Our waitress groaned like he'd put her in harness.

"So how are you feeling about the Bledsoes?"

"Too dirt baggy to get up to homicide."

"Too busy scratching?"

I got the sinus grunt. "Stoners don't kill. Stoners eat Fritos."

"What's that leave? For Katherine Dunbar, I mean."

"Well," Buck said. "We know she went for a walk. On a familiar road. She got maybe a mile from her house. Somebody offered her a ride, I'm guessing, and she took it. Fifteen years old. Not a wild child, as best I can tell. Who would you get in a car with?"

"I like to think I'm careful."

"As best I can tell, she was raised right. Let's assume she was kind of careful too. Who does she take a ride from?"

"Somebody she knows."

"Knows how? From school? From church? From the neighborhood?"

"I guess you've thought about cops. I might get in the car with one of them."

Buck nodded. "Top of the list, but I've got no good candidates. Did your buddy Fig ever say anything to you?"

I shook my head. "Were there relatives around? Cousins or something? Uncles? Aunts?"

"Now you're getting warm."

"Mr. Dunbar?" I was profoundly skeptical. From what I knew of Mickey Dunbar, he didn't come off as a man given to treachery.

Buck didn't think much of Mickey Dunbar as a suspect either. "But he knows more than he's saying."

"That doesn't make any sense. Why hire you and hold you back?"

Buck shrugged. Our waitress brought my soup, Buck's sandwich. She dropped the dishes onto the table from height.

"Spoon?" Buck said and pointed at my bowl.

The girl had a signature grunt of her own, more like a mule than a bear.

"I'm starting," Buck said, "to think it might be a family thing after all."

At first, I thought he was suggesting our waitress had been raised by hyenas or something, but he was just chewing everything Mickey Dunbar had left unsaid.

"There's a reason for the conventional wisdom," Buck told me. "The safe money's on people at home."

"The wife?"

Buck shrugged. "There's no debate that she was a nut. But there's also a son somewhere. Mickey's never even mentioned him."

I nodded. I'd done a little digging on my own. "Matthew. Lives in Pennsylvania. Greencastle, I think." I fished out my notebook and located my scrawl on the matter. "Real estate agent."

"I guess you'll want to go too."

It was as close as I could hope for. "Yeah."

Our waitress pitched a spoon my way. No wonder she'd held it back. My soup tasted like something they might have made accidentally in the sink. Buck's sandwich had come with a piece of cheese wrapper. He plucked it out and showed it to me.

"I guess they get by on the ambience," he suggested.

What else could I tell him? "Right."

Buck

i

I was halfway to my truck when I saw her. She'd parked her Camry up the way a little in the ditch but mostly in the road. A Nationals cap and a pair of sunglasses were hardly enough to disguise her.

P.J. scrunched down as I rolled up on her, though not so far as to get out of sight.

"Want to just ride with me?" I asked her, or asked anyway the top of her near ear and the peak of her ball cap.

Still scrunched, she asked back, "Where are you going?"

"Dog River. East Jesus. West Bumfuck. Somewhere between Alpha Centauri and Wintergreen."

"You buying lunch?"

"Maybe."

She slid full up, tossed her cap on the dash, and said to me, "All right then."

We had what I would discover to be the only sort of chat you could have with P.J. Lamar, which is to say we discussed everything that came to mind pretty much all at once.

I started off by mentioning I'd talked to her buddy Fig. That led to a brief discussion of the politics of the Afghan war and a denunciation from P.J. of the chili served at Earl's. The stuff had made her sick a few months back but not nearly so ill as she'd gotten from eating a dodgy Chesapeake oyster once, which she spoke in detail about as well.

We were halfway to Wintergreen by then, or had reached anyway the junction where Route 6 heads up towards Afton. I stopped in the parking lot of a big, boxy Methodist church to check my map and brief P.J. on who we were visiting and why.

"I've got a lead on some boys. They're Bledsoes. Phelps thought I should chat them up."

"How come?"

"It's complicated."

"I can do complicated."

I ignored her. Tried to ignore her. P.J. thought poorly of getting ignored.

"Got Barry Dan Rivers on the docket too."

"Suspect number three?"

I nodded. I pointed towards a Cavalier Mart a quarter mile up the road. "Too early for crackers?"

She'd pulled out her notebook by then and was doodling away. P.J. had started in on a decent likeness of me but jowlier and balder and a little Satanic, what with the tufts of ear hair and the horns.

"Coffee would be good."

I watched her ink in grease stains on my shirtfront. My trouser fly was at half mast. My pants stopped halfway up my shins.

"That's not very flattering," I told her.

I got a pair of big, bunioned bare feet with nasty, jagged toenails. "Nope," she said. More doodling. "I can't do flattering, but I can do complicated."

"This can't go to the Action/Weather/News! team. Can't even show up on the blog."

P.J. gave me a nod.

"Phelps got in business with some boys who'd been known to snatch their women rather than court them."

"Bledsoes?"

I nodded.

"What kind of business?"

"The usual kind. They paid up to get ignored. Bought two cops -- Phelps and a guy named Lonnie Janks."

"I heard about him. Don't get Fig started."

"Meathead lowlife, by all accounts."

We were back on the road by then. I'd taken 6 north and east and was headed up towards the ridge line.

"You like the Bledsoes for Kiki Dunbar?" She did me the favor of capping her ballpoint and shutting her notebook on her doodle, letting my illusions about myself go uncontradicted for a while.

"I don't know. I've been doing nothing but talking to people for the past . . . what? . . . month and a half, and I'm still only sure she went out for a walk and didn't ever come back."

"But you've put more girls on the list."

"Yeah," I allowed. "Maybe." It all still felt too scattershot to me.

"Where's Rivers?"

"Sherando."

"Is he expecting us?"

I shook my head. "I don't like to be expected."

As far as the police were concerned officially, Barry Dan Rivers was a thief. Unofficially, he was a notorious pervert with an appetite for boys. Not little boys, I'd discovered, but the sort of adolescents that a baby-faced adult could fake if Barry Dan paid him enough. I explained all of this briefly to P.J..

"What's he do?" she asked me.

I gripped the wheel with both hands, concentrated on the road, and told her, "I think he ejaculates on their insteps. Nobody would come right out and say."

"FOR A LIVING!"

"Oh. Fix-it guy. Sorry."

P.J. invoked the Lord.

Barry Dan Rivers' place was no cinch to find. If Google Maps routinely puts the Burger King on the wrong side of the bypass, imagine what it does with a manufactured home where the mailbox is a half mile away back at the place the state maintenance stops and the house itself is sitting up a washed out track in a thicket full of trash that passes for a yard.

I couldn't even locate the mailbox at first. The post it had been fixed on had rotted from the damp and pitched over onto the ground. The dented box itself was sitting in a patch of Virginia creeper. I probably wouldn't have seen it if the red flag hadn't been up.

There was a turn around for the mail truck. Everything beyond it looked like stream bed.

"I guess we're walking from here," I told P.J.

We climbed out of the truck and headed together up the track towards what I hoped would be a house.

"I'm going to tell him you're my assistant."

She nodded.

"No notes. No doodles. No nothing."

"You asking all the questions?"

"Yep. Don't want to hear a peep out of you."

"Best keep your shoes on," she told me.

"You could start now," I said.

We smelled Barry Dan's place before we saw it. The general aroma shifted from lush greenery and moldering leaf litter to something akin to septic drain field married to coyote den.

"Is that music?" P.J. asked me.

It was. Smetana as it turned out. Not what I would have predicted from a guy with Barry Dan Rivers' reputation and about the last thing I'd expected to be hearing in the middle of the woods.

There were a couple of trucks in what passed for the yard. Neither one of them had fenders left. Just ragged edges where the rust had paused for the moment. One of them didn't even have a hood, but they both looked like they'd been recently driven, judging from the muddy tracks they'd made. The near one was still popping and creaking as the engine cooled.

"I'd hate to walk in on anything," P.J. said, which was precisely what I was thinking.

"Hang back," I told her as I approached the front stoop.

It was a rickety, slapped-together perch. Thin, knotty planking that sagged. The aluminum storm door had no glass or screen in it. I located a flat piece of frame and knocked. Nothing. The music was loud and increasingly symphonic. It had been reedy and tinkling for a bit, but the strings had come in by then. I knocked again, harder this time.

The whole house rattled. The front door swung open. Barry Dan Rivers was wearing a flannel bathrobe and a pair of suede mules. His combover was in no proper shape to meet the day. Some of it was standing straight up. The rest of it was flopped in the wrong direction. His pupils were the size of nickels.

He said, "What?" in a tone that seemed mystified and irritated both at once.

"Mr. Rivers?"

He looked past me, found P.J. in the yard. He made an affirmative noise back by his molars.

"I was hoping for a few minutes of your time. I've got some questions."

"Who's that?" he asked of P.J."

"My colleague," I said.

"Come here." He shouted it over his shoulder.

A younger guy. A fit twenty-something in skinny jeans and a belly shirt joined Barry Dan Rivers in the doorway. "Look," was all Barry Dan said.

He did look, like a man who'd missed a few meals would eye an Easter lamb.

"Gentlemen," I said.

They glanced my way. Barry Dan's friend was high as well. Glassy-eyed.

"Get them on in here," Barry Dan's buddy said into Barry Dan's ear. He probably thought he was whispering, but I could have heard him at the mailbox.

Barry Dan tried to open the storm door but couldn't. I had to reach through the space where the glass should have been and unlatch it, swing it open myself. I motioned for P.J. to join me.

I told her lowly, "Stay close," and then preceded her inside.

I've been in a lot of dumps in my life. I've seen people living in hopeless clutter, a few even in outright squalor, and I certainly encountered all over New York City no end of what I'd describe as eccentric decor. Immigrant ware. Family keepsakes and adornments from all over the stinking place thrown in with thrift store furnishings, pictures of Jesus doing everything but water skiing, and knee-high heaps that probably were once tidy piles of the Daily News. All of that mixed in with cat pans and dog beds and topcoats tossed on the floor.

But I'd never seen anything quite like what Barry Dan Rivers had going in his place. Cheap rococo furniture -- side chairs and chintz settees -- thrown in together with fishing gear and fully dressed tailor's dummies. Provided, of course, that latex and chainmaille and strategic rubber fittings even begin to qualify as clothes. There were shoes as well, all over the place. Ladies', men's, toddlers'. Pizza boxes. A greasy chicken bucket. Half gallon orange go cups from UVA football games.

Barry Dan switched off the music. It had been playing on his phone. His buddy dumped junk off a sofa cushion and said to P.J., "Right here, missy."

Instead she plucked a slingback pump off the floor. It looked like a size fourteen. I'll call it teal, with feathers and rhinestones. P.J. glanced from Barry Dan's buddy over to Barry Dan as she tossed the thing back onto the floor, cleared off an ottoman with her foot, and parked herself on it. I claimed the cleared sofa cushion in her stead.

Barry Dan's buddy laid a hand flat against his breastbone as he said to P.J., "People call me Frankie."

"Got it," P.J. told him.

"What do they call you?"

"Nothing when she's working," I told Frankie and Barry Dan both as I handed them each a business card that neither of them looked at.

"I'm following up on an investigation."

"We don't know shit about nothing," Frankie informed me.

Barry Dan pointed at a dinette chair parked against the far wall. It was under the photo of a shirtless model torn from a magazine. A guy in trousers and shoes and a hat even, but nothing else from his navel up.

Frankie looked at Barry Dan like he'd rather not be ordered before he crossed the room and sat.

"What investigation?" Barry Dan asked me.

I told him.

He squinted in a show of concentration. "Dunbar?" he said.

I nodded.

"Where am I supposed to know him from?"

"Her," I told him and made short work of the details of the case.

"And they thought you did it?" Frankie said and grinned. I noticed he had manufactured uppers. A bit too big. A bit too white.

"Guess so," Barry Dan said. "Don't recall."

"Elsworth Phelps would have brought you in."

"Then it could have been any damn thing," Barry Dan told me, "cause he brought me in all the time."

"Why?" That from P.J. She was big on why because she was of a vintage to still believe that everybody did things for a reason.

I didn't even bother to look at her hard to remind her I'd asked her not to talk. What was the point? There was always something sure to need a why flung at it.

"Well, honey," Frankie said. He winked and showed P.J. his choppers. "Police like old Barry Dan. Always think he's up to stuff."

"And hell, I'll say it," Barry Dan added. "I even am sometimes."

"But not this?" I asked him.

He shook his head. "You know what I am?" he asked me.

I sifted through several possible responses before I managed to say just, "Tell me."

"A sumptuary. Ever heard of that?"

Frankie pointed at Barry Dan and said to P.J., "Sumptuary," even if his teeth made him say it a bit wetter than was required.

"You've got the decor for it," I told him. "Even I can see that much."

Barry Dan Rivers' laugh was a throaty, lascivious sort of thing. "My woman ain't been this week," he said. He troubled himself to wink at P.J.

I was about to try a question or two when Frankie asked P.J., "You want something, honey?"

"Got any coffee?" Another instance of P.J. not talking.

Frankie looked at Barry Dan who shook his head and told him, "No."

"Who are all these shoes for?"

I gave P.J. a look, but she'd quite clearly decided to ignore me.

"Now that's a funny thing," Frankie told her. "B.D.'s got a thing for shoes."

"You cum on insteps is the way I hear it?"

Barry Dan grinned and turned my way. "Listen to her," he said.

"Got your sheet right here," I told him. I pulled a copy of his arrest record out of my jacket pocket.

"Ain't never been convicted of nothing," Barry Dan assured me.

"Well," I said, "only twice."

"A man's got to take a plea sometimes, even for stuff he never did. You know how this shit works."

"That foot thing's your business," I said. "I'm kind of interested in this charge here." I scanned his record. "Imprisonment, they're calling it."

Frankie said, "Ha!" and grinned. "Weren't nothing to that. Tell them B.D."

That earned Frankie the sort of look that confirmed who was in charge, a sidelong glance that worked on Frankie like a backhanded swipe. He shrank a little. Dropped his head. Fell silent for a bit.

"Boy owed me some money and didn't want to pay it."

I consulted the printout. "The victim here's named Shirley."

"She was the only thing he gave a hoot about. Had to hit him where he lived."

"His girlfriend?"

Barry Dan winced and shook his head like I was bordering on too foolish to even talk to. He shook his head. "Her girl."

"You took his girlfriend's daughter?"

"Didn't take her. Gave her a ride. Stopped off here for a while. Ate cookies and stuff. You find the crime in that, why don't you tell me all about it."

"How old was she?" P.J. asked him.

He shrugged, held his hand about four feet off the ground.

"How long did you have her?" I asked him.

He shrugged. "A while."

"Get paid?"

Barry Dan grinned. "Oh yeah."

"And arrested?" P.J. again.

"Hell, a week or two went by. They stewed on it. Got pissed. Went over to Waynesboro and filed the charges."

"What did you do while you had her?" I asked him.

"She watched TV or something. I seem to recall I read the Good Book. I didn't touch her, if that's what you're asking. I'll say it flat out -- I don't go in for girls."

"He don't," Frankie added. He glanced sidelong at Barry Dan, not sure if it was time yet for him to chime in, but Barry Dan didn't object. "I do," Frankie informed P.J., followed by a quarter minute of teeth.

"So when this Dunbar girl disappeared . . . '96, remember?"

Barry Dan nodded.

Frankie said, "Up on the mountain?"

"Right," I told him. "Detective Phelps picked you up because . . . ?" I asked of Barry Dan. Of course, I knew the answer already. I'd have done the same thing myself. Phelps had a girl missing and so scooped up anybody with an odor about him.

Barry Dan had a slightly different take. "I missed a payment," he told me. "Don't guess it matters now. Phelps being back in the woods with his beagles and all, but he was a bad one for needing to get bought off."

Frankie nodded. "Ask anybody."

"Hm." P.J. again. At least it wasn't an actual word.

"And those other two guys he picked up?"

Barry Dan shrugged. He plucked a closed heel off the floor. The bow on it was coming unglued. A hint of sadness passed across his features. "Owed him probably," Barry Dan told me, fingering the bow. "Best talk to them."

"Right." I stood from the settee. I would have thanked Barry Dan for his time, but he'd already moved on to shoe repair and didn't appear to need to hear from me.

"Get the glue gun," he told Frankie, who blundered into the bowels of the house.

Halfway to the truck, I said to P.J., "I thought I told you not to talk."

She paused to squint and remember before assuring me, "You did."

ii

We found the Bledsoes. All nine of them. They most decidedly weren't sumptuaries. They were trash. They met us at a park. It passed for a park anyway. It was a clump of woodlands by a roadside with a trio of picnic tables. One open-air pavilion with a slab floor. A few fire pits. A couple of grills. The garbage barrels were all overflowing. There was a dead raccoon in the gravel lot.

"You take me to the nicest places," P.J. told me as we climbed out of the truck.

There were Bledsoes waiting for us back by the far picnic table, the one under roof. Most of them were urinating. The rest of them were finishing off what looked like their third twelve pack of beer.

"Am I not talking again?" P.J. asked me.

"Yeah," I told her.

"Right."

The Bledsoes were chiefly flat-headed unibrows, and the bulk of them were filthy with what appeared to be rust, like they'd been rolling around in a scrap heap for maybe a week or two.

"You him?" one of them wanted to know.

"Probably," I told him.

"Going to cost you," another said. He was the shortest of the Bledsoes and seemed to be in charge. Denny, I had to figure.

"How much?"

"Depends on what you want to know."

If I was on the meter, there wasn't much point in doing anything but getting straight to the nub of the thing.

"Katharine Dunbar. 1996. Know anything about her?"

Denny Bledsoe scratched his chin while he struggled with the math. "I would have been what? Hell . . . twenty-two?"

"Twenty-six," another Bledsoe told him. A young Bledsoe. He looked to be a teen. A Bledsoe with a legitimate knack for figures but -- being a Bledsoe -- no real future beyond whatever graft the whole clan had in mind.

Denny Bledsoe pointed across the way towards one of the battered Bledsoe trucks and said to Einstein Bledsoe by way of instruction, "Go on."

Denny Bledsoe turned his gaze back on me. "Twenty." He gave P.J. a frank once over. The ill-fitting pantsuit. The sensible shoes. Trying to dress older only made the girl look like she didn't know how to put on clothes. Even to a Bledsoe covered with rust who had on coveralls and two different brands of sneaker, P.J. proved enough of a sartorial curiosity to lock him in for a bit. That, or all he needed was a female to get addled.

"Who's that?" he finally asked me.

Before I could speak, P.J. told him, "Going to cost you."

That seemed to delight the man to judge by the joy with which he spat.

"Forty bucks," he said towards P.J., but it was clearly meant for me.

I nodded.

"Heard about it," he told me. "Girl out walking just up and gets gone."

I nodded again.

"Wasn't none of us," he said.

"You sure?"

"Wasn't nobody in these parts. Never heard a peep about her, and you'd better believe I would have. If somebody'd around here grabbed her, it'd get out."

"Phelps says you're not above this sort of thing."

"Not saying I am," he told me. Denny held out his hand, and one of his brothers or cousins opened a can of Busch and put it within reach. "Just didn't have nothing to do with her. Hadn't never heard anything about it."

"All right." I dug out my wallet, found two twenties, and shoved them at him."

"We're mostly in salvage these days," he told me. "Straight life and all that shit."

"Phelps told me pot."

"That man talks too much." He looked towards P.J. "Turn around honey."

P.J. raised a finger and showed it to him with a sneer.

"I'd snatch her," he said.

"I'd have to kill you for it," I told him.

P.J. told me, "Awww," in that way that kind of means "Jesus!"

Denny Bledsoe shrugged like he heard that sort of promise all the time.

"You believe him?" P.J. asked me on the way to the truck.

"Not yet," was all I told her.

Buddy

i

She wasn't anywhere I went for nearly a month. That didn't sit well with me at all, and I took it out on Keith. I didn't just have him do all the grunt work and turn up my nose at the food he brought me, ignore the jokes he made. I even ran down his taste in Jesusy girls and explained why none of them would have him, which I realize now was punishing and cruel. But I was in a mood and grappling and nobody else was in easy reach.

I finally found her in Staunton, at the homewares store. Lisa had signed on as a trainee, was trying to branch out, I guess. She thinks of herself as artistic. She paints and went through a pottery phase. She insists she keeps a journal, but I slipped a look at it one time to find that she skipped whole weeks when it suited her and sometimes just wrote what she ate or shoved polaroids in and let a snapshot do service as an entry. Lisa's lazy at bottom. She'll never admit it, but she's sure quick to point out shiftlessness when she sees it in somebody else.

Lisa was working in plumbing. When I spied her, she was helping a guy with his sink trap. She was handing him fittings and fixtures and lengths of pipe like she knew what she was doing. That's always been one of Lisa's leading gifts. She can fake anything.

I found a spot where I could see her from behind the PVC, and I watched her be all chatty and flirty with one customer after another until I felt like I was wrought up enough to do some good for me.

I waited for her in the lot. I tried to follow her home, but she went all over the damn place. The grocery store. The

CVS. The AutoZone. The day-old bread shop. And even after all that she still didn't go to her house but drove instead to the Golden Corral where she met some beefy guy with a self-inflicted haircut. In front of God and everybody, she stuck her tongue right in his mouth. She had to know I was watching her. She's spiteful that way. That's Lisa all over.

I'm fairly intrepid where it comes to most things, but I'll have to confess to a Golden Corral aversion. There's something about the smell of the steaks and the Texas toast that mingles poorly for me with the stink of the Wonderfall. All that chocolate running down a thing that looks like the Stanley Cup and then getting pumped back up to flow all over again. It's at precisely the temperature where it smells unbearably strong to me, and the odor taints everything else, which already doesn't smell delicious.

So I went in knowing I couldn't stay, that the reek would drive me out, but I'd come to think it would be good for Lisa to see me at the very least. I could have lurked in the lot for a couple of hours, waited for her to come back out and probably take bad haircut home. Lisa had gotten to be loose and heedless that way, had grown to pretend in her pining and heartache that any man at all would do for her after the wreck that we'd become. I wasn't anxious to watch her playact like, so I was being merciful by stepping inside, but she was in the buffet line already, and I couldn't get close to the thing.

It wasn't just the Wonderfall. It was the timberline chili too. Or rather it was the chocolate and the chili in combination with the Bourbon Street chicken that got me wheezing and gagging. Sweating and panting.

Worse still, Lisa saw me struggling and left off spooning up green beans long enough to ask me, "You okay?"

I'm sure to the Golden Corral faithful it sounded like genuine concern. They couldn't know any better, but it sure skewered me. I staggered outside in a fury. My goal is always to hold my nugget close, but sometimes Lisa simply does me in. Pretending like she gives a hoot — that's not at all who she is — is what burns me more than anything. I hate it's only me that sees it.

I raced out of the lot. I went flying out towards the two lane and took it east towards Afton where the damnedest thing happened. A groundhog popped out of the ditch, and I ran him down. He was a meaty one, and my Plymouth bounced over him. I could hear the suspension rattle. I found him in the mirror flopped on his back with his razor teeth pointed towards the sun.

I wasn't sure how I'd feel until the luster came on. I was just expecting to drive along and wish I hadn't hit him when I noticed my anxiety waning and some satisfaction coming on. It wasn't Lisa worthy, but it was enough to ratchet me down, and it got me thinking about what Barry calls countermeasures — those pursuits that let you escape from harm and fight another day.

I'd needed a moment with Lisa, but a groundhog had served until I could have one. I wondered if I could work my way up the scale and feel slightly more defused with each step. I'd try a goat or a cow. A house pet maybe. Perhaps a Congressman. Pretty soon, I was making a chart in my head of Lisa substitutes. All of them lower dosage for sure but acceptable temporary stand-ins for the authentic thing.

Before I knew it, I was back at home and happy enough to be there. I wasn't anxious or agitated. It seemed like a breakthrough for me, and the following week I ended up sharing the news of it out loud.

"You made a what?" Dr. Marlin asked me.

"A kind of chart," I told her. "A table." I tapped my temple. "It's not like I wrote it down."

"I don't quite follow." That was one of Jill's favorites. It was her version of "How does that make you feel?" She trotted it out a little too often. If she didn't, in fact, follow everything she said she didn't follow then she would have needed a keeper and a bib for when she ate.

"I'm trying to organize my expectations," I said.

"Working on yourself?"

I nodded. I'd told her all about Barry.

"Here's my thinking," I started in. It was my fourth or fifth session by then. I'd gotten comfortable enough to let Jill see everything of me right up to the pull shade. That's how I pictured the break between what of me could go out in the sunshine and those urges and impulses I had to hold back in the shadows. Not so much because they were wrong but because they were private and complicated and sure to be misunderstood.

Now I'm aware most people don't break themselves in half the way that I had. Take Hotchkiss and them, for instance. They're flat out all the time. If there's any good in them — and you wouldn't know it by me — it's always out for the taking, but the darker, uglier stuff is reliably on display as well. They don't discriminate. They don't know how to. They haven't bothered to break themselves into pieces.

It's a failure of intellect. Not to sound haughty, but most people are simpler than they ought to be. They're too ready to be satisfied to worry about improvements. They'll let life come to them however it wants to. They don't worry themselves with the idea there's a wider world and better way. They make money to spend it. They get married and split. They buy houses and cars. Resent their children. Quarantine all their regrets in the small hours, wonder what else they might have gotten up to — usually on the way to the toilet.

It's easier to stand pat and stay precisely what you've been. It's a nagging obligation to work on yourself and make improvements.

"I can't always do the thing I want," I told Dr. Marlin, "have the thing I need at hand, so I always want to know what else might work for me instead."

"Give me a for instance." Another crutch for Jill.

"Well," I started, "let's say I'm low, and I know the best thing for me would be a hike out in the woods."

"I see." She made a note and nodded. "A hike can be . . . uplifting."

"It's just a for instance," I told her. I'd as soon build a freighter by hand.

Another note. "I see."

"But let's say I'm a hiking kind of guy. So there I am needing a walk in the woods, but the weather won't allow it. We've got rain or sleet or volcanos or something."

That earned me a smile from Jill, no easy thing to get.

"So I've got to find something to do instead of hike. Wouldn't it be better if I had a chart I could choose the right stuff off of."

"You mean . . . hiking equivalents?"

"Exactly."

"Physically? Emotionally? What?"

"That's why I've been thinking so hard about it." I tapped my head again. I didn't truly intend to or want to tap my head, but I do stuff with my hands sometimes that I can't seem to control.

"Be still when no one else is." That's what Barry likes to say, but I doubt Barry has the nugget of fury I've got.

"Something not maybe as fully satisfying as a hike," I said, "but it hits enough of the buttons until you can go in the woods again."

She made a note. I got a nod. "Sound strategy," she told me. "Maybe you ought to write it all down."

"Like actually make my chart?"

"I would. Some people think about the sorts of things they write down."

"Do you?" I fixed on her notebook. "Awful lot of writing." Another smile. I was mining precious ore.

"Certainly."

I made the brand of noise in my neck intended to let her know I was thinking about it.

"Have you ever kept a diary or a journal?"

I shook my head. "My sister used to." I didn't have a sister.

"You've never been tempted?"

I gave the question what looked like thought. "Can't say that I have." I had a box full of ledgers, the expensive leather kind. I'd filled hundreds of pages. I used a blue Pilot. I print when I write. Tiny and neat. To call those diaries trivializes everything I'm about.

"Just an idea."

My least favorite session phrase. Jill would trot it out when I'd resisted a suggestion or had seen fit to disagree with her. It felt to me like her way of dismissing what she'd told me and ignoring what I'd been stirred to say back. It was her form of deletion, like that bit had never happened.

"Tell me about your uncle, the one who left you his house."

"My sister's diary was all trash and sniping. She said things in there she didn't have the guts to say out loud. It was a book of poison. Kind of put me off of diaries."

Jill smiled, but it was hardly the flavor of smile I had any use for. It was thin and pinched and had the air about it of a woman closing in on being sick.

"Right. Your uncle?"

"Awful things about her friends. About me. Mom and dad." I found myself getting worked up over my catty, fictional sister.

"That can happen." As provocations go, that was a few rungs worse than "Just an idea." Yes, things can happen. It sounded like something Hotchkiss and them would say.

I knew what was coming. It starts for me usually as a spot of inflammation. I imagine my little nugget of rage glowing in my frame. Then I usually come out with, "Oh, I don't know," which is just what I said to Jill.

"Let's move on."

"That can happen?" My jaw did that thing. "What are you saying exactly?"

She laid her pen in her notebook gutter. I'd noticed she tended to do that when I was making her take time on some trifle she'd tried to skirt around and not waste our session on.

"We all approach life differently," she said. "Maybe your sister wrote down her complaints because she knew it would be worse to say them."

"Worse how?"

"Buddy." She said it that way she does when she's trying to steer me.

"If she's thinking it and not saying it, isn't her life just a lie."

"Do you say everything you think?"

I shook my head. "But I don't write it down either. I'm working on myself."

"You keep it somewhere don't you?" Now she tapped her head just like I had.

I couldn't help but feel like Dr. Marlin was having a bit of a run at me. I thought of all the stuff I kept piled up behind the pull shade. I resented Jill for putting her finger on something I knew to be true.

"Maybe," I allowed.

"Girls like diaries." Dr. Marlin smiled. Not thin this time. She picked up her pen. She shrugged.

"Yeah, I guess." I worked on keeping my jaw just where it was.

"Now about your uncle."

"Maxwell," I said. "Everybody called him Bumpy."

"Why?"

I touched my forehead. My cheek. "He had, you know, bumps."

There'd been a time when I would have pitched a fit and marched straight out of the office. Probably knocked my chair over on the way and flung the door open with violence. But this time I only shifted where I sat. I could tell my sessions with Jill were making me better off than I'd been.

Certainly better than most of Jill's other patients. I held the door as I was leaving for a nut bag coming in. She was shifty and twitchy and having a raging argument with herself, such an involved bit of business that she couldn't be bothered to thank me for holding the door. Courtesy is the lubricant that makes us civilized. Barry says that every now and again when he feels unthanked and slighted. Worse still, that woman gave me a look like I was some manner of scum, so I didn't feel guilty when I shattered her driver's side window with a rock.

Her car was full of trash and clutter. Clothes on the floorboard. Grocery bags and mail on the seats. Empty cigarette cartons all over the place. Go cups every stinking where.

I couldn't help but believe that I was probably an oasis for Dr. Marlin given how people, generally speaking, are such a godawful mess.

ii

Barry is a demon for kismet. He's convinced that people get what they've got coming, but Barry is also persuaded we can put ourselves in line for life's rewards.

"Engineer enlightenment," Barry likes to say. "Pilot, not passenger."

I've got that last part written on a scrap of tape I stuck to my steering column. It's dusty and faded and dried out now, but I can see it there puckered when I'm driving, and I know exactly what it used to say.

Lisa has never believed much in self improvement. That just the sort of thing we'd argue about if I were inclined to quarrel.

I went for two weeks seeing her all over the place in her putty-colored Toyota coupe. She was all around Waynesboro, going to spots where I went. The first couple of times, I let it go as homely happenstance. But by the third and the fourth, I had to think Lisa was trying to tell me something. She was never the sort to come right out and make apologies. Air regrets. Embark on overtures. Instead, she'd put herself in front of me until I seized the initiative and spoke up.

That was Lisa all over. At the Rexall, in the Kmart, at the Buffalo Wings place. Even when she had that ginger cop for cover, I knew it was all for me.

I don't like to play into Lisa's hands. Barry and Dr. Marlin are both helping me move on.

"Be content in your skin," Dr. Marlin tells me. "That's all we're really after." Sometimes it's almost like Barry is speaking through her.

"Learn to lean on you," she told me one evening. That might have even been Barry verbatim.

I was her last appointment and had walked her to her car. It was just the two of us out there. Nobody around. It seemed dodgy to me that Dr. Marlin would have an office out in the county when she specialized in unbalanced people. I was going to make mention of my concerns but decided against it in the end.

"Do you feel like we're making progress?" I asked her.

"That's for you to say." Dr. Marlin had that narcotic voice shrinks must cultivate in school.

"I do," I said. That was thanks to Dr. Marlin. I'm usually not assertive and decisive. "I'm relaxed now," I told her. I wasn't actually relaxed, but my nugget of fury was well in check, buried even for the moment, so I could at least give the impression of being at ease.

"That's good news," she said. The voice again. I couldn't help but hear a little Lisa in it. That was the thing about Dr. Marlin. She couldn't keep her Lisa down. She'd be brittle and clinical and business-like, but then she'd lapse into Lisa around the edges.

Women do that. They'll seem like one thing while they're playing at something else. It's just the sort of double dealing that tends to set me off. Thanks to Dr. Marlin, I could choke back my irritation and be suave enough to open my trunk in a completely natural way.

"I've got something for you," I said. "Come look."

She checked the time on her phone. She took a step towards my rear bumper. She glanced from the open trunk to me and stopped. Dr. Marlin had her feelers out, and they were vibrating. I could tell. Everything seemed to pause for a moment while she waited for me to grab her and maybe gave me the room to decide that grabbing her was something I ought not do. She had a look on her face like she could already picture the way I'd lunge at her. That made me feel common and predictable. It made me feel transparent. It reminded me that my progress was entirely for me to say.

I think of it now as a test I was giving myself to see how completely Dr. Marlin (with Barry's help) had taken hold.

"Uh oh," I said. "Must have left it at home. Maybe next time." I slammed the lid and winked at Jill. I looped around to my driver's door and left her standing where she was.

She looked foolish planted there gaping at me, like a woman who'd had her expectations stymied. Like she'd been sure I was one kind of miscreant while I was something else entirely. I was a guy in his Dodge who was going straight home. My progress was for me to say.

Once I'd backed up, I waved. She'd only moved enough to thumb her key fob and make her car beep and blink. The Dr. Marlin who watched me pull out of the lot was almost all Lisa by then. That was satisfying enough to hold me nearly all the way back to my house.

I'll only call it an itch for the sake of convenience since we all know what an itch is. Mine is closer to the marrow and more powerful than that, but imagine poison ivy. A seepy, inflamed patch just starting out. You keep from clawing it at first, but then it gets in your blood and spreads, and you soon enough find yourself pawing and scratching, doing most anything for a spot of relief.

People give you their special remedies. Soaks and poultices and ointments, but nothing works to lasting effect. You can hardly eat and sleep. You wake up in the small hours, prickly and tormented. If there was one sure thing you could do for yourself, one option to bring you peace, there's little doubt you'd find a way to do it.

Now take that dose of poison ivy and make it existential.That's a Barry word. There's ordinary stuff and then larger and forbidding bits of business. I take it as the difference between what you can scratch and what you can't and never will.

I was having a Lisa spell. They get sprung on me sometimes. I'll be watching a video or reading one of my home improvement magazines, and I'll find myself thinking about how they'll probably speak of me in the end. I'd be a fool if I didn't dwell on it a little. I'd planned enough to pack up all my marginal pornography and carry it to the dumpster at the far edge of the county, the one over by the pullout just beyond the day-old bread shop. It's usually half full of fuzzy blue Parker House rolls and wheat bread nobody bought.

I put my discs and my tapes all in a box and took pains to bury it under the bread sacks. I figured some dumpster picker would probably find it or one of those boys at the landfill, so it wasn't like any of my favorites would go to waste. No children. No animals. No corpses. It was red-blooded American XXX, though probably a touch more rambunctious than most. Some scuffling. Some strangling. Quite a lot of spanking, not because I'm especially interested in spanking but because that's mostly what there is.

I had some damning snapshots I'd squirreled away. I finally brought myself to burn them. All the keepsakes I'd taken, I put in a freezer baggie and buried up behind my woodshed. I packed all my ledgers up on a closet shelf. That was the version I hoped they'd see.

Barry likes to say, "If you don't CYA, then who in God's name will?"

She had a grip on me, Lisa did. She was like a breeze across embers. I'd dealt with her enough already to know what was coming up. It was turning into a small world for me and her. She was everywhere I went. That was Lisa's way of tempting me to do a thing about it.

I had Keith problems, of course. There were always Keith problems. Keith just couldn't accept the way he'd turned out and that he was stuck with what he had. I was sympathetic to his way of thinking at first. I imagine everybody was.

"I just want to be normal," Keith would say. Or rather, Perfect Paul would say it.

That seemed a fine enough thing at first. We all want to live in a world where people like Keith can do whatever the rest of us do, are free to want what the rest of us want.

But after a while, I couldn't really pull for Keith anymore. Nobody, women especially, seemed to live up to Keith's standards. The girls he was keen on couldn't just be Christian. They had to be beautiful too. And they couldn't have defects themselves, beyond subscribing to Biblical hokum. There couldn't be so much as a birthmark in a conspicuous place.

I remember a girl with a shriveled arm we came across at lunch one day. She was waiting tables at the barbecue place, the one on the far side of Staunton. We were out there locating power and water lines for a guy trying to site a swimming pool.

Her name was Candy. She was cute and bubbly, primed to chat. She had a ready smile for Keith. I offered to go fetch his talker out of the truck once she'd taken our orders. I had to think he'd want to chat with Candy when she came back to the table.

"Uh uh," Keith told me. He shook his head.

I thought he might be having one of his Jesusy reservations. I'd seen Keith sneer at a girl or two, the sort of tramps who'd clearly fallen away from the Lord. I was on board with that kind of thing. That sort of girl was sure to take advantage of Keith in the end. But Candy seemed something else altogether.

"She had on a cross," I told him. "Pretty girl."

Keith shook his head and made his toddler noise. He was about as stubborn as any living beast I'd ever known.

"You don't like her?"

"Uh uh."

"Why not?"

Candy showed up with our iced tea. She even stripped a straw and stuck it into Keith's glass.

She laid a light hand on Keith's shoulder and told him, "There now."

Once she'd left us, I said, "She likes you."

Keith made his toddler noise again.

I was mystified. I'd seen her shriveled arm. She surely didn't try to hide it. She was wearing the t-shirt they all wore, the yellow one with the pig on the front.

"What's wrong with her?" I asked Keith. I expected him to have some personal reason I wasn't quite tuned into. Like maybe he objected to cute, bubbly blondes the way I objected to blueberries. Everybody else might like them, but they just weren't for him.

Instead he pointed at his own arm. Kieth shook his head and said again, "Uh uh."

I couldn't quite believe it. I'd known Keith for a while by then and expected better of him.

"Born that way probably," I told Keith.

"Uh huh."

"Not like she can help it."

"Uh huh."

"But it's enough to put you off?"

"Eeaah."

It was my turn to make a noise in my neck.

I was already well aware that Keith was neurotic. He was obsessive compulsive, aggressively orderly in stupid, unhelpful ways.

"She seems fine with you," I told Keith.

"Uh huh."

He looked cocky when he said it. Why wouldn't she be fine with him? He was a prize after all. What Keith lacked in muscle control he more than made up for in blind self-confidence.

I leaned across to ask in a voice I felt sure Candy wouldn't hear, "So that arm of hers lets her out with you? Damaged goods?"

"Eeaah."

"Well, isn't that something?"

He shrugged. Candy was subpar, and that was that with Keith.

"I'd feel lucky to go around with her."

Another toddler grunt.

"You know you're damaged goods too, right?" I found myself just blurting it out, even though I knew it was the sort of thing that ought to be left unsaid. Barry was a big one for editorial discretion. "Say what you have to. Swallow what you don't." A little odd for a guy who wrote books and made videos and just generally rattled on as much as Barry.

"Uh huh." Keith didn't appear to take offense at all.

"So a girl's got to take you as you are, but you need to get what you want?"

"Eeaah."

"That doesn't strike you as a little peculiar?"

"Uh uh."

"You're something, Keith."

Keith appeared to take that as a compliment. He grinned. He drooled. "Eeaah."

When Candy brought our chopped plates and said, "Need anything else?" Keith couldn't even bother with his usual chipper grunt — the one I'd seen him use on hairnet ladies at the meat and three, on the guy at the Foodmaster in Charlottesville where we'd stop sometimes for jerky. They qualified for Keith's upbeat chuff. Candy didn't make the cut.

I took out my petty revenge on Keith by refusing to help him with his napkin. I usually tucked one into his collar so he wouldn't slop onto his shirt.

When he pointed at the dispenser, I said, "Maybe Candy'll do it."

That earned me a couple of toddler noises, one right behind the other.

I left Candy a five dollar tip on a seven dollar bill, and I never felt quite the same way about Keith as I had when the workday started. I certainly didn't care what he thought about me, not that I'd confided in the boy. I might have pointed out Lisa to him here and there when we'd run across her, but Keith was too keen on his Christian girls to pay much attention to what I was up too. His plans and desires occupied him in a way I found less inspirational all the time.

I stopped running to fetch his talker when he'd leave it in the truck, made him pick up his crutches when he dropped them. I left his drool to drip and fall. Things got so chilly between us that Keith stopped talking to me about women. It got to the point where a Joan of Arc sighting wouldn't even have led to a chat.

So by the time I was bumping into Lisa all over, I didn't worry about Keith anymore. He twitched and sighed when we followed her to the Buffalo Wings place with her ginger cop buddy. When I spied her Toyota at the Exxon on the by-pass, I whipped in two pump islands over even though Keith groaned and grunted to let me know our tank was little short of full.

"Where have you got to be?" I asked him.

That was the first time I'd known Keith to snarl.

I waited until she'd filled up, didn't even bother with my nozzle, and then followed her through town and up towards

Afton. Keith was in a pout. I tried to tell him we were taking
a shortcut. He didn't drive after all and was usually too
worried about his libido and what the Lord Christ might do
for it to give even passing notice to which way we were going
and where we were.

She parked in the ditch before a dumpy house with a
junky, overgrown yard. A nasty, old dog came around from
the back and nosed her as she crossed the yard.

"Who's that?" Perfect Paul asked me from Keith's talker.

"Girl I know."

Keith moaned and grumbled like he does when he's
hunting talker keys. "Say something to her."

"I will," I told him as I turned our pickup around in the
road and listened to our steering belt whine.

"When?" Perfect Paul asked me.

"When I'm ready," I said to Keith.

In fact, I wasn't quite ready when I finally talked to her.
The truth is I'm not much of a planner. Lisa gets me worked
up. I go to Barry to calm me, but sometimes Barry's simply
not enough. I think I was even trying (as much as I ever do)
to stay away, but Lisa went and put herself in front of me.
She made herself a provocation. That was the abiding
trouble with Lisa. She couldn't leave a thing alone. There I
was not anxious to come across her. There she was in my
way.

I'd stopped in at the Martin's, a place I hardly ever went.
It holds itself out as a gourmet grocery store but never seems
to do much business. Gourmet isn't much of a lure in
Waynesboro. If the locals wanted finer things, they'd have
relocated by now.

The evening I met up with Lisa, the checkout girl spent
probably a good half minute staring slack-jawed at my waxed
rutabaga. She tried to look it up. Flipped through the

produce book they have, but she was wrestling with a bigger problem. Let's call it existential.

"You eat it, right?" she asked me.

I nodded.

She giggled and shook her head. "How?"

I tried to spell it for her, but she wasn't much with spelling. She decided it was a monstrous turnip. "All right with you?"

Turnips were cheaper. I nodded. "All right."

I didn't know Lisa was in the store until I saw her car in the lot. It was parked just beyond my Valiant. There was one empty space between us, so she'd pulled in as good as right next to me, which I was surely meant to notice. Lisa did nothing by happenstance. She always had her reasons.

I wouldn't say I was laying for her exactly. I'd opened my trunk to check my kit. Sure I might have splashed some carburetor cleaner on my rag, but that's the sort of thing that I can frequently permit Barry to undo. I'd more than worked on myself enough to be able to reach for ether and not use it.

But then she came right out, heading my way, and Lisa gave me that look she gives me. It's the one that says, "I know you're standing there, but you're nobody to me." It's all an act with her. I've seen it plenty. She's always out to make me feel inconsequential and small, evermore pretending she's so far past me that I'm as good as forgotten. Before Barry, it used to enrage me. That stink eye of hers. That chin in the air. There wasn't much hope of keeping my nugget at an ember. But then I found Barry and learned from him how to pretend as well.

She couldn't help but look at me. I could see her struggling not to, but that thing between us has got more pull than either one of us can fight.

I looked squarely back at her. I even called her by name.

"I'm sorry, what?" she said. She stopped. Lisa was in one of her blunt moods. I could tell.

"Just hey," I told her.

She shrugged. Whatever. She tried to walk on past me. It didn't take much to tip her into the trunk. Maybe a half minute with my rag. She flailed and shouted as best she could. She kicked and scratched and pinched, but the ether took her soon enough. I shut the lid. Picked up her bag. She'd bought yogurt. A box of Cuetips. Tamari Almonds from the bulk bins. Two dollar water that claimed to be laced with electrolytes.

There was a man pushing a cart across the lot. A woman over at the Martin's gas pumps. There was a labrador looking at me from a Yukon across the aisle. But there wasn't anybody waving his arms. Nobody alarmed or agitated. I guess I should have felt relieved, but Barry doesn't believe in relief. Barry believes in the D and the V — Determined and Vindicated.

I decided I felt a bit of both. I tossed Lisa's bag onto my floorboard. I started my Valiant. I checked my mirrors. I heard her tumble and roll as I backed up. A muffled thump as Lisa finally found a place to settle.

People are everywhere these days, and nobody sees anything.

P.J.

i

You can't really dress for Pennsylvania. Philadelphia maybe, but you're better off thinking of that as greater New Jersey. The keystone state, the part where we were headed, is a gray and dingy place. Cows and WaWa's. Lebanon bologna. More potholes per mile than you'd probably find in some Siberian wasteland. Buck hit one as soon as we'd passed out of Maryland. I thought both his axles might break.

They had a fine rest area as a form of false advertisement just over the border from Maryland. Freshly mopped bathrooms. Vending machines. A place to walk Mabel with complimentary biodegradable poop bags on offer. We stood out in the grass — me and Buck and Mabel — and all looked at each other.

We'd had a long, desultory talk on the way. The first time for me that word ever fit. We'd talk and then we wouldn't — for a quarter hour or more — and then one of us would start back in more or less where we'd left off. That was surely because of what we were talking about. His ex-wife. His estranged daughter. Everything he'd had and lost and how it had all come to unspool. And that laid against what little I knew of people on the planet. If my parents didn't get on with each other, they'd long failed to let me know.

I'd described to Buck an argument I'd seen them have one time.

"My mother wanted to paint the back hall. My father didn't think she ought to."

"Why not?"

"At first he said he didn't want her on a ladder, but she wouldn't stand for that. So he moved onto the paint fumes and how he'd rather pay some guy to sniff them. She threw open the doors and the windows in the house to show him that she could. Then he complained about the color she'd picked, so she gave him the chart and told him to choose. That's when he got mad and left the house, and my mother painted the hallway."

"What happened when he came back."

"He'd stopped for chicken. We had supper at the picnic table out in the backyard."

"What did he say about the paint job?"

"Nothing."

I hadn't needed to pause to recall. My mother and father would disagree. My dad would leave the house and then come back with selective amnesia like they'd never quarreled.

"Did they do that for you?" Buck asked me.

"Don't think so."

"My mom hit my dad with a garden rake once. He had to get sewn up."

"None of that for them. Even at night when they thought I was asleep, I never heard them argue. They'd have their little flair-ups. Dad would wander off and forget."

"Not a bad way to do it. I probably should have tried that."

"You don't seem much of a hothead to me."

I told Buck about my mother's brother, a frustrated musician and part-time bookkeeper who was given to fits and rages. He mostly indulged in them on his own. Some little thing would set him off, and he'd stalk around the yard.

Break something at his office desk. Slam a cabinet in his kitchen. He died in a robbery. A shop he kept books for was getting held up when he dropped in to pick up receipts. That was just the sort of inconvenience he'd get bent out of shape about. The holdup guy was anxious already. The gun went off like they do.

"I'm not a hothead," Buck allowed. "A low simmer with a little boiling over. My ex had a way of talking to me that was ok for a while and then, after a decade or so, wasn't ok at all."

"Talked to you how?"

The whole time we were chatting, we were blasting up Interstate 81 in my Tercel with Mabel in the back seat. Buck was driving. We'd decided at the last minute not to take his truck when I'd held out for taking Mabel along instead of leaving her locked up at home.

"She's windy," Buck had told me.

I'd laughed. "How windy could she be?"

"You'll wish you were dead."

More cackling from me. I'd tossed Buck my keys. Now we were taking turns lowering our windows for a dose of chill fresh air and then raising them again.

"I tried to tell you." If Buck had said that once, he'd said it two dozen times.

"What do you feed her?"

"She scrounges. The deader the better."

We had no warning. She didn't toot. She slept on her back most of the way, with her feet in the air and her nozzle unimpeded.

So that made the chats we were having even more desultory, since there wasn't much talking over the road at seventy miles an hour. I put my window down. I waited. I put it back up.

"Talked to you how?" I said again.

"She'd had a falling out with a girl at work and decided if she'd been honest and blunt, it never would have happened. She convinced herself that being polite and guarded was a poor strategy all around."

"I try to be honest."

"Not like this," Buck said. "Avoiding the unvarnished truth is what makes civil societies civil. What if I told you right now every hard thing I've ever thought about how you think and how you look?" He wiggled a finger at me. "The sort of stuff you wear?"

"I don't like the way that sounds."

"And Janice would just say it. She didn't seem to care if it only hurt and didn't help. And you couldn't tell her anything honest back. That was the hell of it. The woman specialized in getting mad."

"That's not quite fair."

"Thank you!"

That was about as animated as I'd ever seen Buck get.

"So things got scratchy and then worse than scratchy. And then we were in counseling with Darren."

I'd heard Buck mention Darren before. "The same Darren who's Mr. Janice number two?"

Buck nodded.

"Seems unethical."

"Doesn't it though."

"And your daughter stayed with your ex, I guess."

Buck nodded. Then came one of the desultory bits. Our windows went up and down. I shifted around to look at Mabel.

After about ten minutes, I said to Buck, "I think it's maybe half wind and half rotten teeth."

I was hoping that didn't qualify as unbridled honesty. Buck gave it some thought. He nodded. "Vet's been after me on that."

At the Pennsylvania welcome station, Mabel did a lot of sniffing. When she wearied of it, she sat down and licked herself.

"Where does he work?" I asked Buck. "It's Matthew, right?"

He nodded. "Remax."

"And you're sure he's where we can find him?"

Buck nodded and checked his watch. "We're looking at a brick colonial on nearly a wooded acre. Three bedrooms two baths. A screened patio."

"I'm what?"

Buck gave me more thorough study than I was comfortable with. "You'll do for a daughter until we have to tell him what we're up to."

"Well ok then, Daddy."

"Shut up." He handed me the leash and went off to the men's room.

Greencastle turned out to be charming, as far as Pennsylvania goes. It had a handsome town square with a traffic circle and Georgian brick buildings all around. The real estate office occupied one of them.

"What's my name?" I asked Buck on the way in.

I got his squinty, sour look.

"P.J. then."

Squinty/sour with a nod.

Katherine Dunbar's brother was on the phone. He had his father's nose, but he wasn't a big, hale sort like Mickey. Matthew was bony, long but concave. Once he'd cradled the receiver, he gave us both a wan handshake.

"Delighted," he said with no conviction to speak of, like it was a word he'd just made up and was half-heartedly trying out.

"Just up for the day?" he asked us.

I smiled and nodded. I was determined to let Buck do the talking so I wouldn't stumble into making a hash of the thing.

"Yeah," Buck said. "Living down around Afton."

Matthew didn't tell us he was from the same place himself. He twitched. I caught that.

Buck rode with Matthew. I followed them in my Toyota with Mabel and her vapors. The place we were seeing was south of town a few miles in a housing development that gave the appearance of having recently been a farm. There was a fallow cornfield off the side yard, littered with stalks. A spine of the Alleghenies beyond it marred by a high tension line. There was livestock somewhere close enough to smell as soon as I stepped out of the car, and it was early April chilly with frost still in the shade. That place was sure to be ripe come August.

I let Mabel out for a minute, but she just sniffed and licked, so back into the car she went. I cracked windows for her (for us a little too) and went off to join Buck and Matthew. They were walking the property. "Wooded," Buck had told me. That must mean something different in Pennsylvania because I saw just saplings and trash trees. Ironwood. Spindly poplar. Some kind of scraggly pine.

There was a jungle gym out in the back yard, one of those treated timber contraptions. Buck was leaning against it as Matthew explained to him that "nearly an acre" meant about a half acre in real estate listing terms.

"You like?" Buck asked me.

"I smell cows," I told him.

Buck nodded. "A little stockyard." He glanced at Matthew who pointed east.

"Dairy farm," he said. "But he's in talks with a developer."

There was no furniture inside, and it wasn't new construction.

"Foreclosure," Matthew told us.

"Must have a lot of those." Buck fingered a ding in the foyer wallboard as he spoke.

Matthew nodded. "Getting better, though."

He led us into the parlor, I'll call it. The carpet was tracked up. There were pull shades on the windows. Coax hanging from the wall. The place was dreary. So dreary it didn't even need Pennsylvania's help.

The dining room had a built-in cupboard, if you can call four screws in the wall built-in. Matthew tried to show it to best effect, but one of the doors was missing a hinge and so just creaked and hung and looked trashy.

"I'll get somebody on that," he said.

I was dropping into a sinkhole of Pennsylvania gloom by the time we reached the kitchen, which was equipped with the sort of appliances you'd buy if you'd rather save your money for a sofa and a bed. They were cheap and small but went well enough with the linoleum and the press-wood cabinets.

"Jesus, pump him already," I wanted to tell Buck.

He was establishing rapport, I guess. Buck had a peek inside the oven. He asked about the service panel.

"In the garage," Matthew told him and led Buck to a breezeway door.

"I think I'll check on Mabel," I said and got enough of a nod to feel ok about fleeing into the yard.

I even checked on Mabel and dithered while Buck finished with the tour. I saw him in an upstairs window. Downstairs on the side screen porch. Then Buck showed up in the front door and motioned for me to join him. I put Mabel away and went back in.

"Let's talk turkey with Matthew," he said.

We did it in the downstairs den — closer to a rumpus room — where there was only one way in and one way out. Buck had me clot the stairwell. There was a wet bar on a sidewall. The previous owners had left the creaky upholstered stools. Buck took one. Matthew claimed another.

He flipped open the folder he'd been carrying around and said to Buck, "Now."

One of Matthews business cards was stapled onto the sheet of particulars that Matthew shoved at Buck along the bar.

"You're a Dunbar?"

Matthew nodded.

"We know Dunbars in Afton, don't we?"

Buck glanced at me. I nodded. It was Drama Club at best.

"Not so uncommon," Matthew said.

"Didn't you say you're from down around there?"

Matthew looked from Buck to me and back to Buck again. "No sir. Didn't say."

"Funny," Buck told him. "Some way I got the idea you're Mickey's boy."

Matthew stiffened. It wasn't much to see since he went around stiff in the general way of things, but he drew up just enough for me to notice. Buck too, I'm sure.

"You're not here to buy a house, are you?"

"Never any harm in looking." Buck glanced around the room. Cheap paneling. Lousy carpet. Plumbing running along the ceiling. "But I've got to say, this place makes me sad."

"Well." Matthew Dunbar tried to shut his folder.

Buck laid his flat hand on it and shook his head.

"You are Mickey's boy, right?"

Matthew nodded like he seemed to do everything else, which was slightly and hardly at all.

"I'm doing a little favor for your dad."

"Do it somewhere else."

Matthew moved to stand up. Buck laid his folder-holding hand on top of Matthew's shoulder. With no visible effort, Buck made him sit again.

"You're the first one to find me," Matthew said. "Congrats. I'll give you that."

"Talk to me for fifteen minutes and nobody comes looking again."

"You don't get it, do you? Mickey won't quit."

"Can't blame the man for wanting answers. Don't you want to know what happened to your sister?"

"He's got answers already. They just aren't the ones he wants. That's why he keeps hiring you guys."

Matthew shot a poisonous glance my way. Oddly, I thrilled at being included, any chance to feel professional.

"I've got a theory," Buck said.

That was news to me. I thought he had a lot of nothing and a little of not much.

"Want to hear it?"

"No."

"Good. It goes like this. Maybe your sister gets real unlucky. Wrong place. Wrong time. Some bastard grabs her. Possible, but I don't like that much."

Buck paused, but Matthew was hardly the sort with an itch to fill in gaps. He just sat and waited. He gave nothing away beyond looking like a man resigned to not selling a house.

"It's an old saw in the police biz," Buck started in. "I was in homicide for a lot of years . . . and we'd always start with the family. Why kill a stranger when you've got people close by getting under your skin?"

Matthew swallowed. Ordinarily, it wouldn't have looked like much, but given how stiff and closed off he'd been, it struck me as a chink. Buck too, I guess. He bored on in.

"Why don't you tell me about your mother."

Air came out of Matthew like he'd been punched. That was precisely the moment I knew for certain it was all in there somewhere and Buck Aldred was the guy to get it out. Up until then, I'd imagined he'd bought in a little to my theory. A treacherous maniac loose in the landscape, and for a second there I was half persuaded he was putting the two together. I pictured Mickey with a hatchet and bloodletting on his mind. But that was just desperate hopefulness on my part.

"What about her?" Matthew asked. It was less of a question than a challenge.

"How did she get along with your sister?" Buck asked.

Matthew shrugged and looked away. There was a grimy basement window up near the ceiling on the far wall. He appeared to be looking at it until I'd noticed he'd welled up.

"I saw your mom's file," Buck said. That was news to me — state facility and all — but I couldn't say for certain it wasn't true. "She had violent episodes, didn't she?"

That earned a nod from Matthew but nothing else.

"One with you. Three or four with your sister. I lost count of the fits she had with your dad."

"She was . . . sick," Matthew said. "They didn't have drugs like they do now."

"Shock therapy?"

Matthew nodded. "Lithium. Benzidiazepine. She'd never take anything for long."

"Two suicide attempts on the record. Is that close?"

"Close," Matthew said. He sounded like he meant four or five.

"She killed your dog."

That was a charge I'd not expected. I was standing there getting steamed with Buck for sharing none of this with me. It was almost like he didn't trust a twenty-three-year-old Action/Weather/News! team blogger.

Matthew nodded. "Rusty."

"Two cows with a rifle?"

Matthew nodded.

"Who let her get near a gun?"

"She'd seem all right. Even be all right. We'd relax, especially Mickey." Matthew paused. Matthew sighed. "Mom all right was all he ever wanted."

"Then she'd go off her meds and . . .?"

"Back in the bin," Matthew said. "She didn't seem to want to be fixed."

"Sounds dangerous," Buck said.

Matthew nodded. "Had its moments."

"Did you ever think she ought to just stay in Central State?"

"I did. But Dad and Kiki?" Matthew shook his head.

"Were you afraid she might hurt somebody?"

Matthew tried once again to collect his real estate papers off the bar top. Buck stopped him just like he had before.

"I'd sure be."

"You need to talk to my father."

"I've talked to him. He hasn't made his peace with any of it yet."

Matthew tried to push past Buck and head for the stairwell, for me. Buck grabbed him by the arm and sat him back down.

"How did it happen?" Buck asked.

"Kiki?"

Buck nodded.

"I don't really know."

"But it wasn't some random guy on the road. You're sure of that much, aren't you?"

A grim nod from Matthew.

"You didn't see? They didn't tell you? What?"

"I was over at a friend's. I was only eleven. They weren't in the habit of telling me much of anything. I got home, and Kiki was gone. There were troopers and detectives in and out of the house. Dad had dosed Mom pretty good, I guess. She could barely crawl out of bed."

"When did Mickey tell you what happened?"

That got a snort out of Matthew. "I'm still waiting."

"How did you find out?"

"By accident. I was up in the woods behind the house and found one of Kiki's shoes. One of the Keds she used to wear all the time. She got them at Christmas. Kiki loved those shoes."

"Did you show it to your Dad?"

Matthew nodded. "I didn't know what it meant exactly, but I knew it meant something important. I wanted Dad to call the detective. I wanted to get a whole crew up in our woods."

"What did Mickey say?"

Matthew found the grimy window again. "He sat me down in the kitchen. Mom was upstairs crying. We could hear her through the ceiling. You couldn't know if it was grief or just the regular stuff in her head. Back then, Mom was upstairs crying almost all the time."

Matthew paused to piece together, I guess, precisely what his father had told him. "Do you come from one of those families that discusses problems? Votes on everything?"

"Hardly," Buck said.

Matthew looked my way. "Bet you do."

I didn't, but I nodded. "Yes sir," I said.

"I got told what to do, and I did it. That was just the way of things."

Buck waited in silence. I wasn't about to chime in. Matthew took his time. He'd been sitting on this for too many years. It wasn't the sort of thing to just cascade out.

"He said there'd been an accident. Something with Mom and Kiki. He had Kiki's sneaker in his hand." Matthew gestured like Mickey must have. "He said, 'I'm going to put this away now.' Then he asked me, 'We clear?'"

"What did you say?"

Matthew shot Buck a what-the-fuck-do-you-think-I-said look with a snort tacked onto it. "I'm pretty sure I told him just, 'yes sir.'"

"What kind of accident was it?" Buck asked.

"The kind that makes somebody dead."

Matthew was determined to gather his papers this time, was intent upon leaving the house. He made it clear by the way he held himself that he was ready to either get put down or leave.

Buck let him have his real estate papers, even helped him collect them off the bar.

"So you never found out how it went exactly?"

"I can guess," Matthew told Buck. "Mickey must know."

I stepped out of the way to let Matthew have clear access to the stairway. He paused before he went up. "I suppose I've been waiting for ya'll," he said. Then he was up the stairs and gone.

He left us to shut the door and lock the house. We lingered a bit in the yard, sat side by side on swings in the back while Mabel wandered around the lawn and failed to do her business.

"When did you decide it wasn't my guy?" I asked Buck.

"I'm not sure I ever actually decided." He tapped his sternum with his index finger. "I had a pain," he said. "Right here."

"Could have been gas."

He shook his head. "It was my something's-wrong pain. It's served me well. Haven't really felt it for years." Buck looked over and found Mabel in the middle of a squat. "Praise her," he told me.

"You praise her," I said.

We sat in silence while Mabel did her business.

"There is a guy, right?" I finally asked Buck. "For the rest of those girls?"

"The hacked one anyway."

"Big on bodies, aren't you?"

He nodded. "I've learned to be."

"What about Mr. Dunbar? What happens with him?"

"That'll be his call. Accessory after the fact sixteen, seventeen years later isn't something . . ."

Mabel came lumbering towards us. Pleased with herself and five pounds lighter.

"Are you going to tell Fig?" Buck asked me.

I shrugged. "Maybe. Probably."

"This might be enough to keep Mickey from hiring another one of me."

Mabel rubbed snout juice on my pants leg.

"Still want me to praise her?"

"I'll do it," Buck said. He reached over and fiddled with one of her ears as he told Mabel, "That's my girl."

We stopped for supper at the restaurant in Staunton that's famous for its Parker House rolls. They even throw them across the dining room if you're game. We weren't. I picked at my chicken. I picked at my cornbread. I pushed around my slaw.

"What about the others?" I asked Buck.

"Police matter. Talk to Fig. If somebody hires me to look into it, I'll look."

"That's the spirit." I pouted. "I guess I'll go back to blogging."

"Cheer up," Buck told me. "At least it's not repo."

"Right."

When I dropped Buck and Mabel back at Buck's house, he came around to my window to give me a mazel tov and a kiss on the cheek.

I pulled away a little misty, but that could well have been the vapors.

ii

He plays along, but he never likes it. Fig's not a hypothetical guy.

"Who are we talking about?" he asked me. That's what he always asks me.

"A guy," I said. "It's hypothetical."

"Right."

"Play along."

"Go."

"He meant well. Keep that in mind. Maybe didn't know he was committing a crime."

"Ignorance of the law. Blah, blah, blah."

"Be kind of a cop but mostly a human."

"Recalibrating," he said.

We were sitting on a bench in Ridgeway Park. It felt like spring finally, if even only for just a day. The dogwoods and Bartlett pears were starting to pop but would probably get frosted come evening. The South River down below us — it's more in the way of an ambitious creek — had a trio of ducks floating on it and just enough feathery algae to nearly hide the beer cans sparkling in among the rocks.

There was what looked like an octogenarian taking his constitutional on the bike path and a woman with a stroller over by the climbing roses. She was yelling in rapid-fire Spanish at somebody on her phone.

I'd bought lunch on the way. That's what worked best with Fig. I'd stopped at the sandwich shop by Greenwood where they pile their egg salad high on wheat toast and sell the incendiary bottled ginger ale that I can barely even sniff.

Fig insists he loves the stuff, even as the tears are flowing. I brought potato and pickles. A chunk of apple cake. I let him peek in the bag at the precinct. He'd sort of eaten already by the time I got there, but I wouldn't tolerate a no.

"I've got maybe a half hour," Fig told me. "Be hypothetical quick."

"Let's say this guy has a nut in the family."

"Certifiable or just . . . whacky?"

"In and out of Central or somewhere. A diagnosed, authentic nut."

"Medicated?"

"Eat."

He did. A fair bit of his egg salad was even going in his mouth.

"A little out of control." I told him. "And yes, medicated, but off the stuff as much as on."

"Convicted?"

"Never charged. Respectable. Let's say a woman. A mother."

"I'm not smelling a crime."

I shoved a sack of Chesapeake Crab chips at Fig. "Eat."

He shrugged. Surrendered. Ate.

"She's got a teen daughter. They don't get along. Some of that's because the mother's nuts. Some of that's because the daughter's . . . you know . . . a teen. They argue and snipe. A lot of storming around. Plenty of screeching. That sort of thing."

Fig nodded. Said nothing. I like a man who follows instructions, even if only erratically and after being reminded twice.

"So normal family friction with a big dose of bipolar voodoo. And then things go bad in a big way, and it's the girl who ends up dead."

"Am I still just eating?"

"Go on."

"A family blowup that turns into a homicide is kind of routine around here. Sort of the American way. I mean, who doesn't have a gun?"

"Not sure about the gun. All I know is the girl gets dead."

"Witnesses?"

"Don't think so. Father finds out and doesn't call the cops."

"Why not?"

I could think of a half dozen reasons. Addled by grief. Standard-issue shock. Poor instincts or just the typical clannish, Appalachian mindset: You take care of yours, and I'll see to mine.

"Could have been," I said, "as simple as he didn't want to lose them both."

"So hypothetical guy makes a bad call."

"Right."

"How long ago?"

"Let's call it eighteen years."

"What did he do with her?"

"The body or the wife?"

Fig nodded.

"I don't know for sure, and back into Central, I guess."

"Accessory after the fact, if that's what you're asking. Hard to say what else they'd pile on."

"Long time ago."

"No statute on this."

"What do you do?"

"For hypothetical guy? I'd put him with a detective. For Mickey Dunbar? Harder to say."

"What are the chances he'd just get to go home?"

He wiped his mouth. Balled up his napkin. This was the sort of thorny business Fig had been built to be deliberate about.

"Mind if I sit with it for a bit?"

I shook my head.

Fig gathered our trash and chucked it in a barrel. "Got to get back," he told me. "Give me a day."

When I moved in to kiss him, I was aiming for his cheek. Then I recalibrated.

I was low on nerve by the time I got to Afton. I wanted to show up alone, without Buck in tow. I wanted to have Mickey to myself. I managed to knock on his door, but I was relieved when he didn't answer. I drove up towards Swannanoa in an aimless way, just beyond the golf course. That's where I saw Mickey out in his pasture with his cows. They were gathered around him like they were his family now.

Sitting there on the roadside, I called Buck to see if he was planning on making things right somehow. We hadn't talked about anything significant since our day in Pennsylvania. From my my experience with him, I felt sure Buck lived by Fig's sort of moral code, but he was just older and tireder about it. He had more slack to give.

He answered right away. "I'm on a repo," he said. "Call you back." He hung up before I could speak.

I stopped in at the Martin's in Waynesboro to pick up something to drink on the road. The store was huge and empty. I wandered around. The skeevy guy I'd seen at the precinct house was buying a pumpkin or something. I retreated down an aisle towards the back of the store before he could spy me and treat me to one of his creepy, skeevy looks.

I went browsing through the organics where I picked up a fancy water and dropped by the binned nuts to scoop out some Almonds. I figured skeeve would be gone by then. There was nobody in sight but a bored check-out girl. She rang me up, and I headed for my car.

Naturally, he was out there right in my path. He was
lingering at the trunk of his ancient sedan. He'd lifted the lid
and was messing around. The guy was bony and cringing and
taking in everything on the sly and sidelong. To be a skeeve
is to never own up to what you're leering at and why. The
sight of him irritated me. Ordinarily, I'd just shiver, but I
guess a little of Buck's way of going at the world had rubbed
off on me by then.

"All right, slimeball." I think I even said it a little out
loud as I walked on a line straight for my car. Let it carry me
right past him, I decided. He's the one with the malfunction.
Why go out of my way for him?

He had on his khaki twill uniform like I'd seen him in
before. "Buddy" over the pocket. I remembered it from the
station house. I was looking right at him as I closed in.
Being skeevy, he couldn't bring himself to eye me squarely
back.

He made a sinusy noise, and his jaw twitched like a jolt
had shot through him. My plan was to pass as close as I
could and be a living lesson to him. I was right beside
"Buddy" when he threw out an arm and tipped me into his
trunk. Sure I was stunned but not so thoroughly that I
couldn't be indignant, but in that sort of situation,
indignation doesn't help. Better to be desperate and savage.
Best to go utterly feral. I realize that now. At the time, I
opted for insulted instead of wild.

He pressed a nasty rag against my face. I was kicking
and thrashing by then but not enough to matter. Whatever
he'd soaked his rag in made me drowsy quick. I tried not to
breathe, but I was panicked, so I inhaled enough to matter.
It felt like a shade was coming down. Things went dim and
then went dark. I remember being bounced and jostled. The
stink of tire rubber and car grease.

My phone woke me up. I was a long way from anywhere when I first heard it. I got closer as it repeated. I was stuck in a hollow — the spare tire well — and couldn't really move. Light seeped in through a rust hole in the fender, past a run of rotted gasket.

I was groggy still and disoriented. I wondered where the racket was coming from. I wondered how to make it stop.

Buck

i

I decided to give him fair warning. I could have just shown up and knocked on Mickey's door, but instead I wanted him to know I'd need him to string a story together. That it wouldn't be enough for Mickey to try to get off with just a shrug. So I dialed him up.

"I need to see you.

"Well," he said, "all right. How about Toot's? I could do with some lunch."

"Toot's in an hour," I told him. "I rode up to Pennsylvania and talked to your son."

"Might be closer to two," Mickey said. That sounded like trouble. Not a dent.

They were having an April squall on the ridge line. I could see the cap of clouds and the blowing snow from down at the post office where I kept a box.

I'd picked up my bills and my grocery store flyers and was standing out in the gravel lot looking at the blowing clouds and piecing together what I'd tell Mickey when a guy I recognized rolled up in a new diesel truck.

By all rights, I shouldn't have known who he was. I'd only ever seen him naked. I flashed on him in that motel lot. The place up by Afton with the weather-spoiled carpet golf on top of the filled in pool. He was chasing his previous truck to the road without even so much as shoes.

"What the hell's going on?" His lady friend called out to him from their motel room doorway. I could see her lumpy silhouette. The coal of her cigarette.

Now he was driving a massive GM with all kinds of options. Trailer mirrors. Oversized tires. Quit a lot of chrome.

"They getting it, aren't they?" He glanced at the mountain top as he climbed from his cab.

I nodded. "Hammered," I told him. I considered his ride. "Hell of a truck."

"She'll do."

He went into the PO while I considered his ride. Pictured it on the hook and going away.

Mickey was late. I spent about a half hour deciding he wasn't going to come at all. Del was trying not to cook me pancakes or plate me any chicken. Toot jawed at him through the service window, told him to do what she paid him to do, which was stand at the grill and read the tickets, make what people wanted.

His pointed his spatula my way. "He ain't people," he said.

Toot's addled mother shouted, "Poppies!" from her table by the window where she was plucking napkins out of the dispenser and dropping them onto the floor.

Mickey came about the time my lunch platter did. He tossed his jacket in before him and slid onto the vinyl bench.

I let him order, or I let him look at the laminated menu anyway, let Toot come up and say, "Cutlet?"

I let Mickey nod and tell her, "Yes, ma'am."

"So," I said, once it was just us. "Went and had a run at Matthew."

Mickey moved the ketchup bottle. The creamer. Fiddled with the sweetener packets.

"This never smelled right," I told him.

He polished his spoon on his sleeve. Then his fork.

"Matthew told me everything."

Mickey arranged his flatware to suit him. "How is the boy?" he asked me.

"It looked like he was making a go of real estate. He's got an office. I'll bet he's got a phone."

"You have children?" Mickey asked me.

"A daughter."

"You close?'

I made like I had to give it some thought. I shook my head. "Divorce and all. I kind of got the short end."

"Talk to her much?"

"Not as much as I'd like."

"Even though she's got a . . . phone?"

"I get it. Families are complicated, and your business is your business, except that you hired me to find out something you already knew."

Mickey fiddled. He watched his hands move across the worn formica.

"Were you going to keep hiring guys like me until one of us pieced it together? Was that the plan?"

Nothing from Mickey beyond a dyspeptic expression.

"Was there even a plan?"

Still nothing from Mickey.

"Make me understand," I told him.

His cutlet came. On the menu, they called it veal. That sure seemed like a reach.

"Let's eat first," he said and dug and sawed at the breading.

My pancakes were runny and sad in the middle. My chicken was bloody at the bone.

Mickey ate. I mostly watched. Mickey paid. He insisted on it.

"Come on." He pointed at his truck. I left mine in the lot and climbed in.

It was only five minutes up to Mickey's house. We rolled past his driveway and turned off the road on an overgrown, seldom used track into the woods. There was a chain across it. No lock. Just a hook. Mickey stopped, and I got out and opened the way.

As country tracks go, this one was less drivable than most. We bounced over limbs in the rocks in the way. I had to brace myself against the ceiling.

"You going be using this truck again?" I asked.

Mickey told me, "Might."

He didn't say anything else. I didn't bother to talk much either. We rolled into what had once been a pasture. Saplings were taking it over. Thistles and greenbriar were thriving. Mickey stopped the truck and shut off the engine.

"I usually come through the woods, walk up from the house. I keep the cows across the road these days. I guess I've kind of let this go."

"Going wild, all right."

He opened his door. "Come on."

If I had a loose end I wanted to dispose of, I might have brought him to such a place. Pitched his carcass in a thicket.

"Where are we headed Mickey?"

He read me well enough and smiled. Like most men, Mickey couldn't help but be pleased to get taken for a threat and a danger.

"You want to know or don't you?"

Mickey skirted the stickers, forged through the underbrush, and went into the woods. I didn't see that I had much choice but to trail behind him and trust him.

I let Mickey stay about ten yards ahead. I wasn't authentically fearful, just wary. People get funny and a little hard to gauge when they have to own up to their past.

We spooked a doe. We stopped and watched her.

"You hunt?" Mickey asked me.

"Once or twice. I decided I can be cold and drunk in my yard."

"Used to love it," Mickey said and shook his head. "Hadn't wanted to in a while."

Once we'd left the overgrown pasture maybe a hundred yards behind us, we were walking through a typical upland Virginia hardwood forest. White oaks mostly in this one. Stunted by the wind, they'd grown out instead of up. The stout limbs sagged onto the ground. You could walk up one and right into a tree. No climbing required at all.

The matted wood's grass ground cover had kept everything else away. No thorny brambles or suckers. Just the occasional bear-tossed rock.

"Where are we headed?" I finally asked Mickey.

He pointed with one of his blunt, chapped fingers. Mickey had those big, neglected farmer's hands you could have troweled up a flower bed or beat a rug with.

He finally reached where he'd intended to take me and stopped. I drew up beside him. It was hard at first to tell we were anywhere other than just out in the woods. That turned out to be kind of the point.

"I couldn't make much of it," Mickey said.

I looked where he was looking. Instead of mounding up, the ground had hollowed out. The trough had filled with matted leaves and twigs, blown in through the years. It appeared there was no marker until Mickey squatted down to clear leaf litter from a stone. A small slab of basalt about the size of a flank steak, shoved upright into the ground.

"Kiki?" I said.

Mickey stood back up. "Yes, sir."

"What happened?"

"I don't entirely know."

"Tell me what you do know."

"I guess I could."

"Have to."

Mickey huffed and nodded. I would have thought he was hoping to unburden himself. I'd already assumed that was the whole point of hiring on serial investigators to poke around in his tragic business with the goal, I'd decided, of finding out what Mickey couldn't bring himself to own up to and say.

So there he was finally standing with a civilian over his daughter. I didn't need much, but he had to tell me something, and there at first he couldn't even do that.

"Any of your people ever sick?" he asked me. "In the head?"

If I ruled out alcoholics and wastrels, I didn't have a lot of people left. There'd been one second cousin, notorious for her hypochondria right up until she'd pitched over dead of an embolism at the Thanksgiving table. The family took that as her way of saying, "See?" and didn't run her down after that.

"Not that I know of," I said.

"I don't know what they do now for people like Viv. They sure couldn't do much back then."

That was the first time I'd ever heard Mickey call his wife by name or even so much as refer to the woman directly.

"Bi-polar, right?"

Mickey nodded. "That's what they ended up with."

"Was she violent?"

Mickey gazed at the sunken ground before us. "Just the once."

"Had medication but wouldn't take it. That's the way I heard it."

Another nod from Mickey. He gazed towards the racket of a woodpecker hammering a tree.

"So?"

"Kiki went out walking. That part's on the level. Vivian was supposed to drive her, but they had a fight."

"About what?"

"Clothes or boys or hair or something. Those two didn't mesh."

"What was different about this fight."

"Vivian had . . . I don't know . . . hobbies, I guess. The medicine tamped her down. I think that's why she didn't take it. She'd rather just go from knitting to painting to making pots to learning Italian to soufflé making. She'd bounce from one thing to another. It's what she needed. What she liked. She'd gotten onto some kind of Bible study. Fell in a with a pack of Pentecostal fools."

A branch laying across the sunken plot began to trouble Mickey. He tried to kick it clear but then appeared to decide that was unseemly and so bent down to pluck it up and toss it away.

"The Old Testament spoke to Vivian. The way those Bible thumpers read it, the thing was all about saints and sinners. Lot of smiting. Lot of vengeance. Lot of just rewards. Another week or two and she would have likely moved onto something else. Small engine repair. Decoupage. Greek pastry. Who the hell knows?"

"So Kiki went out walking," I said to nudge him.

A nod. "Then Vivian got in the car. I was down by the shed and stopped her. She seemed calm enough. Said she was going to give Kiki a ride."

"Did you know about the argument?"

"They were arguing most all the time. So generally yeah, but kind of no."

"Then what?"

"She didn't come back for probably three or four hours. I even went out looking for her. Left Matthew in case she came home."

"Had she done this before? Disappear for a stretch?"

"A time or two. Her doc said he didn't want her driving, but that was mostly because of the pills he gave that she didn't take anyway."

"So she went where she wanted?"

"It wasn't like I could stop her." Mickey pecked the leaf litter with the toe of his boot. "It was already too late by the time she came home."

I watched as Mickey reached over and poked with his finger between my ribs.

"She stuck it right there. Slotted screwdriver. We kept one in the glovebox. Don't know why she got it out."

"Just stabbed her once?"

Mickey nodded. "She must have hit something that mattered. Then she rode Kiki around the countryside while while the girl filled up with blood."

"Dead by the time you saw her?"

Mickey pecked with his shoe. He nodded.

"And you did this . . . ?" I pointed at the trough before us. ". . . instead of what you should have done?"

"I didn't see how I could stand to lose them both. People do funny things sometimes."

It was my turn to nod. I'd done my share of funny things through the years, though I'd stopped well short of burying blood kin in the woods.

"Why keep hiring guys like me?" I asked Mickey even though I had to think I probably knew the answer.

"I kept hoping one of you'd figure it out. Do what I should have done."

"All you had to do was open your mouth."

"Couldn't," Mickey told me. "Don't know why."

"What do you want me to do?"

"I'm going to leave it to you," he said.

I flashed on what would surely happen to Mickey if I went to the Waynesboro PD. The story would be sensational locally. There wasn't much doubt of that. I could even see P.J. getting it on the Action/Weather/News! team air. Then there'd probably be a plea. Some kind of sentence, mostly suspended, and Mickey would be that guy with the cows and the family secrets and the lies.

"Can't it be enough you told me?" I asked him.

Mickey couldn't say. He lifted his cap to scratch his head. He muttered at me something about justice.

"That ship's sailed." I tapped Mickey on the sternum. "Work here," I said, "on peace."

We didn't say much on the way back to the diner, but not saying much was hardly a rare thing for Mickey and for me.

When Mickey stopped in the lot beside my pickup, he told me, "I thought I'd feel better."

"You might yet," I said.

"I didn't see," he told me one time further, "how I could stand to lose them both."

"You must see it now," I said to Mickey, "since you did."

ii

There's no way to account for what people get up to. No flat standard for how folks might behave. You go in thinking you've seen it all, and then you meet up with a cracker artist. Some fool driven just shy of genius but well beyond lunacy.

It was a second-hand Kia, for godsakes. Dinged and filthy and neglected. You could see the streaks where the guy had wiped the windshield with his hand. He'd been riding on his doughnut in what looked like a semi-permanent way. One of the back windows was busted and taped. When I went up to check the vin, I could see all the damage wayward cigarette sparks had done to the upholstery, and that was in addition to the dirt and the staining and the shin-deep trash on the floorboards.

I was only out there as a favor. The guy who sold that Kia ran a lot where he showcased far finer vehicles, the kind with loans worth calling in. This was a spite repo. The dealer had made no bones about it. The car was worth nothing. The loan was piddling. He should have thrown his hands up and written it off.

"I'm just tired of that asshole driving one of my cars," he told me.

"Good enough." He didn't need a reason beyond that with me. He always threw me work when I needed it.

"Make sure he's passed out or something," was the advice I got. "Never know what you're going to get with him."

So I was careful with this one, even more careful than I usually am. I found that Kia at the Great Value in Crozet. I waited for the driver, and he came out with a box of beer and a pack of hot dogs. He had one of each right there in the parking lot and then took off towards Mint Springs.

I knew where he rented, but that's not where he went. It turned out he had a lady friend over the mountain near Stuarts Draft. She lived in what I'd call a trailer park if it hadn't been chiefly vacant slabs with bits of lattice skirting here and there. Waste drains attached to nothing. Romex standing up all over where it looked like trailers had just been snatched away.

The whole place had been repoed already, and there he'd come by with his Kia which, before the night was out, would get snatched away as well.

At least, that was the plan. I found a spot across the road where a service station had been. Now there was pulverized concrete and weeds. A vacant pump island and a length of rotted air hose. A pile of hubcaps where the actual building had been.

I called my usual guy, Marcus, but he was passing a kidney stone and using Vicodin and Smirnoff to do it. So I called my second stringer, but he was off hunting somewhere. That left Wally. He was always exactly the wrong guy to use. It was a wonder Wally even had a license to drive.

Wally was a prattler. That had probably served him well back in those days when he was picking up people broken down on the highway, but it's rare anymore that a car will strand a driver on the road. Rare enough so that Wally had to shift to repo mostly where his knack for ceaseless talking doesn't serve him well at all. Worse still, Wally has hillbilly ADD. He'll start telling you about a snake he killed or some chesty woman he saw and then branch off into weather because a cloud caught his eye or complain about his itchy socks, wish he'd eaten more for lunch.

I hated to have to call on Wally any time at all, especially there with a sensitive job before me that was entirely spite inspired.

I informed Wally, as was my custom, that I'd entertain no questions from him. That the job was the job, he'd snatch whatever car I told him, and he'd take it where I said he should take it.

"Well," Wally said like usual, "all right."

That didn't mean anything with Wally. It came out of his mouth like breath.

I walked him across the derelict service station lot to where we could get a clear view of that Kia. It was looking especially ratty in what was by then low afternoon sun.

"Who wants that back?"

"What did I just tell you?"

"Can't be worth nothing."

"Wally."

He toed a hunk of gravel with his Florsheim. Wally favored nasty coveralls but, for some reason, he always wore dress shoes. As a kind of avocation, he'd buff his Florsheims on his calves.

"With that new health deal, a doctor can cut you open or not." That was a radio nugget from Wally. How it went from his brain to his mouth, I can't say.

"We're going to sit a while." I pointed towards the trailer park. "Once he gets full of beer and the sun goes down, we'll take a run at it."

Wally nodded. "What have you got to eat?"

Fortunately, I'd long since learned to keep Wally food in my trunk. I handed him a sleeve of saltines and a bottle of Thousand Island dressing.

"You're all right, Buck," he told me.

Wally retired to his truck. He played the radio until I stopped him.

"We kind of want to do this on the sly."

It was always like Wally had never been out of the house before.

"I'm going to make a call."

Wally nodded. He already had dressing on his chin.

I owed P.J. a call back. I'd been putting it off. I felt sure she'd be angling for the sort of news story I didn't much want getting out. I couldn't blame her. She was in the Action/ Weather/News! business, and the whole Kiki Dunbar investigation had taken such a weird, sensational turn that we were probably no longer looking to do the same sort of thing about it.

With a story like that, she'd almost have to put a blonde correspondent in front of it. This was scandal on a scale that would likely have the mother ship sniffing around. At the very least, I could be sure Mickey wouldn't stay just on the blog.

So I'd been thinking about what to tell P.J., running through my range of options. As much as I liked the girl, I didn't see how I could give her my blessing and approval. To my mind, Mickey needed leaving alone. Your Action/ Weather/News! teams don't do much of that. They'd hardly rate an exclamation mark if they did.

I called her up, but she didn't answer. I'd not prepared a voicemail spiel, so I hung up and did some thinking on it and got interrupted by Wally. He had a thing he wanted to tell me about igneous rocks. He'd been reminded of a stone he'd found by all the busted concrete around him.

"Yea big," he said and showed me his hand. "All melty and shit."

"Right."

"Was probably powerful hot way back then."

"Need more crackers?"

He didn't. Wally shook his head.

I called P.J. again. She answered this time and then dropped her phone on the car floor or something. I could hear a roar and a clatter. Somebody talking. P.J. maybe. Garbled and mostly consonants, like maybe I'd caught her half asleep.

"You there?"

Still the roar. What impressed me as a whimper.

"Hello?"

The sort of squeaky girl cry that made me stop and wonder what exactly I might have caught her at.

"Oh, Lord," I told myself primarily. I pictured P.J. all tangled up in passion with that ginger cop.

I had a slight P.J. problem. I was old enough to be her father's older brother, which didn't keep me from being fonder of her in a corner of my brain than I knew in those moral parts of me was proper. The cutter I'd met at the farmer's market had been too young for me too, and she was a decade older than P.J. It had helped that, psychologically, she was too screwed up for guys her age. She was very likely too screwed up for a guy my age as well, but at least I'd run across my share of maladjusted women and so had enough reserve experience to defuse her every now and again.

It was different with P.J. If my choice was between wanting her happy and wanting a time machine, I would have preferred the latter while knowing I'd have to make the former work. So she made me happy and sad in equal measure. I was sharper with her than she deserved. Quicker to correct her and dismiss her suggestions. Always ready to deflate her. It was what I did instead of owning up to how I actually felt. When I was thirty-five, she was a toddler. That was the math I kept running in my head.

So I didn't try to call her again, which left me exposed to Wally. He started in before I'd gotten my phone entirely into my pocket.

"Hear about that ebay boy that killed everybody?"

"I think you mean Craigslist," I said.

"One of them."

Wally had enough cracker crumbs on the front of his greasy coveralls to look like he was getting breaded for the fryer. With saltines and a bottle of salad dressing, Wally was like a cat with yarn.

"Up in Cleveland or somewhere."

"Boston."

"Killed like eight or ten women."

"Two."

"So you did hear about it?"

I nodded. "Did you?"

There was no need at all to worry about giving offense to Wally. He was impervious to insult. I kind of admired that about the guy.

"Damn if I wasn't in the mood for this." Wally gestured with his dressing bottle. He was always in the mood for it. That's why I kept it in my trunk.

I was about to suggest we go on over and try to tow that Kia when the boy who owned it shouted at us from the trailer door.

"Ain't like I can't see you."

We were the only candidates. There were no people about otherwise. Wally was all for shouting back, and drew the breath to prime himself, but I got a hand up to stop him before he could come out with God knows what.

"I said I'd have the money tomorrow, now didn't I? And it ain't tomorrow, is it?"

"What's he talking about?" Wally asked me.

"Maybe somebody floated him a loan. A guy behind on a Kia is sure to be behind on everything else."

"You hear me?"

"What's the plan, chief?" Wally wanted to know.

"You don't come until I whistle," I told him. "Just hold what you've got until then."

Wally nodded. Wally dressed a saltine. Wally shoved it in his pie hole.

I fished a pistol out of the glovebox, chose the Ruger instead of the Colt. It had long been my leading sleepy-time handgun. I'd never shot at anybody with, had never so much as aimed it in fear of my life or in anger, but I had surely knocked it against a human cranium or three. The thing was a sap with a firing pin. Swung at a problem civilian with a full clip, it was as good as having a brick.

"When I whistle," I said one time more. There was no such thing as over reminding Wally.

I decided to walk over. I felt like I could get a better read along the way, not that I believed there was awful much going on beyond a simple mistaken assumption. That guy seemed irritated me and Wally had come to break his legs today when he'd already lied to somebody about having money tomorrow.

I tried to look unthreatening. I wandered over rather than stalked. The guy was standing in the trailer doorway with his woman friend. She was whispering at him from the moment I saw her until I reached her cinder block steps. Her hair was the shade of red you can only get out of a bottle. She was smoking a long, slender lady cigarette. She was all braceleted and ringed up. She had blue lacquered nails except on a couple of fingers where the polish had worn off.

She whispered some more.

"I got this," her boyfriend told her.

She started in again.

He took his eyes off me so he could swing his head around and tell her, "HEY!"

She appeared accustomed to hearing from men that pitch and volume of talk. She didn't even twitch. Certainly didn't retire. She even looked to me like she was fully prepared to whisper again.

"Tomorrow," the boyfriend said to me. "I told him. We worked it all out."

"Second thoughts," I said. "We're going to hold your car."

"That weren't part of it."

"Is now. Change in the weather."

"What the shit does that even mean?" the girlfriend said. "HEY!"

She toked on her lady cigarette and blew smoke out of her nose.

"What if I say, 'no'?" the boyfriend asked me in that way of rough cobs everywhere that does service as a threat. He'd lifted his chin. He'd made two fists.

"Then things'll go poorly for you."

I knew we were at that moment guys reach in every confrontation when you can either separate and come to your regular senses — work things out like grown-ups — or do what men more frequently do and clash in a spitting rage.

He was bound to come at me one way or another. I felt all but certain of that. I could almost smell the gear oil as that guy attempted some strategizing. He settled on a plan and smiled my way.

"Come on in and let's hash this out."

"It's hashed already," I told him. "Keys or tow. Up to you."

"Hell, buddy. I told you, we worked it all out."

"Things changed," I said and whistled for Wally.

I had to know, from long Wally experience, he wouldn't just get in his truck and come.

"That for me?" he shouted from back across the road.

I whistled again while I kept my eyes on Kia guy and his lady friend. He was looking cornered, shook his head in that "Aw shit" way guys like him will.

There wasn't enough beer in the world to make him drunk, but it sure made him predictable. He charged my way. I just had to matador him and give him a shove. He fell hard and hit his forehead on a cement toad that was holding down a Snickers wrapper by way of decorating the yard.

"Stay down," I suggested.

"Sugar!" his lady friend yelled and she came charging out as well.

The woman had grabbed a vodka bottle on her way out. Unfortunately for her, it was plastic. She bounced it off my upraised forearm, tried to claw me with her free hand. I pulled my Ruger out of my pocket and tapped her once with it. She grunted. Her bracelets jangled as she piled up on the ground.

I thought the boyfriend might come at me in gentlemanly indignation. Instead he dabbed at his forehead and examined the blood on the tips of his fingers.

"I'm sort of ok right here," he said.

I whistled again.

"That for me?"

I think I invoked the Savior.

I ended up taking one of those showers I take sometimes when I feel contaminated. It can't be long enough or hot enough to leave me satisfied. I fed Mabel a can of tuna in a bid to be kind to an earthly creature. Then I had a bourbon at the kitchen counter and was nursing a second on the sofa when I pulled out my phone and tried P.J. again. I got an answer this time.

"Hello." A man's voice.

"Who's this?"

"Who's this?"

"Friend of P.J.'s. Your turn."

I could hear voices in the background and could make out enough of them to recognize the brand of crime scene chatter I'd heard countless times before.

"You family?" the officer said.

Buddy

i

I'd dosed her badly. I knew that. Barry would have given me hell. Details, Barry likes to say, are the building blocks of success. One foot in front of the other, Barry likes to say, even when you're doing the tango.

Her phone went off. I heard it. White girls with their ringtones. Their nose studs. Their glitter nails. Their pelvis tattoos. My goodness, it's a wonder I can even locate Lisa. Water runs downhill, Barry likes to say, just like civilizations do. Barry has an inky streak. I suspect he'd be more frankly apocalyptic if he could figure out a way to earn a going dollar by it. Why improve yourself or invest your savings if the world will soon end in fire?

She groaned. I heard her. Lisa wasn't awake, but she clearly wasn't dead to the world either. I'd known her to come around before. It's not my favorite situation because of how desperate Lisa can sometimes get. She struggles in a way that's unseemly. You want Lisa to know what's coming, but you also want her to acknowledge that it's well earned and it's just.

I was going to stop at the package store for schnapps. Lisa has always had a fondness, and I count myself as nothing if not a thoughtful host. I pulled into the lot and climbed out of the car, shut the door like I was going off but just stayed where I was to listen. The ether still had ahold of her sufficiently to keep her from making words, but she jostled and thumped enough to raise the kind of racket that would probably alarm a civilian if one happened to pull up.

I decided to just keep going and do without an aperitif. Lisa usually spits it at me anyway.

It's a bit of a trip from Waynesboro over the mountain to where I live, and I chose to stick to the two lane and take my time getting home. Since Lisa was already rattling around in the trunk, a longer drive wouldn't matter. I'd dosed Lisa carelessly, so it was certain we would talk. Lisa has always been a big one for hashing things out and airing the grievances that have popped into her head.

So I could be certain I'd hear every wretched thing that Lisa thought. Every poor opinion, no matter how fleeting, she'd ever held about me. Once Lisa had decided it was time to have one of her sessions, she could flat hose me off. People had a way of letting Lisa down, of falling well short of her standards, and Lisa liked to point out the chinks and the flaws. It was kind of a hobby with her.

I used to argue back. I used to cobble together explanations anyway. I used to be emotionally invested in what Lisa thought about me. I used to not want to let her down, not serve as a constant source of disappointment. I hated that look she'd give me. Like I was nothing, an inert mass.

I had a hiccup on the ridge line when Mr. Pittman flagged me down. I almost ignored him. Some guy in a truck, waving his arm out the window. Probably trying to warn me of an accident, a cow in the road, or a license check. I was about to turn off anyway and take the cut back down the mountain. Then I saw it was one of our trucks. Cherry red and stickered over. I expected Hotchkiss or one of them hoping to prank me somehow. I'd slow down, and they'd throw a drink can at me or yell something unholy my way.

Instead, who do I see but Mr. Pittman away from a toilet and out in the wild.

We both stopped in the road, nose to tail. Pittman pointed at the empty lot of what had once been a house a pancakes. The place had survived on Blue Ridge Parkway traffic for maybe four or five years. Then it got robbed and caught fire twice, and the IHOP people gave up. Now it was a shell with a busted-up orange tiled roof and bunch of broken windows.

There were motorcycle folks already parked just east of the building. They had those bikes with three wheels and trailers that you need an AARP membership to ride. I followed Pittman to the west side. We had a view of the valley. I parked well away from his truck and climbed out of my Valiant to head him off.

"Problem?" I said as I closed on Pittman. He hadn't stirred from his truck.

I'd been sifting through the possibilities in my head. I'd put off a job or two, but we usually had leeway for that. And there was that woman on Calf Mountain with carpenter ants in her floor joists. We'd sistered up a few of them, but she kept calling us back about creaks. I'd said a hard thing or two to customers lately, but compared to Hotchkiss and them, I'd been a regular saint.

"What's up with you?" Mr. Pittman asked me.

I shrugged. "What do you mean?"

"Keith's not happy," Pittman said. "He's come to me twice. He says you're skipping work, riding around, following people. Doing all stripes of things you shouldn't and only half the things you should?"

"Keith said that?"

Pittman nodded.

"Told you on his talker, or are you just filling in the gaps?"

"I understood him well enough," Pittman said.

"Wouldn't count on it," I said. That was bold for me. I generally yes sirred and right, chiefed Mr. Pittman. I held whatever opinion he did and usually made like he was wise. "Hard to read the boy sometimes."

"He seemed plain enough about it."

"He tell you about his run in?"

Pittman suddenly looked a touch less sure, or maybe his stomach was talking to him. "What run in?"

"He had his eye on a girl. Pushed it with her. She isn't pressing charges, but . . ."

That was just the sort of news to put Pittman in a mood to stalk around, so he shucked his seatbelt, threw open his door, joined me in the lot. "Don't just turn the tables," Barry likes to say. "Flip them over."

"Charges?"

I had a decent solemn nod and used it.

"Keith?"

"He's got kind of a temper," I said. "Frustrated, you know. He's got urges just like us."

Pittman interrupted his stalking to treat me to an appraising look. I took his meaning. There was no 'us'. There was him and his sort, and me.

"What happened exactly?" Pittman asked.

It wasn't a stretch to make something up. I'd seen Keith approach a girl or two. He scared them when he was being polite.

"I don't think he meant to knock her over. Had one of his clumsy fits, you know?"

"Why's he going after you?"

"Probably afraid I'd rat him out, so he went after me first. Keith's kind of cagey."

"Keith?"

"I wouldn't have guessed it either." My more-in-sadness-than-anger voice was always as fine as my solemn nod. "I've only ever looked out for the boy."

Mr. Pittman breathed hard through his nose, just short of snorted really. He laid his hands to his hips and gazed out over the valley. There was a plume of smoke halfway across.

"Me and Keith's mother used to have a . . . thing."

I thought he was telling me more than he was. "So Keith's your son?"

"No! It was like four years ago. I promised I'd look out for him."

"Oh."

"You hear that?"

"Hear what?"

We stood. We listened.

"That."

Thumping. Whining. Lisa.

I shook my head. I did that thing I do when I'm furious. I imagine it looks like a shiver.

We listened some more. I got out enough of a noise for Mr. Pittman to show me his open hand by way of cutting me off.

Thump. Whine. Lisa was begging for stern treatment.

"What the hell is that?"

"Construction, sounds like." I pointed past my sedan towards the shabby motel up the hillside. It was in better repair than the derelict IHOP but not by an awful lot.

Pittman listened some more. It could be Lisa had collapsed and dozed again. All that mattered was there was nothing for him to hear.

"Yeah, maybe," he said.

"I've got an appointment. Dr. Marlin. She's doing me a world of good."

I could tell Mr. Pittman didn't know who I meant. I was just the sort of employee a guy like him would send to a shrink and then forget he'd even bothered with it.

"Marlin."

"Anger doctor. It's going good," I told him. "Me and her have got a handle on things. Not much chance I'll be going back to the guy I used to be."

"Good." I'd seen that look on Pittman's face quite enough to know his gastric system was having a vital word with him.

"Want me to talk to Keith?" I asked.

Pittman was climbing back in his truck. "Give it a day. It'll probably blow over."

That was Pittman's usual approach to office strife. Otherwise, why would Hotchkiss and them still have jobs to go to?

"I'll do that. You have a good night, sir."

A nod and a sour look from Pittman. I watched him wheel into the road and head east down the mountain. Only once he was out of sight did I walk over to my car. I put my foot on the back bumper and rocked my Valiant on its shocks.

I don't quite know what Lisa got up to. Thrashing. Blubbering. Something.

"Is that any way to behave?" I asked her.

Whimpering. Rustling.

"I was having a business meeting."

A choked off sob. Typical Lisa. Her mess spilling out all the time, swamping everybody else's stuff.

"Lisa!" I said, disgusted. I rocked my sedan another time, climbed under the wheel, and left the lot.

We were still a good half hour from my place. It wasn't far cross country, but the roads were all slow going and indirect. I didn't hear much out of Lisa down from Afton on the switchback. No more wailing and crying out anyway. Just the occasional thump and thud.

I passed the time deciding precisely how I'd approach my session with her. For a woman who'd decided everybody else was doing it wrong, Lisa couldn't tolerate advice with any grace. I'd start in, and she'd interrupt me. She'd complain. She'd carp. She'd cry. Sometimes she'd try to run away, and I'd have to chase her down. Lisa can be an exasperating ordeal of a woman. All I ever want her to do is sit still and hear me out. That's fairly threadbare as wishes got. You'd think one time she'd grant it. Not Lisa. Always with the lip. Always with the tears.

"People," Barry likes to say, "will only sit up and hear you if you're making exactly the right kind of noise."

"Almost there," I shouted towards Lisa as I eased off the gravel and road and onto the track to my house. She didn't thump. She didn't whine. No more blubbering. Not a peep.

I parked where I park on Lisa days, which requires some maneuvering and backing.

"Off to change."

I needed to fetch my coveralls off their nail. I used to have a dentist who'd tell me everything he was about to do just before he did it. "You'll feel a pinch." "This'll be cold at first." That sort of thing. It struck me as thoughtful and conscientious. I use it on Lisa sometimes.

"I'll be a few minutes."

Nothing in reply. No noise at all. I took that as a sure sign Lisa had gone sullen. She's a pouter. Lisa will dry up on you if the mood hits. She'll depend on a hard look to say all she needs to say.

I'd lately laundered my yellow coveralls, but the stains had all stayed in. Worse still, they'd drawn up in the dryer and had become too short and tight. I slipped into them and tried to stretch them out but finally accepted that they were ruined. That meant I'd have to resort to my heavier quilted ones that were oversized and fairly swallowed me up. Lisa was sure to have her fun with that. She treated scrawny like a moral failing.

I stood at the back of my Valiant and listened. A bit of vermin-like rustling but nothing else. Lisa was exasperated with me. I could feel it in the air. She was too busy putting her litany together to bother herself with thumping or wailing. I slipped in the key and turned it. I was resigned to getting scorched by her but good.

Lisa didn't scream when I lifted the lid and the air and the light finally hit her. Odd that, because Lisa frequently screams and claws at me in a frantic sort of way. She didn't try to scrabble out the way she does sometimes. She didn't whine and plead. Didn't shrink away. I just gazed in and Lisa — stuck in the spare tire well — gazed out.

"Help me," she said and raised an arm.

Now, I know Lisa is wily. I'm well aware that she's hardly to be trusted, but I couldn't remember when Lisa had seemed so vulnerable to me.

"Please," she said. She touched me. Reached right up and did it without me having to touch her first. And there was no anger in it. No agitation. Her grip was light. Her hand was soft.

I'll confess, that was close to a thrill for me. I'm sure I hid it poorly. I'd been waiting for Lisa to draw towards me instead of pulling away. There she was in need, and I was handy. "Help me. Please."

"Ok," I told her. I didn't want to sound too anxious to forgive Lisa all at once, but if she was willing to soften towards me, I had to be ready to soften back.

She reached up with both arms, and I bent to let her lay them around my neck. It had been so long since Lisa had been anything but sharp and brittle with me, that I'd almost forgotten those times, long back, when she'd been tender, when she'd been soft. Here was Lisa with her cheek right next to mine. Here was Lisa drawing me close.

I made like it was nothing to lift her. That was my job as her man after all. I brought her out of the trunk and held her while she steadied herself on her feet. I waited for Lisa to tell me something grateful and endearing.

"Breathe to live," Barry likes to say. "Let the rest of them breathe to speak." I passed a moment appreciating Barry for all of his wisdom and guidance.

"Are you ok?" I asked Lisa.

She said something I couldn't quite make out. It was soft and sounded tender.

I leaned towards her. "What was that?"

I couldn't believe that Lisa had baited me until she'd struck me twice. In the neck of all places. She'd hit me a third time before I could grab her arm and hold it. Her fingers were wrapped around an uncapped ballpoint pen. A cheap Bic that Lisa had chomped and gnawed the way she does.

The blood that had splashed on Lisa's fingers was as deep and rich a red as any blood I'd ever seen.

"Oh," I think I said to Lisa.

I loosed my grip and wandered off. Lisa stayed where she was and watched me go. Even in my quilted coveralls, I was chilled. I was unsteady. My ears were roaring. I couldn't remember anything I'd meant to do.

"Oh," I think I said again. It was all I could manage. I sat.

P.J.

i

Furious. That's the word for it. There was regret, resentment, some lingering disbelief. Those were handy in their way, but the raw fury is what mattered. I would surely have been done for with anything less.

I'd long since persuaded myself that creeps were just creepy, lacked the nerve to be anything more ambitious or seriously worse. Or maybe that's what I'd been raised to think. We'd had a skeeve up the block when I was little. He gave himself out as a widower and had a snapshot of a woman he showed around. "The Mrs.," he used to say and go moist. It would often earn him a hug, which was exactly what he wanted.

Instead of kids, he had a porky little dog named Augustus. He insisted we all call him Chip, never Mr. Boylen. He was quick with a band-aid if one of us got scraped. He could put his hands more places quicker than any human I've ever seen.

There was a family up the street, the Ketners. They'd moved over from Ohio. There were seven or eight of them altogether, usually a kids and cousins mix that ebbed and flowed depending on who could feed how many when.

They rented, the Ketners did, which people said in a hissed whisper like maybe the Ketners worshipped Satan or killed house cats for sport. My parents and their sort were proud of living in a stable neighborhood where people either owned their homes outright or were doing every damn thing they could to pay the mortgage down. The Ketners were month-to-monthers. They let people pull up and park right in the yard. They had a scandalous amount of junk on their porch. Stagnant water in their wading pool. Garbage they never took to the landfill. Trash they never bothered to burn.

All you had to do was say, "Ketner," on our street and people would shake their heads.

One of the Ketner girls proved to be a grave temptation for Chip. She had blonde curls and dimples, and she was taller than her older sisters, so the skirts and the shorts they handed down to her were always a little too short. She was gangly and happy, and Chip liked the looks of her. Every chance he got, he'd tell us how she reminded him of his late wife. Of course, we'd all seen Chip's snapshot of the Mrs. by then — a thick brunette in a track suit. The two of them likely had the same plumbing, but that was probably about it.

There was no point in calling Chip on such stuff. You'd just get his wide-eye look and a "What?".

So Chip applied his band aids to Gina, her name was, and laid on hands when he could. Gina's mom and dad both worked all day, so the kids ran loose after school. As far as the rest of the neighborhood was concerned, that was a lowlife renter symptom, something else people could shake their heads about.

Then Gina went sullen. It came on her suddenly. One day she was prancing around her yard in her usual way. Shirt too tight. Pants too short. Mop of curls. Bare feet. Quick to shout and laugh. That stopped so completely and all at once that even her father noticed. He wasn't a noticer by disposition. The man worked at a body shop banging out dents and straightening car frames. If he knew one kid from the next when he got home, that was about as good as he'd do.

Gina wouldn't spill the beans. She just shrugged and said nothing for as long as she could. Kids got quiet and

pouty. Everybody let it go for a while, but then Gina
confided in one of her sisters. The oldest one. Rose. She
had six or eight boyfriends in rotation all the time. The kind
of boys who expected something from a girl, and imagined
Rose was just their sort of creature.

"Chip rubbed his penis on her," Rose explained it first to
the rest of us girls in the neighborhood and then to her
mother and father.

Her mother yelled. We could hear her. She was all about
hauling Chip into court for a settlement. She was all about
putting Chip in jail. Gina's dad took a different approach.
He wasn't so keen on waiting for the wheels of justice to
turn. He'd already known a couple of poor outcomes in the
docket, and he felt like he had a fair idea of what Chip
probably deserved.

So Gina's dad took Gina with him to Chip's house at the
end of the street. She was crying and trying to pull away. I
remember watching them go. The whole neighborhood was
probably parked at their windows. The rooting interest was
all with Gina and her dad. It's widely accepted, apparently,
that being a creep is worse than renting.

Chip didn't come to the door at first. In fact, he didn't
come to the door at all, so Gina's dad was obliged to kick the
thing in. Fortunately for us, he hauled Chip out to talk to
him in the yard. I think he extracted a confession. We
couldn't really hear him, but from just watching what went
on, it looked like Gina aired (at her dad's insistence) a
version of events and then Chip took a turn contradicting it.
That earned him a swat from Gina's dad, which led to a
variation on Chip's contradiction. He got a swat for that as
well.

In time, Chip appeared to own up to where he'd rubbed
his penis exactly, and he took a comprehensive pummeling
for it from Gina's dad. From back where I was watching, Mr.

Ketner looked not so much angry as dedicated. He was industrious and thorough. We didn't hear him yell even once. He was content to let Chip do all the wailing. Chip hadn't fully thought through the wages of penis rubbing until Gina's dad had spent a half hour with him and made him concentrate.

Gina was never the same after that, of course. Chip was never quite the same guy either. He kept his hands in pockets around females. He'd flee if he got the chance. Everybody called Gina's dad 'Amos' instead of just 'Ketner' or nothing, and you never heard people complain about renters no matter how many people parked in Gina's parents' yard.

The day after Mr. Ketner beat Chip half to death, my mom and my dad came into my room, sat on my bed, and we had one of our serious talks. That meant my dad told me what he could remember of the things he and my mother had agreed I needed to hear. As he talked my mother nodded and studied her hands on her lap.

I said, "Yes, sir," when prompted, even if I wasn't quite sure what I was saying "Yes, sir" about.

In time, I understood that the thrust of that chat was to open my eyes to skeeves and creeps and morally pliable people, the kind who think it's ok to rub their penises on girls if they do it only just a little bit.

"You can't ever know what they're thinking," Dad said. "You can't know how far they'll go."

"Yes, sir."

"So let them be over there in the dark. You stay where the sun is shining."

"Yes, sir."

Dad glanced at Mom. She nodded.

"Well," Dad said, and they stood up.

So I blamed myself because I'd been warned. My guy was a skeeve and a creep and a cringer. Buddy, for fuck's sake. I should have crossed the lot to avoid him. It was daylight, for Godsakes, in Waynesboro. I'd forgotten what my father had said.

It didn't take much. He just nudged and redirected me. Like most creeps that pucker their sphincters all day, he was a wiry son-of-a-bitch, so one shove was enough to tumble me into his trunk.

I was too stunned to fight back at first. That's what skeeves count on, I guess. He had his nasty rag on my face before I'd even started struggling. The fumes were powerful, and I tried not to breathe them, but I couldn't claw at him with any effect without some air in my lungs. The fighting, then, kind of settled it for me. The more I struggled, the sleepier I got.

It was close and hot and gritty in there. I dreamed my phone was ringing. I dreamed I was in a coal car. I woke up for a half a minute, the way you do sometimes at home, and I kicked whatever my feet could reach. I tried to scream but couldn't seem to. Then I let the fury take over. I remembered Mr. Ketner and what my father had told me while my mother looked at her hands. The fury was for me. Not Buddy. Once I let it wash through me, that's when I settled down.

I had little to work with. A tire iron but not the the big, stout, useful kind. I was hoping for a screwdriver or maybe a hammer if I was lucky, but I could just find in the dark what felt like a brake fluid can, an oil filter wrench, some nasty rags, a tire gauge. I had my notebook and my Bic pen. My phone was somewhere. I couldn't locate it. I was jostled and bounced so that I couldn't do much for a while but brace and hang on.

Then we slowed and turned off the road, I had to think. I could hear grass against the undercarriage. Wherever we were going, I knew we were surely almost there.

I uncapped my Bic with my teeth. I'd decided to jam it into his eye. Stick it anywhere really I could aim it, and run like hell.

Just then I found my phone. There was no signal much. The car stopped. The door hinge creaked. I punched in 9-1-1 as the key went into the trunk latch. The lid swung open. I must have done a convincing job of seeming groggy and half asleep.

"You all right?"

Wasn't that just the way. Throw you in a car trunk. Knock you out. Ride you across the county, and then be all concerned.

I groaned like he'd jerked the covers off my bed.

"Help me." I went all girlish. "Please."

"Ok," he said and reached in to help me. I grabbed him around the neck as he struggled to lift me out. I just hung there. Dead weight. I didn't help him at all. I tightened my ballpoint in my fist. I waited for my chance.

It's funny what you remember and how it bubbles. Not in any coherent way but just in a flash, a moment out of nowhere. In my moment, I saw an actor. A German, I think, whose name I either can't remember or have never actually known. He was in some South American country learning to fight with a knife. It involved quite a lot of dodging so as to not get sliced up first followed up by one quick prick to the base of his opponent's neck. My how the blood spurted when he hit the right spot. Dark, arterial, pulsing blood. That movie was awash in the stuff.

I even remembered the guy who'd bought my ticket and had tried to hold my hand. He had the sort of bangs that needed an awful lot of flinging and a tattoo on his wrist well before that was the general way of things. I'd gone out with him to spite my mother. As is often the case with spite, I was the one who ended up suffering for it.

"Want to go somewhere and mess around or something?" If he asked me that once, he asked it three dozen times. I made a progress from "We'll see" to "Maybe later" to "Not tonight" to "Nope" to "Why don't you take me home."

All of that went through my head in an instant, and I clung to what of it mattered. Once skeeve had me out of the trunk and upright, once he'd said to me, "You ok?" I brought my Bic down on him with all the force I could muster. Then I did it again. And again. And, I think, again.

I'm nothing if not thorough. I wasn't about to stop until he stopped me, and he looked too surprised and disappointed to do much of anything. He just stood there and seeped a little at first. When I hit what I needed, we knew it. Blood shot a good two feet up in the air, and skeeve turned loose of me to put his hand on his wound.

I think he said, "Oh," or maybe he just grunted.

He wandered. I watched him. I kept meaning to run, but I couldn't. He found a tree to lean against. He decided to sit down. I never would have guessed there was so much blood in a scrawny creep like him.

Fig led them all to me. He'd used my 9-1-1 call to zero in on my phone. Fig was probably the only one on the force who was savvy enough to do it. He rolled up with detectives, a rescue squad truck, a fire engine even but it couldn't make the turn. So the fireman came tromping up through the weeds and stood around in their helmets and jackets. One of them even had an ax.

The cops bagged my pen and wrapped a shiny blanket around me. I guess that's in the manual. I guess that's what they have to do.

I wasn't ready to talk about anything. I told one of the detectives as much. The fat one with the flat top and the spearmint gum. He was wearing a dress shirt he'd bought about a thousand burritos ago.

He called me "Honey" and rattled on about one thing and another until I asked him (I like to think sweetly), "Why don't you shut the fuck up?"

They left me alone after that. Even Fig. I sat on the back step of the rescue squad truck from where I could watch the cops going in and out of the house and scouring the yard. They left the skeeve sitting dead for longer than I would have guessed. Some guy in coveralls took pictures of him. Full on and then in detail.

I heard him ask the fat detective, "With a pen?"

He nodded and chomped his gum. They each stole a glance my way. I knew at that moment I'd always be the girl who'd offed a guy with a Bic.

They found what they called a murder pit out in the side yard somewhere, and they went plundering through the house. I could hear them knocking around in there. It was a shack really. Small. Unpainted. Actively rotting in the forest. They brought out bags and boxes of stuff. A sack of leather-bound journals or something. A cop sat one of the boxes on the ground beside me. A carton packed full of self-help books. I recognized the guy on the cover. A quack from California we got press releases from all the time. His caps were far too white, and his rug was unpersuasive. He was a positive-thinking platitude machine.

One of the rescue squad techs wander over. "You know you're in shock, right?" he said.

I might have nodded. I might have asked him, "Do I?"

I saw Buck before he saw me. He came wading up the weedy track, past the trucks and the four by fours. He spied the dead guy first and went over to have a look at him. He scanned the yard and soaked in what he needed. Studied the house for a quarter minute. Buck figured it all out just by looking. He was a higher order of creature. Buck wouldn't have called a victim "Honey" with a pistol to his head.

The only question he asked was, "Where is she?"

One of the firemen pointed me out.

He came over and soaked me in as well. I got a quarter minute too.

"Hey," he said.

"Hey."

He sat down beside me on the shiny steel step.

The sobbing would come later. The panic. The collapse. Just then, he had the only shoulder I wanted.

He knew better than to talk, so I did.

"Told you," was all I said.

Buck

i

Tires again. I couldn't keep air in the spare on my truck, so I carried it over the mountain to Calvin. His wife had fed him tainted potato salad over Easter, and Calvin had decided that was a sign and token of all sorts of things coming apart.

"She's got a man somewhere," was his opening bid. He was using his air wrench at the time, so I had occasion to think about how to respond while he loosened the lugs on a Honda.

"You know it for certain?"

"I ain't met him or nothing."

Calvin yanked off the tire and let it roll against the shop wall. He was just rotating the things, but in his agitation, he'd let them drift all over the place.

"Has she told you about him?" I was doing my straight investigator thing, trying to sift the facts from the wounded guesswork.

"She don't need to."

"Tell me about the potato salad."

Calvin dropped the last tire — the front left — and rolled it rearward. I stopped it from leaving the bay altogether and escaping into the street.

"Poison."

"Made or bought?"

"Bought," Calvin told me. "Fine when she got it, but it sat in the car while she went clear to Charlottesville and back to get her goddamn hair done."

"Hot day?"

"That ain't the point. She put the stuff on the table. It was bubbling and all."

"How did her hair look?"

That earned me a glare from Calvin. I let him lift a tire and hang it on the studs before I told him, "That one goes up front."

He overtightened the lug nuts out of sheer irritation. "I don't know why I tell you anything."

"Yeah," I said. "Me too."

And that's precisely when Mickey Dunbar rolled in. He had a massive tractor tire laying on the bed of his state-body truck. I hadn't seen Mickey in a couple of months. I'd decided how things played out with him needed to be his business alone. P.J. had supplied local law enforcement with a psychotic to hang all their open homicides on. I'd certainly settled on what I'd do if I were Mickey — a whole hell of a lot of nothing at all.

I wouldn't want to depend on a judge to tell me where exactly I'd be living with my conscience.

"Look who it is," Mickey said to me as he stepped into the garage. "She come off the rim," he told Calvin and pointed vaguely towards his truck.

"Give me a minute." Calvin went at that Honda in earnest now.

"How's things, Mickey?" I asked him.

He nodded by way of a "Fine."

We watched Calvin as he worked. "You've got to stop paying," I told Mickey. "I'm not cashing any more of your checks."

"Wasn't sure we were finished."

"We are."

"You get all you need?"

"Yeah," I said. "Did you?"

Calvin picked up his wrench. We waited. Six lugs later, Mickey told me, "Blaming that guy for everything aren't they? The one that chopped up those women."

I nodded. "Let them," I said to Mickey.

"I'm thinking I just might." He sucked some spit through a tooth gap. "Going to walk over to the drug store," he shouted at Calvin. "Back in a while."

Calvin hung the last tire and grunted. I got a wave from Mickey. Then he was through the doorway and out of sight.

"What do you need anyway?" Calvin asked me.

"My spare's leaking. I'm driving to Richmond tonight. Maybe I'll just pump it up." I was heading over for dinner. P.J. was cooking for me and Fig, and she didn't know how. I'd be on the lookout for bubbly side dishes. I'd be pushing stuff around my plate.

"Suit yourself," Calvin told me. "Got two more in front of you."

"Another time," I said. I was standing in a patch of spring sunlight on the gritty cement floor. "Hate to waste any more of this day in here."

Calvin stepped over and joined me.

"She was probably just getting pretty for you. Forgot about everything else."

"I want to believe it. She'd be hard to lose."

"You turn that key. You open that door."

Calvin hooted and yelped. He knew straightaway I was quoting Dr. Barry of Orange County. You can't help a butcher of women self-actualize without getting famous for it in the worst possible kind of way.

"All right, then. Come on back when you want." Calvin scratched his head with his air wrench socket. He pointed towards the wider world. "Going to be a nice one," Calvin told me.

"Already is," I said.

CPSIA information can be obtained
at www.ICGtesting.com
Printed in the USA
BVHW07s2134111018
529904BV00001B/202/P